MORE PRAISE FOR
AWARD-WINNER LISA CACH!

THE MERMAID OF PENPERRO

"Cach's beautifully crafted, erotically charged scenes and light humorous touch will please fans."

—*Booklist*

"A wonderful and engaging tale with unique twists that offer happy surprises . . . [Cach's] ability to create toe-curling sexual tension makes for a must-stay-up-and-read-till-dawn story."

—*Romantic Times*

OF MIDNIGHT BORN

"*Of Midnight Born* passes my CODPIECE test . . . Creative, rather Original, Dramatic, Poetic, Intensely Emotional, Comedic, and best of all, Entertaining."

—Mrs. Giggles from *Everything Romantic*

"A mix of magic, romance and humor, *Of Midnight Born* delights the reader's imagination. . . . [It] kept me glued to my seat, turning pages, till the very end."

—*Romance Reviews Today*

BEWITCHING THE BARON

"With complex and colorful characters, lush detail and a compelling story, Ms. Cach weaves a story rich in humanity and emotional intensity."

—*Romantic Times*

THE SPY WHO WOULD LOVE HER

Rachel was aware of every nerve in her skin, eager to feel him, aching to close the distance. And yet, she was terrified that he *would* touch her, *would* kiss her. He'd know then that she wanted him, and her pride would be humbled. He could laugh at her, and she would have no retort to save her lost face.

She balanced precariously between desire and fear, and swayed toward him. The broadness of his chest and shoulders protected her from the milling crowd, sheltering her, inviting her to touch, to nestle against him and feel the comfort of his arms around her.

He bent his head, his lips lightly brushing her brow, his breath feathering over her skin. He lowered his mouth, his lips hovering above hers.

Warm desire poured through her, urging her to close that small distance. She felt the barest hint of touch, so light it hurt her with the desire for more.

And then her animal sense of self-preservation jerked her abruptly back.

Other books by Lisa Cach:

GEORGE & THE VIRGIN
A MOTHER'S WAY ROMANCE ANTHOLOGY
WISH LIST
THE WILDEST SHORE
THE MERMAID OF PENPERRO
OF MIDNIGHT BORN
BEWITCHING THE BARON
THE CHANGELING BRIDE

DR. YES

LISA CACH

LOVE SPELL **NEW YORK CITY**

To CK, with thanks.

LOVE SPELL®

February 2003

Published by

Dorchester Publishing Co., Inc.
276 Fifth Avenue
New York, NY 10001

ISBN 0-505-52518-6

The name "Love Spell" and its logo are trademarks of Dorchester Publishing Co., Inc.

Printed in the United States of America.

Visit us on the web at www.dorchesterpub.com.

Curiosity killed the cat.
—Anonymous

Prologue

Pha Ngan Island, Thailand

The blonde wasn't wearing a bra under her tank top. Alan could see her nipples hard against the white fabric, visible even in the half-dark. Her wide gestures and too-easy laughter told him she was half-drunk, along with her friend, the both of them sitting at one of the wooden picnic tables on the edge of the twilight beach. A candle in a glass votive painted gold tones upon the blonde's smooth skin. She was luscious, and he wanted to lick her like a popsicle.

Later tonight, she'd likely fall prey to a drunk German or Australian backpacker, and stumble off to one of the cheap thatched bungalows to have sloppy sex.

1

He would save her from that cruel and revolting fate.

He crunched down on the remainder of his breath mint and sauntered toward the blonde's table, already imagining them together in the moonlight on a deserted stretch of beach. She'd be naked, the silvery light turning her breasts into twin grain silos rising above a gentle Midwestern plain.

Unless they were the soft, floppy sort of breasts that were more like sea anemones at low tide, hanging from the side of a rock. Those were nice, too, in their way. He'd take breasts in whatever shape they came, the bigger the better.

He felt a stirring down below. He hoped he wasn't going to get one of those wet spots on the front of his pants from his excitement.

At any rate, he hoped the blonde would "Ooo!" and "Ahh!" when she saw his package tucked inside silk bikini briefs worn a size too small to better show off the goods. It was no larger or smaller than average—he had measured, and compared the results to data from several scientific studies—but some guy in the locker room showers in college had once told him that it was beautifully, perfectly formed.

He'd been horrified at the time, of course, but the compliment had stayed with him. Who better to know, than some gay guy? Whenever he felt in doubt of his sexual appeal, he put his hand in his pocket and touched himself, like a charm.

Beautiful, perfect. It was worth remembering. Any woman would be lucky to have a chance at it.

Ten thousand young Westerners had gathered to dance and drink at the legendary Full Moon Party on Haad Rin Beach. Half a dozen disc jockeys blared heart-shuddering beats of music from the fronts of restaurants and bars all down the shoreline, tempting the young foreign travelers into sensual folly.

At least the female tourists were worth looking at, and the occasional one worth giving a chance in his bed. The males, on the other hand, were a pure waste of oxygen.

Two-thirds of the men on the planet really ought to be put down, he thought, to save the world the misery of their presence. Most behaved with the wit and grace of bull elephant seals, big lardy bellies slapping against one another as they fought for mating rights, barks and brays of idiocy coming from their bloated throats. They always tried to chase away the smaller, more intelligent males, too: the males that perceptive women knew were the better mating choice.

This blonde shouldn't be able to resist him. He was *Dr.* Alan Archer, ship's physician of the luxurious *Golden Waves* cruise ship. The rich old biddies onboard doted on him, comparing him—with giggles at their *au courant* raciness—to Brad Pitt. When he caught glimpses of himself in a mirror or storefront window, he himself was startled by the resemblance.

He fiddled with the diamond-encrusted Boucheron watch on his wrist, which he had borrowed off a corpse in the cruise ship's morgue. The elderly passenger who had owned it wouldn't miss it for the evening.

Gel held his fair hair in place, but even he had to admit that the scent of his bug repellent was overpowering his cologne. Not that the blonde would care, once she got a look at how well he was dressed. He was the wealthiest-looking man here, and everyone knew that women loved money.

He reached the women's table and stopped. The blonde looked up at him. Time for the opening line.

"Hey, baby. Your beautiful eyes have told me everything but your name."

She gaped at him. Stunned by her good fortune, no doubt. Hers was the look of awe that Cinderella gave the prince when he asked her to dance.

She wasn't saying anything, though.

"Er . . . I wanted to ask you . . ." He tried again. "Did it hurt when you fell from heaven?"

She frowned at him.

"Because, you know, you look like an angel. I'm surprised it's not raining, because surely heaven must be crying, it's missing you so bad."

Her frown deepened, and he glanced at the brunette and saw her face was screwed up, giving him the same look you'd give a three-headed sheep.

"Tell you what," he tried again with the blonde, his voice cracking with growing nervousness. "If you buy me a drink, I'll let you kiss me." He'd read that line at a dating-advice web site for men. It was guaranteed to work.

The women exchanged a glance, and then the brunette made a strange snorting sound. The blonde smirked.

Alan's smile faltered, and the blood began to drain from his crotch and creep up into his cheeks. He forced a grin back into place while the women exchanged words in a Nordic-sounding language and snickered.

"You *do* speak English?" he asked, hoping not. He didn't want to think they were laughing at him. Surely they must have noted what a catch he was, how good-looking, how well-off . . . ? "You want drink?" He mimed sipping from a glass.

"Ja, we speak English. You are American, yes?" the blonde asked, grinning.

Alan let out a breath of relief to hear her finally speak. He affected a relaxed pose, resting his weight on one leg. He tucked his chin down and looked at her from under his brows, as if shy and found out. The look worked better without hair gel, when his forelock could fall over his brow. He worried she wasn't getting the proper effect. "Did my accent give me away?"

The brunette turned her face away, putting her hand up over her mouth, her shoulders shaking. A chuff of air escaped the lips of the blonde, and she smiled.

Maybe the gel-stiffened forelock didn't matter. The blonde seemed taken by his charm, by his obvious wealth.

"Your accent, yes," she said, eyes open a little too wide. "First, I thought you maybe are Italian. Very stylish."

"Versace," he said, touching the front of his designer knockoff shirt, picked up in Hong Kong. His eyes moved down to her nipples. Had they grown hard, in excitement? He could suck them right through the cotton. "I'm a doctor," he continued. "A *medical* doctor." He played with his watch, making sure she saw the diamonds.

The blonde made an 'O' of her mouth. "Rikke, you hear?" she said breathlessly, touching her friend on the arm. "He is a doctor, an American

6

doctor! Very rich. Maybe we should *knalde* him."

Rikke's laughter burst forth, as if from a popped balloon. More foreign words stammered out between the gales, and then she lay back on the wooden bench and put her feet into the air, as if in stirrups and waiting for a pelvic exam. She laughed so hard, she fell off into the sand. The blonde howled, tears trickling down her cheeks.

Alan stumbled back, feeling the burning heat of humiliation. What had he done? Why were they laughing at him? He felt the eyes of onlookers going to him, curious about the target of such laughter.

Bitches.

Whores!

Foreign trash. Who did they think they were? Who the hell did they think they were, these slags?

He escaped into the crowd, his face flaming, sweat breaking out all over his body as humiliation and rage fought each other for mastery.

All around him were young, beautiful travelers at ease with themselves and with each other. Couples were making out, groups of friends dancing, laughing people eating plates of bar snacks together. They ignored him.

He didn't belong.

He never *would* belong, no matter how rich or educated he got. Even with half a dozen years' experience over these young twits, he was still their inferior.

He was twenty-nine years old, and still the geek in the corner, watching as big-mouthed college athletes made out with busty tarts on a frat house couch.

Getting turned down for dates.

Getting beat up in the halls of his high school by Neanderthals with brow bones like axe handles.

Lusting after girls from afar, girls who had—with one incomprehensible exception—never given him more than disdain while their eyes looked him up and down.

He wanted women with an ache that kept him awake at night, but no matter what he did, what he said, what he wore, he couldn't make them want *him*.

He hated them for that.

The backpackers' casual clothing suddenly seemed the height of fashion, his silk shirt like something even a pimp would have better sense than to wear to a beach party. He wanted to rip it off and throw it into the sea, but then his flour-white skin would be exposed, and the sad little patch of mouse-brown chest hair that squatted atop his sternum.

Sand filled his tasseled loafers as he trudged down the beach, then up the bank to one of the open-air bars, far from the sight of the blonde and her friend. He shoved his way up to the bar and ordered a vodka with lime.

He shouldn't have come here. His cruise ship was anchored offshore from Samui, the neighboring island, which was where most of the ship's passengers were entertaining themselves. He had taken the local ferry to Pha Ngan, happy to escape for an evening the company of the *Golden Waves*'s passengers, in front of whom he had to behave with perfect propriety.

He should have stayed with them. They, at least, saw him for what he was worth. He was a doctor, by God, and worth ten times any idiot on this beach! Just as he'd been too good for those women.

He sipped his vodka, mentally shutting himself off from the noise and crowd around him, lost in his own thoughts. It was only when he had slurped down the last of his drink and started to chew on the rind of his lime that he noticed the dark little Asian man standing next to him, and the man's interest in his watch.

"Get lost," Alan said, waving him away. Thieving, uneducated little ape.

The man grinned, a tight, nervous expression. "No luck with ladies?"

9

"I *said,* get lost!"

The man's eye twitched. "I help you."

It took Alan a moment to understand what the guy probably meant. Of all the insulting . . . As if *he* would have to pay for it! "I don't want one of your HIV-infected, underage prostitutes. Leave me alone!"

"No, no, mister. No whore." The man opened his hand, flashing a vial filled with a greenish white powder, then quickly stuffed it back into his pocket.

Alan noticed the track marks on the man's arms. That would explain his nervousness: He was probably due for a fix. "I don't want your drugs, either."

"Is not for you. Is for the ladies." The man nodded, eyebrows raised. "Makes ladies hot. Makes ladies . . ." He gave up on words, and gyrated his hips in explanation.

"Right. Sure. And I know how to stop aging and lose ten pounds overnight." He moved away. He had seen this annoying little scumbag's type in every port town in Asia, preying on tourists.

Squeezing through the crowd, Alan walked back out onto the edge of the beach. The strange man followed him.

"No lies," he called. "This medicine, it come from secret place in mountains. Used for many hundred year. We call it 'Yes' in my language, because it make ladies say 'yes' to anything man want."

Alan turned. "And where *is* this secret mountain place?" he asked.

A crafty look came into the man's eyes. "I am not stupid. I tell you; then you go there and take for yourself."

"Mmm." Alan headed for the water, where the crowd wasn't as thick and the walking would be easier. Sand flies bit at his ankles and bounced off his face, ignoring his repellent. The human pest trailed after him, as well, equally immune to DEET.

"Mister, look! See?"

Alan turned, waving away the tiny flies. The man was holding up a silver medallion that he wore on a chain around his neck.

"See? Is from place in mountains. Is real."

Alan took and lifted the silver disk upon his fingertips, the light of the full moon catching it and revealing a design of a mountain range with the rising sun behind it.

Or were those raised knees, and a starburst of pubic hair? He couldn't tell. It was like a psychological vision test: Is it a young woman, or a hag? A vase, or two profiles?

He'd seen nothing like it in all the cheap souvenir shops of Southeast Asia—and he'd been in plenty of them during the port calls of the cruise

11

ships he'd worked on. This embossing was done by hand, not stamped out by a machine.

His interest sharpened. New drugs were being found in the jungles of the world all the time. There was the slightest possibility that this strange man spoke at least a grain of truth.

And if there *was* a grain of truth in what the man said, Alan would be a fool to brush him off. There were millions to be made from new drugs. And a true aphrodisiac for women, one that made them the active, willing sex partners of any man . . . ?

It would be world-altering.

And in that new world, *he* would be king. No bull seal would be more powerful than he. No cow would be able to refuse him.

He showed his teeth, trying for a friendly smile. "I'm Alan," he said, putting out his hand. "What's your name?" he asked, as they shook.

"Durga."

"Maybe we can do a bit of business after all, Durga."

He would have to do an initial test of the drug, of course. And he already knew exactly who his guinea pigs would be.

That blonde and her friend would soon be paying the price for their laughter.

Chapter One

Kathmandu, Nepal, two years later

"It's going to be hard to say good-bye," Fritz said in his German accent, holding her hand and stroking its back.

"It always is," Rachel replied, affecting her best Ingrid Bergman in *Casablanca* stance. Fritz was a middle-aged member of the tour group she had just led on a two-week trip through Nepal: fourteen days during which she had had to deflect his frequent amorous advances without offending him.

In every group, there always seemed to be one person who made it his goal to sleep with the guide. A sort of souvenir experience, she supposed. A little notch on the old passport.

He wasn't a bad-looking man, and she might have considered taking him up on the offer this last night of the trip, but he smelled funny and never cleaned the wax off the hair in his ears. Even desperate girls had standards.

"My flight isn't until tomorrow afternoon. We have many hours," Fritz suggested, not quite willing to give up the battle.

"You see, the problem is," Rachel said, lowering her voice and leaning in close, "I've got two boyfriends here in town who've been waiting for my return. I already don't know how I'm going to handle both in one night, and if I throw in a third—you—well, I'm afraid I'm going to get terribly worn out, and I've got a lot of paperwork that's due in the morning. Have you ever tried to do paperwork after a night like that? It's not easy, I promise you."

Fritz stared at her, as if not trusting his comprehension of her English.

"You do understand, don't you?" she asked.

"You are joking?"

She raised her eyebrows. "About my stamina? It's embarrassing, I know, at my age. I should be able to handle three, four times a night. Maybe I need to eat more protein."

He choked out a laugh, looking at her with a mix of wariness and disbelief. "You are a good joker. Ha."

She patted his arm. "I'm sure you'll find others who aren't already booked up for the night. The club stays open until two A.M.—drink, dance, have fun!" She smiled and sidled away, quickly engaging a Danish girl in conversation.

This was the farewell party for her group of ten, held at a noisy restaurant and jazz club that called itself "New Orleans." The restaurant served jambalaya and blackened catfish, a fact that never failed to amuse her. Who would ever expect to find Cajun food on the edge of the Himalayas?

Then again, one would not have expected Internet cafés, either, in a land where goats, chickens, and water buffalo were routinely sacrificed to the gods, and foreigners had been forbidden to enter until the 1950s. The modern world's hold on Nepal was firmest here in Kathmandu, but she need only wander away from the tourist district and the main thoroughfares to be reminded how close to the past Nepal truly still remained. Neither electricity nor plumbing were things to be taken for granted.

Her group ate and drank at a table on a wide balcony, looking down over the crowd of Western tourists in the open-air portion of the restaurant. Strings of small lights drooped in catenaries above them, but if she tilted her head back she could see the real stars twinkling in the black night sky above, barely dimmed by the low-voltage street lamps of the city. The stars reminded her of chilly nights with her father, stumbling out onto the lawn in bathrobes and jackets to look for meteors or the fuzzy blob of a comet. A wave of sadness washed through her at the memory, bringing a sting of tears to her eyes.

"A toast, to our leader!" lecherous Fritz declared, standing with a glass of Chinese beer in his hand. "One more lovely we could never have hoped to have—pink hair, nose ring, and all!"

Rachel lowered her gaze from the heavens and forced a smile, just as she forced away thoughts of her father and mother.

"Nor one more resourceful!" a British girl added.

"Wily as a dingo," an Australian man agreed. "Like how she dealt with that hotel manager in Pokhara. I thought he'd be offering the rooms for free when she got done with him."

Rachel smiled sincerely this time, as they all raised their glasses and drank to her.

"Here's to a great group, with remarkable powers of endurance," Rachel proposed, raising her own glass and feeling a fleeting fondness for the lot of them. "Only three of you got lost, eight ill, one bitten by a dog, and I give special honors to Annette for sitting with the goats on the bus from Pokhara."

They all laughed and drank.

As every group did on their final night together, this one started retelling the best of their travel horror stories from the past two weeks. Rachel listened with one ear, a half smile on her lips, feeling as she always did, as if she were on the outside looking in, somehow immune from their excitement and from the connections they had made with one another.

Kathmandu had been her home base for a year now. She led tours for Courageous Adventures, an Australian company that catered to young travelers with more spirit than dollars. She was hoping to be transferred to Malaysia soon, but Courageous Adventures seemed oddly reluctant to move her. She didn't understand why they needed her here so badly, when tourism was doing so poorly in Nepal.

The country had become like an old friend— an old friend from whom one needs a break. She was growing restless and a bit bored, and that left her with too much time to think.

Even if she wasn't transferred to Malaysia, she wouldn't quit her job and go back to her life in the States, though. The merest thought of walking the familiar byways of home, empty now of those she had loved most, wrenched at her heart with a pain she could not face.

No, it was much better to wander unknown Asia, where little touched upon memory, and where she could skate along like a water skipper on the surface of a black pond of grief, safe from the drowning depths.

A touch of envy lay against her heart as she looked at her tour group. They seemed so happy, so easy in each others' company. So apart from her.

She tried to shake off the melancholy. On the bright side, hanging out in Kathmandu nightclubs beat the grind of graduate school, and at least she no longer had her nut-flake older sister, Pamela, to contend with. She was free to do as she wished—and to do it whenever, however, wherever she wished. Curiosity, whims, and fancies were her only commanders.

Her attention was caught by a waiter down below, pointing up at her group. The remnants of her morose mood dissipated when she saw Beti standing next to him, nodding. The small Nepalese woman moved through the restaurant, headed for the stairs up to their balcony.

Curious, Rachel excused herself from the group and went to meet the woman at the bottom of the stairs. Beti was no more than 4' 10", and slender as a child; but hidden inside that tiny

18

package was a wealth of knowledge and intelligence. She had an advanced degree in history and was a teacher, though the economy of Nepal forced her to earn extra money as a local city guide. Rachel had often hired her to lead walking tours of Kathmandu.

"Beti, what a surprise! Everyone will be so happy to see you again."

"Forgive me if I do not go to say 'Hello.' It was you I came to see," she said, unsmiling. Beti was naturally reserved, but she and Rachel had built a small friendship over the year Rachel had lived here. Her serious tone was unexpected.

"What is it?" Rachel asked, a flutter of worry beginning in her chest. "Is something wrong? Has something happened?" There were so many possibilities. A few years ago half the royal family had been massacred. Maoist rebels routinely killed members of the police and army. Bombs went off in the city, organized strikes and marches sometimes led to violence in the streets. It was rare for foreigners to get caught up in the country's strife, but it was not unknown. She might have to move her group back to the relative safety of the hotel, quickly.

"Nothing has happened," Beti said, betraying now a trace of tension in her voice, "but there is someone who needs your help."

"What? My help? Who?" Rachel's disquiet

went up a notch. As a foreigner in a strange land, *she* was the one who usually asked for assistance, from the locals.

"Can you come with me?" Beti asked.

"Do they need first aid? I left my supplies back at the hotel."

"No, no, it is not so urgent as that." Beti's smile was small, and she nervously pushed her glasses higher up the bridge of her nose. "No one is bleeding, no broken bones."

Rachel hesitated and glanced up the stairs toward her group. She shouldn't leave them so early: They were still her responsibility. "But you do need me right now?"

"Within the half hour?"

Rachel nodded. She could get away by then.

"The Nepalese Kitchen. We will be in the bar."

"We?" Rachel asked.

"You will come?"

Rachel nodded, more puzzled now than worried. She sensed Beti did not want to be pushed further for details, though, so she would have to hold her curiosity. Impatience never got you anywhere in Nepal.

The narrow, dust-covered street was quiet outside the centuries-old Newari House that was the home of the Nepalese Kitchen. Lantern light flickered on either side of the wooden door and glowed orange from inside the upper windows, persuading her for a moment that she had stepped back in time. The facade of the building was redbrick and dark wood, the windows carved bays and grills that had graced the house for hundreds of years.

Rachel stood for a moment, listening to the distant sounds of motorcycles and cars, and the barking of a dog. There was never silence in Kathmandu, and one learned to appreciate different degrees of relative quiet in this city that was struggling to find its place between the medieval and the modern worlds.

The owner of the restaurant, Rajendra, greeted her from behind the foyer desk as she entered. He was a handsome Nepalese man, tall and broad-shouldered.

"Your friends are waiting for you upstairs," he said, coming around the desk. He was gorgeous, his features more Asian than Caucasian, his skin a perfect, poreless, warm-toned brown.

Rachel had been here many times, and she considered seeing Rajendra as much a lure as the food. He figured regularly in her sexual fantasies. Pity he was married.

"It's only Beti that I know," Rachel said, letting him guide her up the narrow, rickety wooden staircase. She knew better than to say she could find her own way: Rajendra was nothing if not courteous, and would insist upon escorting her. Who was she to protest?

"Ahh," he said.

There was something to that "Ahh" that gave her pause. She cast a look over her shoulder at him. He was smiling. "What is it?" she asked. "Why do you look so amused?"

"I think your friend has plans for you."

"What sort of plans?" she asked, suspicious.

"Very nice ones."

"Everyone is being very mysterious tonight," Rachel muttered.

Rajendra only smiled and gestured for her to continue up the stairs. At the top landing Rachel bent down and removed her sandals, leaving them with the other shoes shoved against the wall, noticing a pair of black men's dress shoes, expensive and dust-free, set neatly amidst the worn, dirty footgear of others.

The "bar" was an attic room, low tables scattered far apart, cushions around them for customers to sit upon. She felt the embrace of the warm light cast by the oil lamps, the dark wood of the roof beams and lattice windows adding to the sense of quiet, relaxed comfort. It was late in the evening, and only a few tables yet had customers.

Rajendra led her to the far corner, his broad back blocking her view until she was standing right in front of the table where Beti sat . . . with a man whose beauty made all thoughts of Rajendra vanish from Rachel's lusting head.

She stood and stared, gape-jawed, at the male anomaly who was climbing to his feet, his hand held out to shake hers.

Where the heck had *he* come from—a European perfume ad? Good God. He couldn't be human. He looked like he should be driving a convertible down a seacoast highway with a long-haired blonde in the seat beside him. He was even wearing a tuxedo, for God's sake, the bow tie undone and hanging around his open collar.

"Rachel Calais?" he asked. "I'm Harrison Wiles. It's a pleasure to meet you."

Rachel put her hand in his, still incapable of speech. Glossy black hair, light brown skin, Caucasian features, tall, lithe, graceful . . . and he had a British accent, indecently seductive when spoken in such a deep voice. His ancestry could have been anything from Indian to mixed Asian, Spanish, Italian, Arab, or even French with a tan.

His hand was warm and dry, engulfing hers. A faint scent of cologne came off him, just enough that she wanted to lean forward and breathe more deeply.

She saw his dark eyes quickly take in her pink hair and the small gold disc on the side of her

23

pierced nose, then come back to meet her gaze. He was still smiling, but he couldn't completely hide his dismay at her appearance.

He was the sexiest man she'd ever met, and she immediately felt her own beauty lacking in comparison. Fluorescent hair suddenly seemed gauche next to such practiced suavity. She felt the heat of a blush burning her cheeks, then spreading up over her forehead. A sick mixture of desire and inadequacy made her gut churn.

Even in the soft lamplight Harrison Wiles would be unable to miss her blush, and the knowledge embarrassed her anew. It annoyed her, as well: She was already at a disadvantage, without even speaking a word.

Wiles released her hand, and Rachel looked away, feeling awkward and at a loss for what to do with herself. Rajendra's familiar voice broke into her dazed state.

"I will bring you your usual, yes?"

She looked at him, grateful, wishing that he could stay and be her safety blanket. "Yes, please, the usual."

The amusement in Rajendra's eyes and the bare hint of a smile at the corners of his mouth told her what he thought: that Beti had brought this man as a prospective husband for Rachel. Rachel widened her eyes at Rajendra and shook her head.

He winked at her: a big, slow wink that he had learned from his foreign customers, and that was as obvious as a drunk elephant sitting on the table singing Madonna tunes. Rachel's blush deepened as he left her to her fate.

"Please, sit down," Wiles said, genial and at ease, and gestured to the cushion across from where he had been sitting. He went around to take his own place again, failing to look silly without his shoes on.

He should have a hole in his sock. Lint on his pants. Something. And for God's sake, he should button his shirt to the top. Men like him shouldn't leave that hollow at the base of the throat exposed. It was indecent.

Rachel glanced at Beti, looking for clues to what this was all about, but the Nepalese woman was looking even more nervous than before, refusing to meet Rachel's gaze and playing with the edge of her glass of mineral water.

Rajendra hadn't been right, had he? This man could not be a blind date. It *would* explain his faintly detectable disappointment upon seeing her, though.

She sat down with a conscious effort at grace, folding her legs neatly to the side and arranging the long skirt of her silk tunic in a smooth drape over her legs. This past year she had taken to wearing *shalwar kameez,* the long tunic and loose trouser outfit that was as popular in Nepal as the sari.

She would compose herself and pay no attention to the indecent good looks of Mr. Wiles. She may not have ever met anyone as sexually appealing as he—was the man exuding some unnatural level of pheromones?—but good looks did not a superior man make.

"Thank you for coming on such short notice, Ms. Calais," he said in his luscious accent. "Beti tells me you had to abandon your tour group to do so."

"They'll manage to get toasted just fine without me," she said with a quick smile. "Most will probably even find the hotel again. I doubt that more than two or three of the most drunken ones will sleep on the streets tonight."

"Are you sure it is safe to leave them alone?" he asked with concern.

She made a face. "I was kidding."

"I see." He didn't smile.

God's sake, did Mr. Gorgeous really take himself so seriously? Maybe he was stupid. Yes! That would make her feel better. Pretty but stupid.

A waiter appeared with Rachel's "usual," a bottle of Sprite. He popped the top off the small green bottle and poured the contents into a glass of ice, the three of them waiting silently for him to finish and leave. Rachel pondered reaching under the table to fondle Wiles's knee.

"So. What's this all about?" Rachel asked, smothering a giggle as she imagined his look of shocked offense at a pawing hand. She sipped from her glass to cover her grin, looking over the rim first at Wiles and then at Beti.

The Nepalese woman made a murmur in her throat before sitting up a bit straighter. She glanced at Wiles, then at his nod turned again to Rachel. "Before I begin, may I have your promise to keep what is about to be said in confidence?"

What the . . . ? Rachel lowered her glass from her lips. This didn't sound like the beginning of a romantic introduction. "Of course." She hoped she wasn't about to hear about something illegal.

"Thank you." Beti pushed her glasses up her nose and fixed her gaze on Rachel. "We have a job for you. We need you to lead a trek into the Himalayas, to search for the legendary city of Yonam."

Rachel's lips parted as her eyes widened. She set her glass on the table with a thud. "You *what?*"

She turned her gaze to Wiles, who appeared as serious as Beti. "Is this your idea?" The man must be some species of rich idiot, fancying himself a real-life Indiana Jones, chasing after fairy tales. After Shangri-la.

27

"No. If I had my way, you wouldn't be involved at all," Wiles said.

Rachel looked back at Beti, disbelief and confusion muddling her brain.

Beti said, "What do you know about Yonam?"

"Just what you've told me in the past. It is a legendary city in a hidden valley of the Himalayas, a paradise where beautiful women cater to every wish and whim of the men. A *male chauvinist's* paradise, I should say." She glared at Wiles.

"Paradise for the men, but likely a hell for the women," he said.

She tucked her chin down in surprise. It wasn't what she would have expected him to say. Shouldn't he be smirking about what a wonderful world that would be?

"What if Yonam were real?" Wiles went on. "And what if the secret to the subservience of the women were a drug?"

"Then I should think that it was a very good thing that the city was lost," Rachel said. "I certainly would not go searching for it."

"Someone has already begun the search. And he not only knows that the drug is real, but he has the knowledge and resources to synthesize it and bring it to the world marketplace in great quantity. You've probably heard of Rohypnol and GHB, the date-rape drugs?"

Rachel nodded, her skin going cold.

"Victims of Rohypnol have no memory of what has happened to them. Those who take GHB go unconscious. How much worse, do you think, to be fully conscious, lucid, and an active participant in one's own abuse? This drug takes away a woman's ability to follow her own will. She becomes completely subservient to the man who has drugged her."

"It only works on women?"

Beti answered. "As far as we know. And the woman is somehow bound to the specific man who drugged her. We speculate that it has something to do with his unique scent. When the drug wears off she is herself again, but for as long as it is in her system she has no will of her own, and is possessed by strong sexual urges."

Rachel frowned at Beti. The woman's background was in history and anthropology. How much could she know about the chemistry of a drug? "When you say 'we,' " she asked, "are you speaking only of yourself and Mr. Wiles?"

"We are speaking of B.L.I.S.S.," Beti said.

" 'Bliss?' What the heck is 'Bliss?' "

"It's an acronym for an international secret service organization composed almost entirely of women," Wiles explained without cracking a smile.

Rather remarkable, that he could keep a

straight face. A women's secret service organization, Rachel's lumpy ass! What, were they headed by Wonder Woman and all lived on a magical island? "Have you had a sex change operation? Why do *you* work for B.L.I.S.S., if they're all women?"

"Not all, just most," he clarified. "Even the superbly able women of B.L.I.S.S. occasionally have use for a man."

"I'll bet," Rachel said, and snorted. "Whose government?"

"I beg your pardon?"

"Whose government does B.L.I.S.S. work for?"

"We, ah . . . operate outside the confines of any one specific government."

Rachel raised her brows. "Do you, then. My mother did not raise a fool. Is this 'organization' one that hides its funds in offshore bank accounts?" This so-called "Bliss" could be a drug cartel or an arms-trading organization, for all she knew.

"We know you are no fool, Ms. Calais," Wiles said. "No one who begins work on her Ph.D. at age nineteen could be unintelligent. She would, indeed, need to be a person of extraordinary gifts."

Rachel's breath left her, and for a moment she felt her heart had stopped. What did he know of her? How? She'd never told Beti about her abandoned studies.

A dozen questions warred for prominence, but what came out was a harsh "Why are you checking up on me?"

"The head of our organization gathered information on all foreign guides currently working in Nepal," Wiles said. "Your advanced coursework in anthropology and paleethnology were of particular interest to her, as well as your experience leading trekking groups." He smiled, showing off a dimple. "In this case, it also helps that you're an American woman."

She shook her head, stunned. They knew what she had studied? What else did they know? Just who the hell *were* these "Bliss" people, and why were they so determined to have her help them? "Surely there is someone better qualified, through one of the other trekking companies? Leading groups along well-traveled trekking routes, as I do, is hardly the same as exploring off the beaten path."

Wiles showed his first signs of discomfort, his jaw tightening. "As I said, it was not my decision. The head of B.L.I.S.S. says you're the best choice."

Rachel narrowed her eyes. As thoughts clicked into place, she slowly shook her head in denial. "A woman should be the last person to go stumbling off in search of a land where all women fall prey to men. It sounds like someplace I should stay the hell away from."

Wiles winced at her vehemence, and she wondered if he was offended that a lady should say "hell." Prissy Brit. Or maybe he was upset that she'd ended the sentence with a preposition.

"Something that Harrison has failed to make clear," Beti interjected, clearing her throat nervously, "is that although B.L.I.S.S. would like you to lead this expedition, the expedition itself is not B.L.I.S.S.'s endeavor."

Rachel raised her brows. "Then whose is it?"

"A countryman of yours," Beti said. "One Dr. Archer. He is the man who is going in search of Yonam, in hopes of finding the so-called 'Yes' drug."

"Wait a minute. . . . You want me to *help* some guy find Yonam? *Why?*" she cried. These two were bonkers. She should get Wiles drunk, drag him back to her hotel room, and get the only use from him he obviously had to offer the world. Thinking certainly wasn't his forté.

Wiles answered. "Archer is the only one with any idea how to find Yonam. He has a map, or information—something that gives him the confidence that he can find this city, and upon which we have been unable so far to lay our hands. He doesn't trust foreigners—seems to hate them, in fact—but he needs someone to organize and lead his trek. He's been searching. If *you* are that person, then you can carry a satellite tracking device to keep B.L.I.S.S. apprised of your location, and when you find Yonam we'll send in a team to destroy the drug and the means of producing it."

"And Archer?"

"If he returns to civilization with so much as a gram of the drug he'll be able to synthesize it in a lab, and this will all be for naught."

"So, what—you want me to kill him? Maybe with my highly trained kung fu moves!" She slashed her hands through the air in her best imitation of a martial arts expert, then dropped them into her lap. "This isn't the movies, you know. And I'm not going to shoot anyone."

Wiles sighed at her antics, and for a moment she thought he was going to roll his eyes. "We wouldn't ask you to," he said. "But if by some chance Archer gets away from Yonam with a sample, you might be able to . . . ah . . . remove it from his person."

"Steal it, you mean."

"Just so."

Did she look like a thief? "And the reason you'd like it to be a woman who leads this expedition into folly is . . . ?" she asked. "Is it because I'm supposed to be able to charm him?" Such an expectation would explain Wiles's dis-

33

may upon seeing her. He probably thought she lacked the appeal necessary to snag a doctor.

"Something like that," Wiles admitted, and she heard a touch of resentment in his tone. "Archer will be off his guard with you. The information we have on him suggests that he is a loner and feels threatened by other men. He isn't going to trust a man not to steal his research or the potential profits to be made from it. Our best chance of getting one of our people on his expedition is to send him a female candidate for a guide. Unfortunately, we have no B.L.I.S.S. agents with trekking experience in Nepal."

Rachel tilted her head to the side and stared at Wiles.

"Yes?" he snapped, short temper showing through.

"You wanted to lead this trek yourself, didn't you?" she guessed.

His expression went flat, his lips closed in a hard line. There was no question that she'd struck a nerve.

Perversely, it gave her confidence. Beautiful Spy Boy was under someone's thumb, someone who called the shots and didn't think he had exactly what it took to get this job done. He might look perfect, but he wasn't.

She had an impish, evil urge to rub his handsome face in it.

"Perhaps I *would* be the right person to do this," she said, watching the man. "I mean, how hard could it be?"

"This isn't to be taken lightly," he said, his lips barely moving, his skin darkening with a betraying flush of anger.

"Since I am the one who has been chosen for this task, I should think I would be trusted to take 'it' however I saw fit." She raised her eyebrows, as if asking him to accept the logic of her words. She took a sip of Sprite.

Beti made a murmured sound of distress.

Wiles glared and muttered under his breath.

"What was that you said?" Rachel asked sweetly.

Wiles continued his dark regard, and her confidence began to crack. He looked ready to refuse her help, whatever his superiors might have ordered him to do.

Suddenly, the thought bothered her.

However crazy this quest for Yonam might be, it had at least the promise of intrigue and adventure to it. It sounded a heck of a lot more interesting than leading another group of tourists around to places she'd seen a dozen times before. Whatever other emotions may have been caged in the darkness within her, curiosity still thrived and ran free. It was all that kept her going.

"I am to take it, then, that you are willing to

join us?" Wiles asked, sounding just able to get the words out without spitting.

Relief washed through her, which she hid by taking another sip of her soft drink. He wasn't going to toss her on the street for being a snot. She set her glass back on the table and stifled a small belch. As nonchalantly as she could manage, she said, "Yes."

"Dr. Archer is interviewing prospective guides sent to him through a local trekking agency," Beti said, sliding a piece of paper to her with the name of the agency, the contact person there, and a job description. "The Hotel Harati, starting at ten o'clock each morning. He'll be in the garden. Go talk to him tomorrow."

Wiles began to get to his feet. "I'll call you a taxi."

"But—" Rachel said, taken off guard. "I have so many questions! You can't just throw me out there like this!"

"Better you know as little as possible," Wiles said, on his feet now. Rachel scrambled up. "Just go to the interview as a guide looking for a job," he continued, "ignorant about who Archer is and what he is really looking for. You'll come off as genuine. If he hires you, we'll fill you in on everything you need to know."

"Like what the B.L.I.S.S. acronym stands for?

I'd like to know who I'm working for, you know."

"In good time," Wiles promised. Rather arrogantly, she thought.

Wiles gestured for her to precede him toward the stairs. Rachel obeyed, looking back over her shoulder at him. "What about my job with Courageous Adventures? What—"

"We'll deal with all that when we need to."

She turned to face him fully and put her hands on her hips, planting her feet and refusing to budge. "I don't understand why you're rushing me out like this."

He sighed and ran his hand through his thick black hair. It fell back into place even more charmingly arranged than before. "I've got to get back to the Yak and Yeti. I promised to teach my date how to play baccarat."

That explained the tuxedo. The Yak and Yeti was a hotel housed in a former palace and was the lodging of choice for visiting luminaries. Rock stars, movie stars, heads of state: They all stayed there, well insulated from the real life of Nepal.

"So your date is more important than this little adventure we're organizing," she snapped. She was appalled at the spurt of jealousy she felt, and that leaked into her tone. Lord save her, she wasn't truly attracted to this pompous tight-ass, was she?

No, surely not.

Was she?

Damn it. How embarrassing.

"His date is a member of the royal family," Beti said quietly.

"Oh," she said, and chewed her upper lip. Curses. He was dating a friggin' princess. "Well, I guess it really *wouldn't* do to keep her waiting."

"It's not a bridge I want to burn," Wiles agreed dryly.

Rachel didn't know if it was the networking opportunity he didn't want to destroy, or the possibility of the woman's more private favors. She'd guess both. She'd guess as well that the woman would be happy to oblige him in whatever he sought.

Thank God he wouldn't be on the trek. No telling what humiliation she might bring on herself if she were in his company for too long. She'd follow him around, brush imaginary dust off his shirt, try to draw him into conversation, sneak glances at his butt, and try to resist the urge to squeeze it. Sooner or later he'd realize she had the hots for him, at which point he'd run away screaming.

She smiled to herself. He might run, but she wouldn't let him get away untouched.

Chapter Two

"I've got to go on that trek," Harrison said, watching Rachel Calais's taxi bump away down the street.

"It's been discussed. You know Y decided against it," Beti said, referring to the head of B.L.I.S.S.

"*She* can't be left to handle it on her own. That girl is an ill-mannered flake."

"That *woman* is the most intelligent person, male or female, I have ever met."

Harrison raised an eyebrow, grinning down at her. "Present company excluded?"

Beti frowned up at him. "Present company *in*-cluded."

39

He sighed. "She certainly didn't act like the genius she is supposed to be."

The Nepalese woman shook her head. "I do not know what was happening in her head. I have never seen her behave so. Never." She narrowed her eyes at him. "Nor have I seen you so unable, or unwilling, to charm a woman."

"Here now, I take offense at that! My charm is always in place, and it *never* fails." He grinned.

Beti rolled her eyes.

The second taxi they had called pulled up, and Beti slid into the backseat of the small, beat-up Datsun. Harrison handed money to the driver. Moments later that taxi, too, had rattled away on bald tires; he was alone on the street with his welter of emotions, all of them focused on Rachel Calais.

He went around to the back of the building, to where his borrowed Toyota Landcruiser was waiting. He unlocked it and slid into the driver's seat.

The file he had been given had led him to expect a quiet, studious, awkward young woman. The college photo had shown her as overweight and mousy-haired, with the shadows of an insomniac under her eyes. She had looked sufficiently bland and timid that Archer would feel at ease with her and never suspect she was a spy.

The Rachel Calais in the file was *not* the Rachel Calais he had met tonight.

Nothing had prepared him for the slender, pink-haired, nose-studded, smart-mouthed, disrespectful female who had appeared at their table. If not for the elegant *shalwar kameez* she wore, he would have thought she had walked straight out of an American high school.

His eyes had gone again and again to that shocking hair, with ragged bangs and spiky, flipped-out ends that brushed her neck and shoulders. They had talked for half an hour, and yet if she appeared before him as a brunette he doubted he would recognize her, he had paid so little attention to the features of her face.

All he did know was that her eyes were pale green with silver flecks, uptilted, and set off to startling effect by a heavy line of black eyeliner and lavender eyeshadow. Theatrical, true—but stunning.

Throughout their conversation, however, he had been thinking, "*This* is who Y trusts to deal with Archer? Instead of me?"

Appallingly, she had picked up on his thoughts. She knew he resented her being offered leadership of the mission. She knew it, and she laughed. She probably had agreed to help just to annoy him.

Bloody hell.

And yes, it rankled that she had been so thoroughly immune to his charms. He could barely even admit that to himself, but when a guy was fawned on all the time by women—however much he might dislike that fawning—he noticed when he got the opposite reaction.

He slammed the door and started the engine, then backed out and turned down the road for the Yak and Yeti.

Rachel Calais's file listed her school records, and that she had quit her studies just before finishing her Ph.D. No explanation was given for her abandonment of what appeared to be a promising academic career, and he could only assume she had gotten bored with hard work and chosen instead to indulge herself with aimless, pseudo-hippie wanderings.

He felt a burst of annoyance. The concept of noblesse oblige might be outdated in many minds, but he firmly believed that those who had been gifted with wealth, health, and education had a duty to use those gifts in aid of others. To squander such gifts, as Rachel was doing, was an insult to humanity.

He pulled up at the hotel and let a valet take the car. He retied his bow tie and went in.

Twelve-year-old Kamina, his royal "date," was probably done with her dessert by now and anxious for her baccarat lesson. The girl's uncle, the new king, had asked Harrison to keep her entertained for the evening. One did not deny the requests of kings—not that he'd want to, in this case. Kamina was a sweet, shy girl who needed encouragement to spread her wings.

It wasn't Kamina who saw him first when he reentered the ballroom where the dinner was being held, though; it was her older sister, Samina, who had long ago spread her wings both wide and bright. She sashayed toward him in a Western evening gown, its fabric pouring down her body like red paint. She was beautiful and had made it clear she was available, and her eyes as they met his reinforced that promise.

He panicked and ran to hide in the men's rest room.

Women like Samina always unnerved him. Why couldn't she sit down with a cup of coffee and tell him a little about herself, rather than shove her breasts at him first thing? Although they *were* great breasts.

He found a clean stall and locked the door, savoring the peace and safety. His friends had always laughed at his reserve with women, never understanding how being chased could disappoint him, rather than fill him with ecstatic joy. It was hideously old-school of him, but he always felt that women who chased him were debasing themselves. They should consider themselves a prize to be won, not a free sample to be shoved into the hands of a stranger. *He* wanted to think of them that way; why couldn't they think of themselves as such?

He shook away the thought and took his cell phone from his pocket. He had more pressing concerns than Samina. He had to contact Y and make fresh arguments against Rachel leading the mission.

He told himself that his determination to join this trek had nothing to do with offended pride about being passed over as leader. Nor did it have to do with Rachel having gotten under his skin, prickling and annoying like a brush with stinging nettles. Not at all. He was more mature and self-aware than to take her taunting attitude as a personal challenge.

It was the mission he was concerned about: He wanted to help save the women of the world from the Yes drug.

He didn't give a brass farthing about looking again into Rachel Calais's stunning green eyes, or about proving to both her and to Y that he was a man worthy of the trust and admiration of women.

After her taxi deposited her in front of her hotel, Rachel stood for a moment outside the entrance, then turned around and headed back up the street. A few of the Internet cafés were open past midnight, and she found one of the smaller ones on a second floor, tucked away up a dark cement staircase.

The place stank of cigarette smoke. A few tank-top-clad backpackers were occupying terminals, silent but for the clicking of their fingers on the keys.

She sat down at a computer in the corner of the bare, fluorescent-lit room, feeling fairly certain that no one she saw was the infamous Dr. Archer. No one here looked like a doctor.

She logged on and went to the Google search engine and entered "B.L.I.S.S."

Over a million results came back, all of them ignoring the periods between the letters. There were Bliss day spas, Bliss music companies, Bliss bridal shops, a toy store, a charity for premature babies, etc. etc.

She narrowed her search to "bliss secret service," and got ten thousand hits.

"Caroline Bliss" came up. She was one of the actresses to play Miss Moneypenny in the James Bond films.

"Richard Bliss" had been accused by the Russians of being a spy.

Nothing, though, that sounded more than coincidentally related to the B.L.I.S.S. of which Beti and Wiles claimed to be members.

A search on "Dr. Archer" turned up too many hits to look through. She wished she knew his first name.

"Harrison Wiles" had been a landowner in Indiana in 1877. The only other hit was on someone's home page. She clicked on the URL, and found herself on a gallery page. The Internet connection was painfully slow, and she sat back to wait for the photos to appear, line by line.

Five minutes later the page was complete, the photo with "Harrison Wiles" in the caption appearing at the bottom of a page of "friends and family" pictures.

It was a young Wiles she saw, no more than sixteen years old, in a line of five young men with their arms over each others' shoulders, all wearing muddy rugby uniforms. Wiles hadn't yet filled out, his body still holding traces of boyish slenderness, his face softer than it was now.

She wondered if his friends had razzed him about his pretty face. She wondered if they'd envied him his easy time of it with girls, for an easy time he must have had.

She leaned close to stare at the photo, Wiles's face blurry on the old monitor.

What was she hoping to discover? She didn't know. There were no secrets revealing themselves, no hint of who he was, of what besides his dark good looks might make him different from his paler, unremarkable friends.

She clicked on the "home" button at the bottom of the gallery page.

The owner of the page, Geoffrey Shelton, was a banker in London. Married, new baby. Enjoyed football: soccer, she assumed. Judging by another photo, he owned a midsized home in what appeared to be an average suburb.

He was a resoundingly average man. Normal.

The contrast to the dashing Harrison Wiles left her wondering all the more: Who on earth was he?

Chapter Three

Hotel Harati

Rachel nervously rubbed her finger over her front teeth. It wouldn't do to interview for a job with flecks of magenta lipstick marring her smile. She used the back of her hand to blot any traces of shine off her nose, and with shaking hands flicked her fingertips through the hair around her face.

She took a deep breath and smoothed her palms down the front of her petal-pink, silver-embroidered tunic. The matching organza scarf lay against her throat, the ends trailing down her back all the way down to her knees. She was as ready as she would ever be to meet The Villain.

In the course of her travels in Nepal she'd effectively dealt with minor league scam artists, pickpockets, corrupt officials, and drug dealers. The encounters had tested her wits and occasionally ticked her off, but they hadn't frightened her. No one had meant her harm; they'd only wanted money.

She'd fended off dozens of men who assumed that Western women were of loose morals and wouldn't mind being fondled in public. Once corrected in their impressions—an angry shout and mention of their mothers in their native language worked wonders—they'd left her alone.

What Dr. Archer was after was a whole different ball of yak hair. The thump of her heart and the dampness of her palms said she was far from confident she could handle him.

What had she been thinking, to agree to this? Was she nuts? She didn't want to end up helplessly throwing her legs in the air for some creepy megalomaniac, all because she'd been unable to resist a bit of adventure.

Or unable to resist the chance to see the gorgeous Harrison Wiles again.

She grunted in disgust. She was an idiot, getting mixed up in something like this. Perhaps her mother had raised a fool, after all. She should turn around and go back to her own hotel, and forget she'd ever heard of B.L.I.S.S., Archer, or Harrison Wiles.

Instead, as if already under the power of the Yes drug, she stepped off the covered patio at the back of the Hotel Harati and started across the lawn toward the youngish man sitting at a white-painted table. He was fair-haired and slender, and gesturing in frustration to a waiter with a tray of tea things.

A veneer of calm settled over her. Her stomach continued to churn, her armpits to dampen her clothes with sweat, but on the surface she forced herself to relax. She donned a mask of confidence and ease, consciously releasing the tight muscles of her face and shoulders.

She told herself she was a laid-back, capable guide, interviewing for a job that she didn't particularly care whether she got. Archer was just another confused tourist, looking for help and, likely, a meal he could stomach.

She could do this.

The "garden" of the Hotel Harati looked like a large backyard in the States, casually edged with conifers and flower beds, and scattered with wooden lawn furniture. The only other guests present were a tanned, middle-aged woman engrossed in a book and a young couple who still looked half asleep as they sipped their coffee. The single man arguing with the waiter had to be Archer.

Birds chirped. A yellow butterfly fluttered past.

Green, volleyball-sized citrus fruits weighed-down the branches of the tree that shaded Archer and the confused waiter from the morning sun. It was an incongruous setting in which to meet a man bent upon subjugating the women of the world.

"Separate, separate!" Archer was saying, gesturing to the waiter.

"You want milk with your tea?" the waiter asked, concern on his young face, as he started to lift the pot off his tray.

"Yes! Separate! Not in pot! Not *that* tea!"

"Cup of tea? No pot?"

"Black tea. Separate, separate! In pot!" Archer practically shouted.

She felt a faint sense of recognition. Had she met this man before?

"Excuse me," Rachel said, joining them. She looked at the waiter. "A large pot of black tea, no sugar, no milk. Please bring hot milk in a separate pitcher. Please bring a bowl of sugar."

"Ahh!" the waiter said, nodding in relief.

"Dhanyabadh," Rachel said, using the Nepali word for "thank you." She could have given all the instructions in Nepali, but wanted to teach Archer by example how to properly make his request. Like many foreigners, he had mistakenly assumed that deeply fractured English was more comprehensible than clear instructions. Nepalis

51

these days began learning English in grade school.

"Thank you!" Archer said. "That moron kept trying to give me a pot of tea with the milk already mixed in."

Rachel faked a smile, still trying to place him in her memory. He sounded like a typical, impatient American, angry because a country halfway around the world didn't operate exactly like home. Maybe it was just his "type" that she recognized. "It's the way they drink the tea here," she said. "They see no reason to add the milk separately, if you're going to have it anyway."

"I wonder if it even *is* milk," the young doctor grumbled. "God knows what it might really be made of."

Mission or not, she had no interest in engaging in a whine-fest with the man. Time to change the topic. "Rachel Calais," she said, and extended her hand. "You must be Dr. Archer? I've come about the position for a trekking guide."

"Rachel Calais," he said dumbly. "I once knew a . . ." He stared at her; then his eyes widened and he stumbled to his feet. "Rachel?"

A deep uneasiness squirmed in her belly as she looked more carefully at his eyes, the shape of his nose. No, it couldn't be. No, no, no!

"It's Alan! Alan Archer!" he said. "Don't you recognize me? I didn't recognize *you*. No *way*

52

did I recognize you! My God, what are you doing here?"

Crap! How the hell . . . Of all the . . . Crap!

"Alan. I can hardly believe it." She stared at him, stunned into stupidity. "You've bleached your hair. Filled out. I almost didn't know you."

He laughed. "You've changed your hair, too. But I'm glad you didn't forget me completely. You didn't, did you?" he asked eagerly.

"How on earth could I?"

He chuckled. "Yeah. I guess it's not the type of thing one does forget. I certainly never did." He looked into her eyes. "Never."

Oh, God. Of all the people in the world, B.L.I.S.S.'s alleged villain had to be the guy to whom she'd lost her virginity.

She had never thought to see him again. Not in the States, and certainly not in a far-flung corner of the world like Kathmandu. What were the chances? She'd been sixteen at the time, to his twenty-one.

"You really do look different," he said. "You lost weight." His eyes strayed to her breasts, which she knew were about three cup sizes smaller than the last time he'd seen her.

"Thirty pounds. It just sort of falls off you when you live in Asia and walk everywhere. But look at you! A doctor now!"

He shrugged, turning his head shyly. "Yeah. I

had to sell my soul to the air force to pay for the degree, but it was worth it."

"*You,* in the air force? I don't believe it," she said, sitting down. She needed to get off her wobbling knees.

"I hated it." He retook his own seat, still gazing at her in delight.

She laughed, the sound strained. "I imagine you would. No friend of Pamela's could enjoy being in the military."

"How is your sister?"

"Same as always. Finding new causes to fight for. She spent six months living in a tree to protest logging, but at the moment she's focusing her efforts on genetically modified food."

"And your parents?"

She waved the topic away. She was *not* going to discuss that. "Tell me what you're doing here, what this journey is about! God, of all the places to run into you!"

"You know, I'm terribly embarrassed that you saw how incompetent I am. I can't even order tea for myself." He ducked his chin down, a lock of hair falling onto his forehead, and looked at her with clear blue puppy-dog eyes.

She couldn't believe it. *This* was the dastardly Dr. Archer that Wiles and Beti were so concerned about? His gaze held no guile beyond the hope that she might still like him. He was about six feet tall, with sloping shoulders and a body that had been wiry when she knew him, but now had gone soft and full beneath his yellow polo shirt. He didn't look the least bit like a man bent on dominating the women of the world, or even capable of it. He looked more like a golfer.

"I don't know anyone who does get their tea the way they like it, their first week in Nepal," she said, smiling. "Not unless they're a tour guide and know the secret password."

Her chair was too deep to sit back in without slouching, so she settled for leaning an elbow on one of the broad arms and folding a leg up beneath her. The position canted her to the side, leaving her leaning forward intimately, as if she wished to be close to him.

Kee-rist. She'd already been as close as a girl could get.

What she felt most of all was disbelief. How could a man she'd gone to bed with nearly ten years ago possibly be someone who would try to bring a date-rape drug to the world market? Was she such a poor judge of men? She couldn't be. So, Wiles and Beti must be liars, or mistaken. It was on the tip of her tongue to tell Alan everything they had said.

The words were on the verge of spilling out, but then a natural caution exerted itself. It wouldn't hurt to hold her peace for a bit and see if he was the same man he had once seemed to be.

Although, come to think of it, he'd been a little odd even way back when. She'd get some information from him and then decide whether he should be warned about B.L.I.S.S.

She made small talk with him until the waiter returned with the tea. Alan poured her a cup, and as he handed it to her she was aware of his eyes tracing over her face, then down again over her chest.

He hadn't gotten any better at hiding that checking-out of the goods, with age. Twice in five minutes. Charming. She was glad that the neckline of her tunic came almost to her collarbone, and that her bra was thick enough to hide any trace of nipples. She wasn't going to put on free shows for leering men of any degree of familiarity, thank you very much. They could buy her dinner first.

"So what are you *doing* here, Alan?" she asked. "Why do you want to go tromping off into the Himalayas? I never figured you for an outdoors type of guy."

"Would you believe I'm looking for the cure for cancer?"

She shook her head and grinned. "Nope."

"If I stumbled upon one, I wouldn't be disappointed," he said, with more apparent sincerity than she had expected. "Most of the medicines we have now, for both cancer and AIDS, have come from plant sources. You never know what you'll find in the wild. The next billion-dollar medication might be growing on a rotten log somewhere." The speech had a practiced feel to it. Rehearsed?

"So that's really what you're doing? Prospecting, hoping to strike it rich with one lucky plant?" Maybe the Yes drug came from a plant.

"I'm a doctor, Rachel," he said, reproving. "My training is as an internist. If I'd wanted to make millions, I'd have become a plastic surgeon."

"Taking a trek through the mountains seems a haphazard way of finding new plants. Don't drug companies have their own scientists they send out into the wilds? Don't they usually go to rain forests or something? You may come back with nothing of use, or something that has been found a dozen times over, already."

"You let me worry about that," he said, smugly patronizing.

Had he been like that before, smug? She thought he'd been more timid when she knew him, less confident.

She smiled and blinked, trying to look trusting and bubble-brained, and did her Yosemite Sam impression. "So maybe there *is* a cure for AIDS somewhere in dem dere hills." The word "hill" jogged forth a memory. Beti had once told her that legends of Yonam described a mountain with green skin. Was the green skin actually a unique plant?

Alan shrugged, pouring himself more tea. "If there isn't a cure for AIDS, then at least there will be fewer worries about overpopulation. Damned planet's too crowded as it is."

She gaped at him.

He glanced at her, caught her expression, and grinned. "Kidding! I'm just kidding! Jeez, what do you take me for? You know me better than that!"

But she had a feeling he had meant what he had said. She really *didn't* know him that well, either. That's why she'd chosen him to rid her of her virginity in the first place: no ties, no expectations. He'd been "safe" in that she knew circumstances would soon part them, and that with any luck they wouldn't see each other again after those brief two weeks together.

Better to bring the conversation back to safer topics than the virtues of killing off half the planet. "Which districts do you have in mind to visit in this drug search?"

"That, ah, hasn't been quite finalized yet."

Now *that* sounded suspicious. Rachel chewed

her upper lip for a moment, frowning. "If you'll pardon me for saying so . . ."

"Yes?"

"Well, it's just . . . You *do* know, don't you, that there are some areas that are restricted to foreigners? If the places you wish to visit are within them, you'll need special permits from the government. You'll have to get them before the trip begins—if you can get them at all."

He waved away her concern. "There's no problem with any of that."

"No?"

"I know the secret password," he said, using her term. He smiled and tucked his chin down again.

She raised an eyebrow. "Money?"

"I have carte blanche for wherever I wish to go." He sounded pleased with himself.

"I'm impressed," she said, and to some degree meant it. She had yet to fully master the art of the bribe, herself. The flat gazes of petty officials always made her too nervous to pull it off gracefully.

He shrugged, and she could tell he was trying not to smile at the compliment. She smiled herself, pretending to warmth and a shy attraction. She looked down, then raised her eyes and held his gaze.

He put his free hand over hers, the delight in

his regard flaming into something brighter and more intense. She had the impulse to pull back, but quelled it.

"Think what a great team we'll make," Alan said. "How could I ever find anyone better for a guide? If you want the job, it's yours."

Heaven help her, Rachel thought. She was hired.

Alan ran his finger over Rachel Calais's name on the résumé she had left him. Stroking it. Possessing it.

It was his heart more than his head that had made him offer her the job so quickly. He hadn't been thinking, hadn't been cautious, but he had been powerless to do any different.

He'd been looking for a female guide anyway, though. Once Yonam was discovered and the truth of what he sought revealed, a woman would try to stop him from fulfilling his plan. Conveniently, she would be utterly helpless to do so.

The thought made him giggle.

What a shock to have Rachel Calais come strolling across the lawn and back into his life. Never in a million years would he have expected to see her here, and never would he have thought she'd turn out to be such a stunner. She had been sort of cute at sixteen, in a plump, studious sort of way, and a wild thing when it came to bed. She had wanted him to do *everything* to her, as if she thought their few times together would be her only chance ever to experience sex.

He felt a flush of embarrassment at just how little he'd had to show her. Twenty-one-year-old guys did not make the best lovers.

Then, too soon, she'd been gone from his life, their lives taking them elsewhere. She'd remained a goddess of his sexual fantasies, though, for both her enthusiasm and her big breasts.

Pity the breasts had shrunk.

Other than that, though, Rachel was everything he could want. She was attractive, and smart enough to see his true value.

She'd have to get rid of her nose stud, though, if she wanted to become his again. And the hair. She'd be a knockout as a blonde. Wouldn't they look great together, with matching hair? The ethnic clothes she could keep: They showed she possessed the natural modesty of a true lady, at least on the surface. There was something in their flowing foreignness, too, that made him think of harems.

He imagined Rachel lying on a bed of pillows, naked but for that long, filmy scarf, the fabric half hiding her pink nipples and the bare folds of her sex. He'd shave her pubic hair for her, and she'd moan while he did it.

He half closed his eyes, the image bringing a warm flush of pleasure. He knew what he'd be thinking about in the shower tonight.

When this trek was finished, he would be a king in this world. There would be no woman who could keep her legs closed against him. Every king, though, needed a queen, a "first wife" in the harem, whose loyalty and adoration were unquestioned. If she proved worthy of the role, Rachel Calais might be lucky enough to become that queen by his side.

He could barely wait for the expedition to begin.

Chapter Four

"What the hell am I going to need *that* for?" Rachel cried, staring in horror at the black stun gun in Beti's hand. Beti, Wiles, and she were in her hotel room. This was the first time she'd seen them since she got the job with Archer two days ago, and they'd arrived bearing gifts.

The saying about gifts and Greeks appeared to apply as well to Nepalis and Brits. Beware, beware, beware.

"It won't kill anyone," Beti said, and pressed a button. A bolt of blue electricity zapped between the two metal prongs at the end of the device, and reflected in the lenses of Beti's glasses.

Rachel's opinion of the woman as a quiet academic was undergoing revision. The prongs looked like the mandibles of a robotic insect, and Beti seemed unnaturally fascinated.

"It will immobilize him for several minutes," Beti said. "It will not feel good, but there will be no damage."

Rachel shuddered. "I don't know if I could use that on anyone. It's like a shock collar on a dog, or a cattle prod."

"You could use it," Wiles said. He was sitting cross-legged on the second twin bed in the small room, a duffel bag full of further goodies beside him. Today he wore chinos, a faded navy-blue T-shirt, and a black plastic expedition watch on his wrist. It was the costume of a hundred Nepalese young men, but he failed to look average in it, or to blend into the scenery.

She couldn't help noticing that the hair on the back of his forearms was so fine as to be nearly invisible, and every time he gestured with his hand she could see the fine muscles and tendons at work.

Curse him. She was a sucker for well-toned forearms.

Curse him as well for looking so good in casual clothes. Some of his handsomeness should have been due to the tuxedo and lamplight of the other night, but daylight was just as kind. If anything, daylight made him look younger. She guessed him to be no more than a year or two older than herself, maybe twenty-six or twenty-seven.

It was perverse and insane, she knew, but with every pulse of attraction she felt for him, she felt an even stronger need to push him away. She'd rather he thought she loathed him than have him pick up on the girlish, hormonal flutterings of her heart. Such physical appeal as he possessed scared her silly.

Which left her acting as if she had the social skills of a middle school boy suffering his first crush.

Rachel took the stun gun from Beti, feeling the weight of it in her palm. Nausea roiled in her belly at the thought of using it on a living creature. "I'm not bringing this. It's unnecessary, and too heavy to pack around."

"If Archer attacks you, wouldn't you want to have something with you?" Wiles asked.

"He wouldn't do that. He likes me." These past two days had been spent shopping with Alan, gathering the supplies and equipment they would need for the trek. He was proving himself to be both an attentive companion and an occasionally annoying one, especially given his xenophobic tendencies.

She hadn't yet mentioned to Wiles or Beti her past history with Alan. It had occurred to her that B.L.I.S.S. likely knew of her past association with the man, and the coincidence of her knowing their "villain" was too big for her to swallow. She wanted to see if either Wiles or Beti would admit to their knowledge.

Also, on the remote chance that B.L.I.S.S. did *not* know, remaining mum seemed the wisest course. Rachel needed time to figure out what everyone was really up to.

" 'Liking you' may be just the reason he tries such a thing," Wiles continued. "If you aren't open to his advances, he may force the issue. This isn't a man who patiently woos women, content to suffer obstacles and rejection on the path to his true love's heart."

The Brit's patronizing tone made Rachel grind her teeth. Was he trying to prod her into admitting she'd slept with the guy? "I'm a big girl. I know how to handle men who make passes."

"Or maybe he doesn't want to make one," Wiles said, musing almost to himself. She saw his gaze flick to her hair. "You may not be his type."

"You think he couldn't desire me?" she snapped. She narrowed her eyes and leaned forward across the slim gap between the beds, pointing her finger at him, stabbing him on the chest with it. It was a very hard chest. "No matter your own opinion, I am not a gap-toothed hag that no man would ever want."

From the corner of her eye she saw Beti gaping at her, eyes round as coins.

Wiles gently grasped her stabbing finger, stopping her. "I never said you were unattractive," he said from between tight lips.

She jerked her hand out of his hold. "You didn't have to. It was clear enough on your face when we met."

"I was surprised by your hair, but any other interpretation is purely your own. If you assumed I thought you ugly, then you have your own hang-ups to blame, not me."

"Oh!" she gasped. "It's a good thing you're not going to be on this trek. I would shove you off a mountain before half a day had passed."

A slow smile spread across Wiles's face. Beti cleared her throat. A cold wash of panic ran down Rachel's body. No, surely not. . . .

"As a matter of fact," Wiles said, "the question has been reviewed, and I am indeed to accompany you—in the role of a mountaineering expert."

"No," she said, in a denial born of fear.

"It's not for you to decide."

"Isn't it? Dr. Archer has given me complete authority in the hiring of support crew. You're not coming." She sounded weak even to her own ears, like a whining three-year-old.

"Use your brain, Rachel. I know you have one,

if your school records are any indication. You'll be far safer with a trained professional on your side, than alone with this Dr. Archer in the wilderness."

"You're not helping your case by bringing up my school records or the file your B.L.I.S.S. has on me. You wouldn't like me to start talking about your school days in England or some of your rugby chums like good ol' Geoffrey, would you?"

He stared at her in blank-faced surprise, and she felt a spurt of triumph.

He didn't take her bait, though. Instead, he leaned back on his hands, one eyebrow raised. "I've been wondering, since we're on the topic. Why did you give up on your Ph.D.? Precious few people have ever been in pursuit of one at such a young age. I would think that it bespoke a certain devotion to school."

The question took her off guard, and she stared at him with no words with which to answer. It wasn't the Ph.D. she had given up on, so much as everything else. If he didn't know what had happened, though, she wasn't going to illuminate him. "It's none of your business why I quit my studies," she answered.

"I'd like to know whom I'll be following, since you are so adamant on being the leader," he pressed, unperturbed.

She hated him acting so calm and collected.

"Follow my orders, and you'll be just fine."

"That's a useful attitude," he retorted.

Was that a bit of dander going up? Good! She'd gnaw on any Achilles' heel she could find. "You're the one who insisted on coming on this trip. If you want to know more about me, consult your file."

His jaw tightened, but he didn't say anything. Perhaps that file on her was thinner than she had thought. And maybe, even if the powers-that-be at B.L.I.S.S. knew about her previous relationship to Alan, they had chosen not to tell Wiles.

Her lips curled in a cat-in-the-cream smirk. She liked that thought, although it created its own host of new questions.

Wiles was staring at her, and she began to feel uncomfortable under his gaze. It was as if he were trying to read her mind. He spoke slowly, seeming to find the words as he went. "Most people who leave their own countries to wander for years in other parts of the world are running away from something. Is there something you're avoiding?"

She suddenly saw the faces of her parents in her mind's eye. *No, no, no!* She would not think of them. No! But, with her caught unaware like that, her eyes began to sting; hurt clenched at her chest.

She forced her thoughts onto cinnamon rolls.

A new backpack she wanted. A paperback she'd been reading. Anything, anything to distract her. Nothing captured her thoughts, though; her parents' faces slipped back into her mind.

Desperate, she set her eyes on Wiles's crotch. Maybe *that* could distract her. She imagined him sitting there naked. What would he look like, *down there*? Was it all shrunken up and floppy right now, nestled against a fluffy bed of black hair? Maybe it was silky hair. Maybe he trimmed it, or used conditioner. She'd done that once, to herself, but it hadn't seemed to make a difference.

The threat of tears left her eyes, all thoughts of her parents pushed away.

Was he circumcized? Did he have darker skin at the top, or freckles along the sides?

Did he play with it?

She silently sniffed back the running of her nose, feeling much better. He was probably quite lovely down there, and she wouldn't mind meeting it in person.

She glanced at Wiles's face and saw him frowning at her. He pulled the edge of the duffel bag over his crotch. She made herself meet his gaze full-on, her shoulders tense, willing any last trace of trembling from her mouth. She knew her eyes must have the red-rimmed look of incipient tears.

Alarm lit his face. He lifted a hand as if about to reach out to her.

The last thing she wanted was for him to feel sorry for her. "My past is not germane to this discussion," she snapped, her voice squeaky. "And I'd appreciate it if you refrained from any further mention of my private life."

He said nothing, then nodded, once, and dropped his hand. She thought he'd probably agree to anything as long as it kept her from crying. Cliché as it sounded, men never could stand tears.

Silence stretched, broken at last by Beti. Rachel had almost forgotten she was in the room.

"You do need Wiles on this trek," the Nepali woman said. "You're not trained to handle Archer on your own, especially not if he truly *does* like you. His type is prone to obsession, and you'll want a friend with you."

A friend. Was that supposed to be Wiles? "He'll just overstep his place, and tick Alan off," she snapped.

"It's 'Alan' already, is it?" Wiles asked.

"Oh, for God's sake. You see what I mean?" she said to Beti. She turned back to Wiles. "We're American. We can hardly call each other 'Dr.' and 'Mz.' This isn't going to work if you keep treating me as if I'm incapable of doing anything on my own. I survived quite well up till now without your help, thank you very much."

"You just sounded rather familiar with him, for two days' acquaintance. Almost cozy."

She raised her eyebrows and looked expectant, waiting for more. Was he going to confess his knowledge now? "Didn't someone once say that you should keep your friends close, but your enemies closer?" she asked.

"Sounds a foolish plan to me," he retorted. "A smart woman would keep her friends by her side, to protect her from her enemies."

Arrogant ass! "A *smart* woman." Oh! "At least Alan treats me with respect and trusts me. Strange qualities, don't you think, for a man allegedly bent on subjugating the women of the world? And what do I really know about your B.L.I.S.S. organization, anyway? Why should I be trusting your version of events? Maybe *you* are the bad guy, and maybe there really is no B.L.I.S.S."

"Archer is an evil man behind a fair face," Wiles said, his ire showing. "If you can't see that, then God save us all from the poor judgment of women like you!"

"Oh!" Rachel was so angry, she couldn't speak. This freakin' male chauvinist! Women like her, huh? Her grip tightened on the stun gun that was still in her hand, and electricity zapped between the prongs. "Oh! I could just—"

Wiles's eyes widened, and he scooted back on the bed. "Wait a minute, just wait a minute—"

She grinned, lifting the stun gun in front of her. "Wouldn't I like to! Wouldn't I!" She pressed the button, electricity zapping again. "No lasting harm, after all!"

Wiles held up his hands. "Now, Rachel . . ."

She feinted toward him. He jerked away, lost his balance, and fell backward off the bed with a scramble of limbs and a thud. Soft cursing came from behind the mattress.

The top of Wiles's head appeared over the edge of the bed, cautiously peeking.

Rachel shook her head and tossed the stun gun onto the mattress where he had been sitting, the anger gone now. She was disgusted with the whole scene. "I told you I couldn't use that on anyone."

"That wasn't funny," the man said, emerging from the space between bed and wall. He got to his feet and brushed off bits of carpet fuzz, looking like an offended cat trying to preserve its dignity after falling in the toilet.

A hint of mirth curled Rachel's lips. She wondered if Wiles ironed his T-shirts and got his nails manicured. She wouldn't doubt it, given the way he was trying to bring his disarranged fur back into order.

He saw her amusement, and glared. "That was simply childish of you."

Her smile broke free, and she grinned. "Yes, wasn't it? I feel *so* much better now, thank you."

It might not be so bad to have Wiles on the trek, after all. How she'd love to see him dealing with the dirt and sweat! "Do you actually have any mountaineering experience?" she asked sweetly.

"I do. I've done considerable climbing in both the Alps and the Himalayas," he said, chin high. "How about you—do *you* have any mountaineering experience?"

"Of course not. Do I look like a nut? That type of sport is for adrenaline junkies. I have no intention of going anywhere that requires either ropes or pickaxes."

"It's not just about adrenaline. It's about pitting your abilities against the challenge of the mountain, about discovering something inside—" Wiles began, then cut himself off. "Why bother explaining? You would have no desire to understand." He frowned at her, as if expecting her to dispute his statement.

She raised her eyebrows and let the statement lie.

"And they're called *ice* axes, not *pick* axes," Wiles added. "Just so you know."

"Whatever. I'm not going anywhere that requires them. Nor those gawd-awful ice cleats," she said, enjoying herself. Seeing him fall off the bed had done wonders for her humor. She was feeling almost civil toward him.

"Crampons," he grumped.

"Sounds like a feminine hygiene product."

He winced.

"Anyway," Rachel went on, "I don't know why Alan should believe that we need a mountaineer. No one lives at the altitudes where mountaineering is done, so why would we need a mountaineer to find Yonam?"

Wiles sat back down on the bed, using exaggerated care to move the stun gun far from Rachel's reach. "This is a hidden city we are trying to find. There's a good chance that we may have to go over a mountain to get to it. It may be at the bottom of a valley that is unreachable through any known pass, and thus its long isolation from the world."

"Damn. You're right."

He looked at her in surprise.

"Hey, I can admit when you have a point," she said.

A reluctant pleasure joined the wariness on his face and she almost smiled, recognizing a similar soul. He liked being right as much as she did.

Beti spoke up. "The legends about Yonam always speak of a series of obstacles that must be overcome to reach the city. Most scholars believe the obstacles are symbolic of stages of spiritual growth."

"But you believe they are literal?" Rachel asked.

Beti waggled her head from side to side, non-committal. "That is for you and Harrison to discover. The obstacles vary from tale to tale, but a river of ice is usually mentioned. Sometimes a wall of fire. There *always* seems to be a yeti."

"The abominable snowman. Terrific. This is sounding like more fun every moment."

"If it *is* literal," Wiles said, "it's probably nothing more than a statue or a carving."

"Let's hope so." With Rachel's luck, it would be as real as the hill people claimed.

"Has Dr. Archer shown you yet a map of where he intends to search for Yonam?" Beti asked.

"No. He's being quite cagey about where he wants to go. I think he wants to keep our destination to himself until we've left Kathmandu. It's making it difficult to prepare properly, when I don't know how long this trek will take, or what conditions to expect. I'm going to end up with a whole pack full of trekking maps, to cover all the possibilities of where we might end up."

"Perhaps you can use that reason to push him for more information," Beti suggested.

Rachel sighed. "I've tried."

"Try harder," Wiles prodded.

Just when she was starting to feel friendly toward him, he had to go and be jerky again. She rolled her eyes, to show him how well he intimidated her. "Give it *up*, already. You don't scare me. You have no control over me. I'm not part of your little 'B.L.I.S.S.' army," she said, making quotation marks in the air with her fingers.

"You still haven't grasped how real this is, have you?" Wiles asked in disbelief.

The look on his face pricked her with uncertainty. She backed off and tried to keep the smart-aleck tone out of her voice. "Why don't you try convincing me again? Tell me how you even know that Alan is pursuing this mythical Yes drug. He told me he was looking for new medicines for things like cancer and AIDS."

Wiles sighed and ran his hand through his hair. Rachel was temporarily distracted by the glossy black waves, and the muscles in his forearms. His hands weren't bad, either: They were large and strong, and of that same perfectly even skin tone of his face and arms. They were hands a woman would enjoy having upon her skin.

Vague, half-formed thoughts of how those hands could touch her flitted through her mind. A wash of desire spiraled down into her loins, and was as quickly followed by a frightened sense of vulnerability.

She revised her opinion that it would be amusing to have Wiles on the trek. She behaved like a bad-tempered teenager whenever she was around him. It was defensiveness, obviously, but she couldn't stop herself from doing it. She was attracted to him, but with his perfect looks and dashing career he was obviously out of her league. If she valued her pride and fragile sense of self, she would keep all the mountains of the Himalaya between them.

"This all started about two years ago, in Bangkok," Wiles said. "One of our agents started hearing stories about a drug that made sexual slaves out of normal women. Usually it was a tourist who gave it to the woman; a foreign businessman, someone with money to spend, and with the urge for something 'cleaner' than the usual prostitute.

"The source of the drug was traced back to a Nepalese man named Durga. Rumor had it that he used the money from the drug to buy heroin. Before our agent could locate him, though, he had left the city.

"His trail was picked up again a year later, on Kho Samui, off the coast of Thailand. There are lots of tourist dollars there, and Durga went to where the money was. By the time our agent found him, though, he was dead."

"What?" Rachel cried, startled out of her reverie on Wiles's sex appeal. "How?"

"Heroin overdose. Maybe. Or a morphine overdose, administered by someone with a ready, pharmaceutical-grade supply."

"You're saying Alan killed him?" She couldn't believe that.

"When our agent located Durga's hut, there was someone coming out of it carrying an old backpack. She decided to follow him, in case he was going to drug some woman. She followed him to a bar, and then back to the pier, where she heard one of the hands call him by name: Dr. Archer. He boarded a tender and rode it out to his ship where our agent couldn't follow.

"When she returned to Durga's hut, she found him dead. There was no visible cause, and the authorities assumed it was an overdose."

"So you still don't know how Durga died," Rachel suggested. "Alan may have just come upon his dead body."

"It would be an unlikely coincidence," Wiles said.

"No more unlikely than that Alan murdered him, I should think."

Wiles shrugged, obviously unconvinced, and continued. "Durga's belongings, or what was left of them, were scattered around his hut. Our agent found no trace of the Yes drug, nor any piece of identification. Archer had obviously stolen everything he thought was of use.

"There was nothing B.L.I.S.S. could do about Archer at the time except keep tabs on him. We didn't know if he had any of the drug, or intended to either use it or synthesize it if he did. For a while, keeping tabs was all that we did.

"Then Archer started asking a lot of questions about mountain villages and willing women, in every port into which he sailed. He eventually quit his job with the cruise line and showed up here, in Kathmandu.

"It was Beti who put the pieces together for us and explained about the legend of Yonam."

Rachel chewed on her lower lip. "So, for all you know Alan might have some 'Yes' with him?"

"We're guessing not," Wiles assured her. "Perhaps Durga had sold all he had. As I said the other night, all Archer needs is a gram of the stuff—about a teaspoonful, if it is a dried plant, as we suspect—to be able to chemically analyze and reproduce it. There would be no need to go to the trouble of finding Yonam if he already had some of it in his possession."

"Unless his goal is to destroy the possible source of future competition," Rachel said. "He may have synthesized the drug already, and be working solely to ensure his monopoly."

"It's possible," Wiles admitted. "But not likely. Pharmaceutical companies can use samples of the drug he produces to copy it for themselves. His monopoly will last only a short time, no matter what."

"He won't have some sort of copyright on it?"

"Patent. He'll likely apply for one."

"Seems like a strange thing to do, for a drug that will be outlawed," Rachel mused.

"Outlawed in the U.S. for certain, but permitted in most other countries, and even in the U.S. they may find a use for the drug, unrelated to the granting of sexual favors. A patent will protect his right to sell the formula, and to sue those companies who try to steal it.

"If he's smart," Wiles went on, "he'll hit the market large and fast. Even if he's copied, he'll make his fortune before the companies in India or South America start churning out their own versions." Wiles leaned forward, his expression intent. "But our goal is to stop this from getting anywhere *near* that point. We have a unique opportunity to stop a disaster of worldwide proportions right at the start."

"Why not ask the Nepalese government to help stop him?" Rachel asked.

"Would you trust a group of men to completely destroy such a drug?" he asked back. "Especially when there is the potential for such vast profit?"

He had a point. "Then why not just shoot him and be done with it?" Rachel asked, half serious.

Wiles smiled, sitting back again. "The John Wayne answer. Americans. 'Just shoot him!' So much for your 'I couldn't hurt anyone' policy." He shook his head.

Rachel tightened her lips, annoyed at getting caught in such an obvious contradiction.

"The agents of B.L.I.S.S. are not murderers," Wiles explained. "Whatever information Archer has on the location of Yonam, using it is our best chance to find the source of the drug before some other yahoo gets the clever idea to go look. If Archer is looking for the city now, someone else surely will be looking for it later. Information like this doesn't just disappear in the modern world. And besides . . ." Wiles trailed off.

"Yes?"

He grimaced. "Technically, we have no evidence of Archer's intentions to synthesize 'Yes.' We can't do him harm on speculation alone."

"So, for all you know, he really could be looking for a cancer treatment," she said.

"It's unlikely."

"He could even be looking for Yonam for purely anthropological reasons," Rachel argued, pouncing on the possibility although even she did not believe it. It was definitely more comfortable to believe that Alan might be innocent. That kept away the fear, and the undigestible thought that she'd slept with such a total creep. "Maybe he's been dreaming of seeing himself in his own PBS special on the lost city of Yonam."

"We don't think so." Wiles laughed without humor. "And absence of evidence is not absence of guilt."

"But how can Alan be that evil?" Rachel asked plaintively, not even expecting an answer. "How could anyone consciously release such a drug onto the world market?"

Wiles smiled bitterly, his expression saying he had expected no different from her. "We can't sense evil in a person, much as we might like to think we can," he said. "We like to tell ourselves we'd know a murderer if he sat down beside us, but the truth is we might think him an exceptionally well-mannered gentleman, a kind, cultured fellow with whom we'd like to have tea."

His words unsettled her, his expression telling her she was foolishly naive. If she couldn't count on any natural ability to tell the good guys from the bad, though, then how was she going to make the right decisions? Could she really be so unable to sense evil in a person, even one she had been so close to?

Beti seemed to sense how she was feeling. "You won't be alone on the trail with Dr. Archer, not now that Harrison will be there. He will, as you Americans say, 'watch your behind.' "

"Will he? I hope he enjoys the view. No touching, though—at least not before the first date."

"Her *back!*" Wiles corrected Beti, with a glare at Rachel. "I'll watch her *back!*"

"Or you could say he'll 'cover my ass,' " Rachel continued helpfully, "although that may hold connotations he's not ready for, the poor prudish dear."

Wiles waved his hands in the air, apparently embarrassed. It was an Achilles' heel to remember. She *did* so enjoy seeing him squirm. And maybe the best way to hide her attraction was to lust and leer, to pretend it was all fake.

"Your 'ass' is different from your 'behind', yes?" Beti asked, a delicate frown of concentration between her eyebrows.

"It's pretty much the same piece of equipment."

"Then I shall use 'back.' I think 'ass' is perhaps not such a nice word."

"Men seem to like it well enough, in both the literal and figurative senses. Don't they, Wiles? Or are you a breast man?"

He made a small, strangled sound.

Who'd have thought he'd be so shy on sexual

topics? Rachel wanted to clap her hands, she was so delighted.

"Here, you need to see the rest of your equip—er, stuff," Wiles said, digging determinedly in the duffel bag beside him, his cheeks red, obviously attempting to change the topic. He pulled out a pair of what looked like short binoculars attached to head straps. "Night-vision goggles." He passed them over to her.

"You've got to be kidding. Why on earth would I need these?" she asked, finally distracted from the ass conversation. She hefted the goggles' weight in her hand.

Wiles stood in the space between the beds, took the goggles from her, and started to jam them onto her head.

"Ow! Hey! What are you doing?" She cried out as straps went behind her head and another caught the tip of her ear, folding it down. She reached up to bat his hands away, but he ignored her and kept shoving and adjusting.

"Now wait a moment," he said as she blinked through the lenses, the weight of the goggles pulling her head forward.

He jogged over to the window and yanked the curtains shut, then jogged back to her and flipped a switch on the side of the apparatus. There was a quiet electronic hum, and everything went green. Already looking down, Rachel saw her hands in that dull green shade familiar from watching CNN reports of night battle excursions. She raised her head. Wiles was looking at her with the luminous eyes of a demon.

"Bweh!" she cried, jerking back.

"Cool, aren't they?" he asked, with the eagerness of a little boy. She realized that it was the reflective back of his pupils she was seeing, much the way one saw the eyes of a cat or dog "glowing" in headlights.

She looked at Beti, whose eyes were also lit up behind her glasses. The Nepali looked like the incarnation of a particularly malevolent Hindu goddess.

"Okay, so the goggles are cool," she admitted, "but what use are they on this trek? I sure as hell don't want to lug them around for no reason."

Wiles took them from her and slipped them on over his own head, sounding not in the least put off by her lack of enthusiasm. "We like to prepare for *all* eventualities."

"Huh. Are you sure you don't want them just because they're a fun toy?"

Wiles took off the goggles and tossed them onto the bed, opened the curtains, then dug again into his duffel. "We'll take the goggles. But if you want to talk about fun toys, look at this!" He handed her a black plastic device with a thick antenna stuck on its side.

"A cell phone?" she said, taking it. And a rather large one, at that.

"Satellite phone. It will work almost any-where, as long as you have an unobstructed view of the sky. But that's not all." He sought out a latch in the phone's side, his fingertips brushing along her own. She watched the movements of his fingers, and the flexing in the back of his hand, losing herself in the motions and the brief touches to her own skin. She could feel the warmth of his body as he leaned over her.

"There!" he said, and opened the phone like a book, revealing an LCD screen on one half, and a small keyboard on the other. "We can stay on-line wherever we go. Not only that, but there's a built-in global-positioning system. B.L.I.S.S. will be informed of exactly where we are each time we connect to the satellite. There's a digital cam-era and microphone . . . here," he said, touching a set of small holes at the top end. "We can also download images from space of the terrain we are crossing. You won't need to rely solely on that rucksack full of maps."

"I'll keep the hard copies, just the same," she said. She did not trust the infallibility of com-puters. Pressing the power button, she watched the screen as the computer came alive. She could shop on eBay with this thing. Maybe she'd sell Wiles. Post a digital picture of him and see how high the bidding went. "Anything else in that bag?" she asked.

"These," he said, taking a small cardboard box out of his bag of tricks. "Standard issue. For emergency use." He tossed the box to her, then looked away.

She caught the box and, curious, turned it so the label faced her.

For a long moment she couldn't understand what she was reading. The words were in plain English, but they came as too much of a shock for her to take in the implication.

And then comprehension *did* come.

A cold white rage froze her belly and sent icy fury through her veins. She pitched the box back at his face, the corner catching him above the eye and digging a bloody nick out of his forehead.

"You frickin' pimp! I am *not* going to need a box of condoms!"

Chapter Five

"You should not hate him because he is beautiful," Beti said softly.

Rachel was lying on her back on the now-vacant bed where Wiles had sat. She lowered her arms from over her eyes and rolled her head to the side to stare at the woman she had thought was her friend. "Tell me you didn't just quote a shampoo commercial to me."

"I beg your pardon?"

Rachel sighed. "Never mind."

"His face, it is like looking at someone very ugly, or of another race."

"An alien race," Rachel muttered, "from Neptune."

Beti made an impatient sound. "When you become familiar with such a person, you stop seeing the surface. You start seeing who he is beneath. Then you forget the scars, or the different nose, or the lighter skin."

"I don't hate Wiles because he's handsome," Rachel lied. Handsome, sure of himself, possessed of purpose and conviction. All things she lacked.

She rolled onto her side and propped herself up on an elbow. "I hate Wiles because he's arrogant and thinks I'm a slut. Condoms, he gave me! Wouldn't you be insulted?" Thank God he didn't seem to know about her history with Alan.

"Bringing them on the trek is like bringing antibiotics. You will hope there is never a need, but will be happy to have them if there is."

"That's not a straight answer, Beti. Tell me you wouldn't be insulted."

Beti looked down at her hands for a long moment, her lips tight, and then she met Rachel's gaze. "I would not have the courage to go on such a mission. The dangers are real. I would not put myself within reach of one such as Dr. Archer."

Beti's fear was contagious, and she felt a quiver of uncertainty about her judgment of Alan. Not for the first time, Rachel wondered what she was getting herself into. It would be safer if she forgot she had ever heard of

B.L.I.S.S., and went back to her regular tour guide duties.

Safer, yes. But bo-ring.

"I doubt Wiles will do anything to keep me out of Alan's sleeping bag if he thinks my being there will help him get to Yonam," Rachel said.

Beti shook her head. "You underestimate Harrison and his moral sense. He will do everything in his power to keep you safe and your honor intact."

"You could have fooled me." Not that she'd ever been particularly bothered by traditional versions of female "honor." She had let impatient curiosity prompt her to seduce Alan when she was just sixteen, after all. The difference was that she'd wanted to go to bed with him then, whereas the thought held no appeal now. To her, sex was honorable as long as it was something she honestly wanted to do and the guy was single.

"I am sorry, Rachel, but you are wrong about Harrison," Beti said quietly. "Did you read in the *Kathmandu Post* about the prostitution ring that was broken in the Terai?"

The Terai was the hot, flat region in the south of Nepal, bordering India. It was known that young, poor Nepalese girls were sometimes taken through the Terai into India to become prostitutes. A large ring of such traders in human flesh had been arrested last week. "Yes, I read about it," Rachel said.

"Harrison was one of the B.L.I.S.S. agents who infiltrated the group, and was crucial in breaking the ring. That's why he was invited to the party at the Yak and Yeti."

"Oh."

What did one say to *that*? So not only was Harrison disgustingly handsome, but he was a hero, too.

Rachel was a coward at heart, who had run away from what was left of her life. Wiles had been right about that.

Whose bright idea *was* it, anyway, to send her on this mission?

"Beti, who is it who runs B.L.I.S.S.? Who chose me for this?"

Beti was silent for a few moments, then reached a decision in her head and answered. "We call her 'Y.' I do not know her real name."

Rachel blinked. "You don't? Have you never met her?"

Beti shook her head. "I've spoken to her on the phone a few times. She must keep much secret for B.L.I.S.S. to be a success. I think she may have a public role and could be recognized."

Rachel chewed her lip, searching the uncertainties of her heart. "I would feel better if I could meet her, or at least talk to her."

The Nepalese woman smiled slightly but said nothing. Rachel took it to mean that she could not yet be trusted with firsthand knowledge of the esteemed Y. It did nothing for her confidence. "I don't know if I can do this, Beti," she confessed softly.

Several seconds of silence passed, and when Beti spoke it was in a slow, serious tone. "Of all the foreign guides I have met, you are the only one I know to be capable of this mission. You have your head glued tight to your shoulders, Rachel. I am not fooled by your wild hair or your joking manner. You are stronger than you think, and braver. Do not tell me that I am wrong in my judgment of you. I will not let you disappoint me."

Rachel grimaced at her friend. How could she disappoint Beti? "If you put it that way, I don't have a choice, do I?"

Ready or not, a spy for B.L.I.S.S. she would become.

She spent the rest of the day finishing up the arrangements for a Nepalese trekking guide and four porters, asking the former to choose men he had worked with before.

The Nepalese guide was a necessity, as he could ask questions of and receive favors from locals that a foreigner like herself could not, even with her middling command of Nepali. She had worked before with the one she chose, Min. He had a few personality quirks, but she trusted him to get them to wherever they wanted to go.

She had had a brief fling with him herself half a year ago, too, but that shouldn't be a problem. They had remained on friendly terms, both having taken it for what it was: a romp for the fun of it. She'd been lonely and stereotypically easy, and he'd been more enthusiastic than tender or skilled. He'd always been gentleman enough to remain quiet about it, too.

With those chores done, she had a couple of hours free before dinner. She, Alan, Min, and Wiles would be meeting at Fire & Ice, an Italian restaurant that served the best pizza in Nepal. She was hoping that good, familiar food would help Alan digest that Wiles was to be part of the team. Alan had a phobia about the hygiene in restaurants run solely by Nepalis.

He probably kept his mouth closed tight in the shower, and only brushed his teeth with bottled water, too. Rachel smiled to herself. He'd get the runs sooner or later, no matter his precautions. Everyone did.

The satellite-linked phone/computer sat on her bed beside a growing pile of crumpled tissues, brochures, and receipts. Beti had shown her how to use the gadget, and assured her that all connection costs would be absorbed by B.L.I.S.S.

Could Rachel assume that B.L.I.S.S. would not pry into her e-mail and track her as she wove through the Internet, though? Not if she had a brain cell left in her head, she couldn't.

She shouldered her day pack, wrapped a pashmina over her shoulders against the chill of the evening, and headed out. Five minutes' walk through streets still crowded with honking cars, pedestrians, motorcycles, and rickshaws, and she found another out-of-the-way Internet café. She logged on to Hotmail and then sat staring at the screen in indecision.

Her previous attempts at gathering information on B.L.I.S.S. had been a bust, but there was yet one source she had not tapped: her nutty, brilliant sister, Pamela.

Pamela had a wide and unusual circle of friends and acquaintances, gathered over her years as an activist. Not all of them were fruit loops. Some were professionals, a few were in law enforcement, others came from wealthy families with political ties. If anyone Rachel knew could find out about B.L.I.S.S., it would be Pamela pulling the strings of her wide network.

One e-mail was all it would take.

One e-mail, explaining everything she knew, and for the first time in years asking her sister for help. Not that she could count on Pamela to give it.

When their parents died, Pamela had been a wailing, emotional mess. Claiming herself too distraught, she'd left Rachel to do the hard work of making funeral arrangements. While Rachel had gone into their parents' closets to choose the clothes in which they would be buried—weeping as she held her mother's favorite blouse, her father's favorite tie—Pamela had sat in the living room, talking to friends, absorbing their sympathy and caring.

Pamela had left her to deal with the lawyer and insurance agents. To sell the house. To settle debts and close accounts and sweep up all the detritus of two lives abruptly ended.

She'd hugged Rachel and whispered in her ear that they'd "get through this together," but had been precious little help in doing so.

The uselessness of her sister had felt like an abandonment on top of the loss. Rachel had come away knowing that there was no one left to count on, no one left in this world to take care of her but herself.

Knowledge, though, was power. She would be wise to go as well armed as she could manage into the wilds, no matter that she had to go to Pamela to do so.

She opened up a new letter and addressed it

to her sister. For the next forty minutes she typed in all that she knew, and all that had been planned. When she was done she sat back and read it over, corrected a few typos, and then moved the cursor over to the "send" button.

And paused.

This e-mail, if sent, might bring her the information she sought.

It might also spread the story of Yonam far and wide. Pamela would see no reason to keep secrets, if she thought a cause could be best served by broadcasting facts or suspicions. She was fond of conspiracy theories, and saw it as her duty to expose evil cabalists to the public eye.

Such publicity was the last thing Rachel wanted. On the off chance that the Yes drug was real, the fewer people who knew about it, the better.

Rachel highlighted all but one paragraph of the e-mail, and hit "delete." On the nearly blank page she wrote a cheerful account of her latest minor adventures and then added:

Guess what! Alan Archer is here in Kathmandu! Do you remember him, from way back? He's a doctor now. I'm going to take him on a trek into the Himalayas. Should be fun! He asked me to say hi.

She asked Pamela general questions about her own battles against the genetically modified food companies and Congress, and then, in the post-script, wrote:

P.S. I met someone who claimed to belong to a nongovernmental organization called B.L.I.S.S. I'm not sure, but they might do some sort of international work related to women's issues. I've never heard of them. Have you?

There. Nothing to raise alarm, or invite any "constructive" criticism.

She sat back and hit "send."

Chapter Six

Harrison slouched against the wall at the busy entrance to Fire & Ice, waiting for Rachel, Archer, and Min to show up. Voices speaking Western tongues came to him from the outdoor seating area, along with the mingled scents of Italian food and cigarette smoke.

Despite his slouched posture and dull expression, he was aware of everything going on around him. He detected nothing out of the ordinary, no one besides himself who lingered longer than he or she should, but such an absence of obvious threat was no reason to relax his vigil. Archer's quest for Yonam may have aroused the interest of other entities than B.L.I.S.S.

Rachel and the doctor came around the corner, walking so close to each other that their arms brushed. Rachel was talking and laughing, Archer looking down at her with entranced attention.

Harrison narrowed his eyes. Did the woman still not understand the danger with which she played?

Likely not. In his experience, women rarely did until it was too late. As long as the man said "please" and "thank you," bathed regularly, and had a good job, she thought he was a fine fellow. His own mother had been one so easily duped, and he, helpless as a child, had watched her pay the price again and again for such naïveté.

It had driven him half mad to see her hurt, and his fury had driven him to acts that had destroyed forever any chance at leading the life he had wanted since a boy.

Rachel smiled and touched Archer's forearm.

Harrison clenched his jaw. If Rachel was just pretending at liking Archer, she was doing a hell of a job of it.

A disturbing thought cast its shadow in his mind. He wasn't jealous, was he? Of Rachel, paying attention to Archer?

He dismissed the thought as ludicrous. It meant nothing that Rachel was friendly to that monster, while she treated Harrison himself with all the welcoming warmth one would give a tax inspector.

No, come to think of it, she'd likely be more courteous to the inspector.

He tried not to care that Rachel's deep magenta *shalwar kameez* was lovely against her fair skin, or that the filmy gold scarf lying against her throat brought his eyes to the bare flesh between it and the tunic's neckline.

He told himself that he wasn't interested in the light of fierce intelligence he had seen in her eyes, or that he had seen as well a streak of tender vulnerability beneath her prickly demeanor.

It didn't matter that he had long dreamed of meeting a woman who stood up for herself, refused to trust him on his say-so alone, and had no compunction about giving him a hard time if she thought he deserved it. Someone who would never let a man take emotional advantage of her, not even if she loved him.

Of course, Rachel was miles away from loving him.

She was a dropout genius, with no goals or values, and that was all. He didn't like her. His interest in her was related only to the mission.

He stood straight as Rachel and Archer approached. Rachel caught sight of him, and he watched as her eyes lit with recognition, a moment of pleasure, and then her expression turned sour so quickly that he wondered if the moment of pleasure had been in his imagination only.

Then even the sourness was gone, hidden under what he imagined must be the face she used when meeting her new groups of tourists: blandly pleasant, friendly, expectant.

"Wiles, there you are!" she said.

Rachel turned to Archer. "Alan, I'd like to introduce you to Harrison Wiles, our mountaineering expert. Harrison, Dr. Alan Archer."

He could almost see Archer's hackles rise as the good doctor took in his greater height and muscled body.

Harrison slumped his shoulders, extended his hand, and mumbled a greeting in a milder version of his native British accent, tinged with Nepali. He gave Archer's hand an effeminate shake, left his mouth hanging open, and then sniffed loudly and wiped his nose on the back of his hand. From the corner of his eye he saw Rachel make a moue of startled distaste. He ignored her and tried to look less intelligent than one of the sacred cows out in the street standing in a pile of garbage and eating plastic bags for supper.

Archer scrutinized him while Harrison continued his impression of a mouth-breather and did his own subtle scrutinizing in return.

He had seen Archer from afar several times, and had studied the photos in his file, but meeting the man was disconcerting. With a static photo to stare at, it had been easy to ascribe evil thoughts to the mind behind the pale blue eyes and Nazi-fair hair.

The living version of Dr. Archer, though, came across as awkward, nervous, and vaguely helpless. Most disturbing of all was that there was nothing about Archer to tell you that the man was likely a murderer and rapist. He looked instead like someone who needed mothering, and Rachel looked eager to fill the role.

Women were so blasted blind to the evils of men. Yes, they did their man-bashing, but it was always after the fact. He'd yet to meet a woman who was able to steer clear of a guy she found charming, however loudly his red warning flags snapped in the wind.

"Is Min here yet?" Rachel asked, apparently unaware of the sizing-up going on between the two men.

Harrison shrugged and scratched at the skin beneath his nose, as if surreptitiously trying to reach a bit of dried snot. He dropped his hand and pretended to wipe his fingertips against the thigh of his pants.

Rachel frowned at him, her nose crinkled. Archer caught her expression, and some of the tension left the doctor's shoulders. When Archer glanced again at Harrison, his expression was marginally more friendly. As long as Rachel was repulsed, Archer would tolerate him.

"Ah, well, I'm sure Min will find us. Shall we?" Rachel asked, and gestured toward the interior of the restaurant. Archer took her hand and placed it on his forearm as they entered, leaving Harrison to follow behind like a lackey.

They were being seated when a short Nepalese man with the muscled body of a gymnast bounced up to them, a wide grin stretching his features.

"Rachel! You took a long time. I have eaten three bowls of ice cream, waiting! But you are looking very beautiful, so I think it was good to wait."

"Min! Do you never stop?" Rachel said, laughing, and then introduced the man to Archer and to him.

"I will never stop so long as there are beautiful women asking to go into the hills with me." Min's cheerful grin softened his lechery, but Harrison watched the man's eyes flick over Rachel's body, then take a side trip to trace over the bodies of a group of foreign women who were standing up to leave, their shoulders bare and their breasts on display beneath the thin, tight cotton of camisole tops.

"I would say you will have no appetite for dinner after all that ice cream, only I know better," Rachel said, oblivious.

"One of my cousins has just started work here. He gave me the ice cream." Min drew his eyes back to her, and made a conspiratorial face. "Shhh! Don't tell the boss!"

A belated flush of failure shot through Harrison. How had he missed Min's arrival, been unaware that the man was here the whole time he himself was slouching by the door? Some professional he was! He'd been too preoccupied with thoughts of Rachel to do his job right.

They placed their orders with the waiter, and then like a grammar school teacher Rachel asked them all to introduce themselves. There was a communal groan. No one looked happy, and no one volunteered.

"Oh, I know everyone hates to do this," Rachel said, "but humor me. You always end up finding out something interesting.

"I'll start," she said, as the waiter set down a basket of bread, a bowl of salad, and plates. "You all know that I lead tours here in Nepal. What none of you know is that I used to have a pet rat. Miranda."

"You did not!" Min protested. "My lovely Rachel, no. Not a rat."

"A beautiful white rat, who slept beside me on my pillow at night. She was a wonderful friend, and would give me little rat kisses right on the lips." Rachel puckered up and leaned toward Min, making kissing noises. He shied away, a look of horror on his face.

Harrison chuckled despite himself, and heard Archer do the same.

"Your turn, Min," Rachel said.

"I am Min, and I started as a porter when I was thirteen, working with my older brothers. For five years now I have been a guide, but I am still fastest and strongest on the trail!" he declared, and put up his arms to either side and flexed his muscles. "I am very strong! Feel, feel," he said to Rachel.

"I've felt them before, thanks."

"Women like muscles. Feel! They are bigger from last time."

Rachel rolled her eyes, and gave his biceps a squeeze.

"Oh, oh, you hurt me!" Min squealed, and pulled away, cradling his arm. "Now let me feel yours."

"He flirts outrageously," Rachel said, slapping Min's hand away from her arm. "He's always going after the female tourists."

"And sometimes they fall in love with me," Min said, grinning.

"Love, or lust?" Archer asked.

Min shrugged. "Does it matter?"

"To some, it does," Archer said, and Harrison saw his eyes go to Rachel, to check her response to this bit of gallantry. Her attention was on the salad bowl.

Rachel piled lettuce, tomato, and cucumber on her plate, then glanced up at Harrison as she poured olive oil over her greens. "Your turn."

"I've been mountaineering for fun since I was a teenager. My father is a Gurkha, so I spent a few years living in Brunei, and was sent to England to school," he said in a semitruth. It was his grandfather who had been a Gurkha, but claiming that his father had been one provided an easy explanation for both his fluent English and Nepali. "I am thinking about starting my own mountaineering company, here in Nepal, but need more local experience before doing so. At least, that's what Father says. I don't know. I think I'd do okay."

Harrison took a bite of bread, chewed with his mouth open, and tried his best to look like a sleepy water buffalo. He swallowed, then reached into his mouth with a finger and dug gummy bread out of his teeth. Archer grimaced, then turned his attention back to Rachel.

Good. Mental dismissal was exactly what Harrison was aiming for.

"Alan?" Rachel said.

"Oh, I imagine you all have already been told

about me," Archer said in false modesty. "I'm an internist—that means I do adult medicine—but I've worked all over the world. First with the United States Air Force, then for Golden Cruises, but next year I want to work with Doctors without Borders. There are so many people in this world who need help, and it's unfair that only the rich can get the medical care they need," he said, defensiveness entering his tone. "Maybe that's just me who feels that way, but I have to act on it. Call me an idiot for it if you want." He stuck out his jaw and glared at the rest of them, as if expecting an attack for his noble stance.

Harrison looked down at his salad plate, fearing his contempt would show. The lying piece of—

"The world needs more doctors like you," Rachel said softly, and from the corner of his eye Harrison saw her lay her hand on Archer's wrist.

"My colleagues say I'm crazy," Archer said, an affectedly plaintive note in his tone. "They think the only way to be a doctor is to specialize and pull in piles of money. Then they donate some to research charities as a tax write-off. They don't care about *people*. They don't see the suffering of the poor and the ignorant in the third world, not like I do."

Rachel made a soft tsking noise and shook her

head, her eyes big and sad as she looked at Archer.

Harrison couldn't stand it. The man was a sociopathic hypocrite, and Rachel was eating it up. Angry words of refutation burned in his throat. Some protest had to be made.

"Third-world people are not stupid," he said. "Look at the people in the hills, here. Sure they're poor, but they have their own medicines, made from the plants around them. They do not need your Western science." It wasn't a statement he completely agreed with, but he had to say *something,* and it might segue to the topic of Yonam.

"I know they have medicines, and some might even be useful," Archer acknowledged in a patronizing tone. "But I doubt that most of them work. And considering the number of infants and children that die of disease and dirt, I don't think you ought to be praising the all-powerful pharmacopoeia of the forest to the exclusion of Western science. What is the average life expectancy here in Nepal? Forty-two?"

"Maybe it is a better life, though," Harrison proposed. "Focused on family instead of TV and expensive athletic shoes. These people are happy, until they see the Western tourists with their riches and start wanting things they cannot have."

"So you would stop them from seeing the outside world?" Archer challenged. "You would play God with them, deciding what was best, and not allow them the freedom to choose for themselves?"

What a thing for Archer, of all people, to say!

Rachel answered before Harrison could. "But that's an eternal human problem, isn't it? We can be happy with our circumstances, whatever they are, until we see someone who has a little more."

"You'll be exposing more hill people to rich foreigners if you start your mountaineering company here," Archer said to Harrison, scoldingly. "It's rather hypocritical of you to complain about corrupting Western influences if you're going to be profiting off them, yourself."

Harrison felt his face flush, and had to clench his hands under the table to keep from springing at Archer and pounding the man's fair head into his oil-drenched salad. The man dared call *him* a hypocrite?

"He has a point, Harry, don't you think?" Rachel asked sweetly.

Oh, she was going to get a tongue-lashing when he had her alone. "Maybe I will have to think about it," he said, faking a look of defeat.

Archer reached over and slapped him on the shoulder. "That's my boy! It's always good to admit when you are wrong." Archer smiled at him as if he had discovered a spot of fondness for him.

"Min, what do you think?" Rachel asked, as the waiter shoved aside their salad plates and set down three thin-crust pizzas.

Min sniffed at the pizza nearest him, shrugged at Rachel, and said, "I want to buy a car."

"There you go," Archer said to Harrison, still acting the fond parent instructing the ignorant. "You can't stop the modern world from reaching people and showing them the possibilities out there. And you can't keep the women stuck in the rice terraces and the kitchens, however quaint you think it is."

Dr. Archer looked at Rachel.

Rachel smiled in approval, eyes soft. "I wish there were more men like you."

Oh, for God's sake!

He'd kill Archer, when the time was right. Just for the satisfaction of wiping that smug look off the man's face. Better yet, Harrison would humiliate him in front of Rachel, give him a good thrashing, and *then* kill him.

"But here's something you don't know about me and Rachel both," Archer said. "I used to date Rachel, way back when she was sweet sixteen."

What?

A ringing started in Harrison's ears, and the

world went blurry. Rachel and Archer? They had a *history* together?

Bloody hell! Why hadn't Y told him?

Why hadn't *Rachel* told him?

He gaped at her, silently screaming the accusation. Didn't she trust him? Rachel let her gaze skip past his, not pausing to so much as shrug in apology. She grinned nervously, poked at her food with her fork, and looked at no one.

"Rachel! You and the doctor, you were boyfriend and girlfriend?" Min asked, and then unaccountably began to laugh. "It will be very strange to travel with an old lover, yes?"

"Oh, Alan and I only dated for a few weeks," she said with a brittle brightness. "Alan was older than the usual boys I met, which made him more interesting. I don't know what he saw in *me,* though, an immature teenager." She laughed, the sound near a hysterical screech. Harrison wondered at it. "He grew tired of me very quickly."

"Don't listen to her," Archer said, gazing at her with possessive adoration. "I never grew tired of her. She left town for some sort of summer study program, and from then on she was more interested in school than in guys. We lost touch."

"Now you find each other in Kathmandu. It is

a very romantic story," Min said, grinning. "Maybe a story of true love."

"Oh, I don't know," Rachel said with a strangled laugh. Her eyes met Harrison's for a moment, widened at what she saw there, then danced away.

She was going to get it, when he had her alone. What type of partnership was this, if she wouldn't tell him something so important to the mission? She would pay, pay, pay for her sins.

How close had she and Archer gotten in those few weeks of youthful infatuation? Kissed, certainly. Had Archer touched her more intimately? The thought pumped a red fog of anger into Harrison's brain.

They ate in relative peace for a few minutes, Min struggling with the unfamiliar food, watching how the others attacked such fare. Rachel and Archer picked up the slices to eat. Harrison worked at his with knife and fork, imagining it was Archer's body he was dissecting, and shrugged at Min's questioning expression.

"Either way to eat it is fine," Rachel said to the local guide. "Both are polite."

Min piled salad onto his slice of pizza, rolled it into a log, and ate it like a burrito. With his mouth full, he spoke to Archer. "Where are we going?"

Harrison's eyes met Rachel's for an instant,

the both of them surprised by the blunt question, the issue of the past relationship momentarily shoved aside.

"We are going someplace that your friend here," Archer said, pointing at Harrison with a pizza crust, "would approve of. We are going to gather samples of hitherto unknown medicinal plants, in the hopes that they may yield something of use to mankind."

"So the ignorant third-world plant-users are not so ignorant, after all," Harrison said.

"If there *are* plants with medicinal properties up in the hills, I've no doubt that either they are being used in methods that negate the majority of their chemical properties, or they are being used for the wrong purpose altogether."

"Where are we going?" Min asked again. "We have to order a car, or buy bus tickets. Or plane tickets?" He raised his smudged brows in expectation.

The three of them looked at Archer, waiting for an answer.

Archer chewed his upper lip and frowned. "Err . . . well, truth be told, I'm not really sure where the best place to start would be."

They all stared at him.

Archer fidgeted, then spoke again. "Um . . . Someone *did* tell me that there was a monastery in the mountains, where the monks have considerable healing skills. I suppose we could go there, first."

"Wonderful!" Rachel said. "What's the monastery's name?"

Harrison leaned forward, ears straining to catch the information.

"I, uh, forgot." Archer smiled sheepishly, tucking in his chin, his forelock falling over his brow.

Rachel pursed her lips and frowned teasingly. "That does make it a little difficult to find."

"But not impossible," Archer said, smiling boyishly. "There is a monk here, in Kathmandu, who is from that monastery."

Harrison struggled to keep the amazement off his face. Could it be a monk from Yonam? Here, in Kathmandu? Good God, they might not need to take Archer on his quest, after all! If this monastery was in Yonam, and the monk could lead them . . .

"Really!" Rachel said. "Where is he? Have you talked to him?"

"I don't know his name."

Rachel's lips fell open in surprise, just as Harrison felt his own do. Where had the man gotten his information, a psychic channeler of Durga's dead spirit?

"I do have a picture of the monk, though," Archer went on. "A fellow I met in a . . . er . . . bar gave it to me."

115

"You do! Great! Can I see it?" Rachel asked, already reaching across the table. "Is he Tibetan? Maybe he's at Boudhanath."

Boudhanath was the largest Buddhist *stupa*— a huge white dome housing a relic—in Nepal, and around it lived a community of some sixteen thousand displaced Tibetans.

"It's not a photo," Archer said, opening up his small backpack and rooting around inside. "It's actually a drawing."

A drawing? The man couldn't be serious. Harrison had a sudden dread that he would be spending the next fifty years wandering the mountains, in search of a legendary city that had never really existed. They'd be sucked into the mountain mists and disappear forever.

For a moment, he even doubted that there really was a Yes drug. Perhaps it was as mythical as the Fountain of Youth, and this quest as doomed to failure as the search for El Dorado.

"Here it is," Archer said. He pulled out a piece of paper and handed it to Rachel.

Harrison and Min strained to see it, and Rachel held it out so they could. It was a photocopy of a drawing, the faint lines of the ruled school paper on which it had been drawn still visible. The artist—had it been Durga?—had both talent and an apparent love of pornographic doodling: The central drawing was the face of a monk, but around it were dozens of monkeys engaged in a series of sexual acts that would put the *Kama Sutra* to shame.

"Did your friend give you any idea where to find this monk?" Rachel asked Archer.

Archer shrugged. "There can't be so many monasteries here in Kathmandu."

Rachel laid the photocopy on the table, a thoughtful look on her face. "Min, when you think of monkeys, what do you think of?"

"Hanuman," he said, naming the Hindu monkey god. There was a royal palace named after him, in the palace square at the heart of Kathmandu.

"Hanuman, yes. But if you were thinking of Buddhist monks, as well as monkeys?"

Harrison caught her thought and nodded.

Min obviously caught it as well. "Swayambhunath!"

"What?" Archer asked.

"The Monkey Temple," Rachel explained. "At least, that's its nickname. It's more than twenty-five hundred years old. According to legend, an important Buddhist had his hair cut there. Trees appeared where his hair fell, and his lice all became monkeys. The place is crawling with them."

Archer's lip curled. "Charming."

Rachel shrugged one shoulder. "Charming or

117

not, it's the best place to start looking for this monk."

Archer's sneer of disgust softened into a smile, as he realized she was right. "Good work, Rachel! I knew you were meant to be on this expedition with me, knew it from the moment I saw you."

Pink touched Rachel's cheeks, and she made a little "pshaw" sound, waving away the comment with the tips of her fingers. "Let's not get too excited yet," she said. "We still have to see if the monk is there. I could be wrong."

"I doubt it. You're a brilliant woman," Archer said.

Harrison couldn't stand it. He had to interrupt. Remembering the role he was supposed to be playing, he pushed back from the table and stood, all dim-witted eagerness. "Let's go!"

Rachel and Archer both blinked at him. "Go?" Rachel asked. "Go where?"

"The temple!"

"It's a little late in the evening, Harry," Rachel said. "I think tomorrow morning would be soon enough."

He stood a moment longer, fidgeting with false anxiousness. "He might be there, right now! We could talk to him!"

"Have some ice cream," she said, as if pacifying a little boy.

He caught the twitch of a smile at the corner of her mouth. She was enjoying having him play the idiot.

How had he managed to get himself stuck in this role? A week ago he was being fêted by a king.

He slowly sat back down. Let Rachel laugh at him and withhold her trust. When they were out on the trail and dear *Alan* showed his true colors, she would be grateful to have Harrison there to save her. Archer was not the attentive, harmless suitor she remembered from her teens. She would obviously have to find that out for herself.

Besides, he didn't need Rachel clinging to his arm and looking up at him with adoring eyes.

He didn't need Rachel cooing that the world needed more men like him.

No, not at all.

Not him.

But perhaps he should warn her to keep her head in better control of her heart, in regards to Archer. All in the interests of a successful mission, of course.

Chapter Seven

The route Rachel chose to the Monkey Temple led through a neighborhood different in flavor from the tourist district. Instead of shop after shop selling pashmina shawls, T-shirts, or bulky turquoise and amber jewelry, here was where the average residents of Kathmandu lived.

The open fronts of shops revealed open bags of grains and flat platters piled high with tomatoes, peppers, and apples. Barbers in shops no larger than a Western bathroom massaged scalps and wielded straight-edge razors on their customers. Pieces of butchered goat lay on wooden counters in the sun, flies crawling over the white and red flesh.

Bits of trash were trodden into the potholed

mix of dirt, rock, and asphalt that served as a road, the street peopled with women in saris and *shalwar kameez,* the men in Western-style pants and plastic sandals. Dogs, cows, and the occasional chicken roamed at will.

Alan would have preferred a taxi, Rachel was sure, but with four of them it was easier to walk. Going by foot was probably just as fast, anyway; or faster, given the traffic.

They crossed a concrete bridge, the shallow river below lined with heaps of garbage, its banks an unofficial dump. The ripe stench of it wafted to them on the bridge, and as quickly passed away as they reached the other side.

"Disgusting. I'm going to have to burn my shoes when I leave this town," Alan said.

Rachel glanced up at him, the bright morning sunlight glaring in her eyes and turning Alan's falsely fair hair into a halo of light. She wondered if this was how Lucifer had looked before being cast from heaven: a golden child, with potential for both good and evil. She didn't know yet which way he would fall.

"I'd imagine any hint of dirt would be anathema to a doctor," she said.

"Anathema to anyone with any sense of personal pride," he said, casting a sneering glance at the people around them.

Rachel felt a twinge of discomfort, and debated whether to comment. It was a fine line she had to walk with Alan: He wasn't here to have his mind broadened, although he would find his stay in Nepal far more pleasant if he was willing to bend a bit, and to look with open eyes. "The garbage on the banks of the river is a pity, true, but I've seen the same along highways and rivers at home. I should think Americans had less of an excuse for it."

"Hey, I'm not prejudiced about it," Archer said with a quick grin. "I think the redneck slobs back home are just as bad as anyone else, whatever the country or race."

She murmured a noncommittal noise, and chose not to point out the carefully washed laundry hanging outside houses, the swept and scrubbed front stoops, or that all the women had clean, neatly arranged hair—no matter that it was long and must take great trouble to tend, especially when your bathing facilities consisted of a bucket of water and a scoop.

She wondered what Wiles thought of their surroundings, he with his cover-boy good looks, immaculate clothing, and plummy accent. She cast a glance back over her shoulder.

Wiles and Min were in the midst of an animated conversation. As she watched, a child playing a version of hackeysack with a bundle of rubber rings kicked her toy into the road in front of Wiles. Without even pausing, he scooped it into the air with the toe of his shoe, bounced it thrice on the inner arch of his foot, then kicked it in a soft arc back to the girl. The child let it fall at her feet, putting her hand over her mouth to hide her shy smile and giggles.

Was no female safe from his charms?

She turned back to Alan. "So. You haven't told me how your love-life has been these past years. Did you ever get close to marrying?"

He laughed, short and bitter. "Hardly."

"Oh, come on. A good-looking doctor? They'd be after you like a pack of dogs after a lamb."

"No one is looking for lambs. They all seem to want the muscle-bound wolves with long hair and sports cars."

"I don't believe that," she said gently.

He shrugged, and she saw years of rejection hidden in the gesture.

"Well, *I* think you're a sweetie. Women are idiots if they pass you by, and they deserve the losers they get if they go after the wolves instead of you."

Her words coaxed a smile onto his lips, and she felt the better for it.

The temple was just ahead, atop a wooded hill that rose to nearly five hundred feet above the valley floor. Three hundred steps led straight up the front, lined on either side by animal statues representing the vehicles of the gods. "Consider this as practice for the Himalayas," Rachel said to Alan.

Min jogged past and started running up the stairs, taking them two at a time. He turned and shouted over his shoulder, "You are slow! So slow! You will not last in the mountains!" Obviously not wanting to be too badly outdone, Alan picked up his pace. Rachel followed more slowly, with Wiles taking up the rear.

Wiles quickly caught up to her and matched his step to hers. His closeness sent a shiver through her, and when her arm brushed against his the shiver turned to a wave of electricity, shooting to her heart and down her body. She cursed herself and tried to put more distance between them, but as if they were two celestial bodies drawn by gravity she again found herself nearly touching him.

With Alan, any such closeness was faked by her. It vexed her that she could not equally fake disinterest in Wiles. Next she'd be tossing her hair and wetting her lips.

God help her.

"I thought I warned you about being too cozy with Archer," Wiles said softly.

She wrinkled her nose. Too bad he was such an arrogant know-it-all. There were some things even a handsome face couldn't make up for.

"Just doing my job," she said.

"Is that all it is?"

She frowned at him. "What do you *think* is going on?"

"Unless I'm a poor judge of behavior, I *think* you really like the guy."

Thank heavens Alan hadn't blurted out that they'd slept together. She'd never get a moment's peace from Wiles if he found out.

Not that that was the only reason she wanted to keep it quiet. A secret part of her worried that Wiles would find her unappealing—dirty, even— if she claimed Evil Alan as a past lover.

She wondered how he'd feel if he knew she'd slept with Min, as well. Best to keep that to herself. Guys seemed to like thinking that any woman no longer a virgin had only had sex once in her life.

"I wouldn't be doing my job well, now, would I, if it appeared even to the average, unintelligent observer that I didn't like Alan?" She shrugged. "We *do* know each other from way back, after all. Besides, it's a basic tenet of human behavior that he'll be more likely to like me, if I seem to like him first."

"But *do* you like him?"

She couldn't answer that. Alan had many more unpleasant opinions and traits than she remembered from her teens, but that didn't necessarily make him a bad person. She'd learned from leading groups of tourists that even annoying, bad-tempered, closed-minded people usually had good hearts under there somewhere. "What difference does it make if I like Alan, as long as I do my job? Whatever I feel about him will not change what I do if we find this semimythical Yes drug."

"It could bias your actions at a critical moment."

She laughed. "*What* critical moment? I can't see Alan holding a gun to anyone's head. The worst that'll happen is you'll have to tackle him and pry a vial out of his hand. Or do you think he might get the best of you in a fight?" she teased, a smile in her voice. It was fun to picture the two men rolling in the dirt, punching each other.

"I just want to be sure you're not standing there with a stick, ready to conk me from behind. I want to be sure where your loyalties lie."

"They lie with the women of the world," she said. "Not with you, Wiles. But not with Alan, either. And not with B.L.I.S.S. You'll have to take that as your answer, because I've got no other to give you."

He nodded. "I can accept that."

She glanced at him in surprise. "You can?"

The corner of his mouth pulled into a smile,

revealing a hint of dimple in his cheek. "You have no reason to trust me any more than you do Archer—maybe even less, since you already know him. Beti and I have told you that we're the good guys, but you don't have any proof of that. You're wise to be wary. I just wanted to be sure that you're equally wary of Archer. I thought he might have held the appeal of the underdog for you, with all we've been saying about him."

"If he's the underdog, does that make you the alpha dog?"

He frowned at her. "I didn't say that."

"Not directly, but you implied it," she said. "You must be used to being the best of the pack."

"Is that what you think?"

"It's not how I see you, if that's what you're asking." She was taunting him. It was fun to poke a stick at the bear.

"I frankly don't care how you see me," he said, sounding offended.

"If you didn't care, we wouldn't be discussing it," she said, biting her lips to keep from smiling.

"That is utter codswollop!"

She burst out in laughter. "I beg your pardon? *Codswollop?*"

"It means, 'That's nonsense.' "

"I know what it means. But *codswollop?* My

God, where did you get that? From a maiden aunt?"

"Would you rather I be crude and say 'bullshit'?"

"And take away the fun of seeing you be a priss? Never."

"I am not a priss," he muttered.

"Most people wouldn't find it macho for a guy to avoid swearing in favor of words like 'cod-swollop,' " she said, and elbowed him in the side.

Oh, God, there she went, finding an excuse to touch him. Damn it! She was such an idiot!

"I don't need to say 'bullshit' to prove my Y chromosome. I was brought up not to use words like that in front of a lady."

"Glad to hear you consider me one."

"All women are ladies until proven otherwise."

"And if proven otherwise?"

His dimple flashed again on his smooth cheek. "Then you still treat them as ladies."

She narrowed her eyes at him, fully aware that she might fall into that latter category. "How chivalrous."

"I do try."

"Smart-ass," she said, half smiling.

"Better than a dumb-ass," he said, grinning.

"Not always."

"Yes, you'd like a dumb-ass to push around, wouldn't you?"

"Are you saying I'm bitchy?" she asked.

"A priss like me would never use a crude term like 'bitchy.' 'Difficult,' I might say. 'Domineering,' perhaps. 'Authoritative.' 'Imperious.' 'Despotic.' "

She lowered her eyebrows. "I will stand by my original statement, since it seems to please you. You *are* a very smart ass."

He laughed, the sound carrying to Alan and Min, who had paused up ahead and now turned to look down at them. Alan had his camera out and had been looking through the viewfinder. Rachel guessed he had needed an excuse for a breather from the climb up the stairs.

She could tell that Alan was examining both her and Wiles, so she deepened her scowl for effect and said a harsh, "Mind your manners," to Wiles, hoping Alan would hear it, and then hurried up the remaining stairs between her and the doctor.

"Is everything okay?" Alan asked, putting his hand on her shoulder. His palm felt damp and soft, the heat of it uncomfortable through the thin fabric of her tunic. She resisted the urge to shrug it off.

"Fine," she said, flashing him a smile. "That clod has the sense of humor of a donkey, is all. When God handed out brains, he was too busy in the bathroom admiring his reflection to get in line."

Min snickered, then took a piece of candy from his pocket and started playing keep-away with a small monkey perched on one of the animal statues.

Alan squeezed her shoulder. "You're sure we need Wiles on this trek?"

She shrugged. "He had good references. You know how it is: Dim-witted people can be very good at physical tasks. He's probably as good in the mountains as a yak, and it would be best to have him in case we need him."

"Just be sure to let me know if he starts getting . . . well, you know. A bit fresh. I won't have you harassed."

Min snorted. Rachel glared at him, and he made an innocent face.

"Thank you, Alan," she said, and tried to look grateful. "I'm fairly sure I'll be able to handle Wiles on my own."

Alan brushed the back of his finger against the side of her cheek, his gaze intense. "I'm here if you need me."

"Thank you," she said again, and shivered as he released her. Something about the way he looked at her made her more nervous than reassured. Maybe Wiles was right, and she had recaptured a little more of his interest than was wise.

The monkey screeched and scampered off into the brush on the other side of the rail. Min was still smiling, still holding his piece of candy. He shrugged when he saw them looking at him. "He didn't want it."

Or Min didn't see the beasts as too holy for teasing. She wondered what he'd done to scare if off like that, but then let the thought slip away as they started up the last stairs to the top.

The Monkey Temple was, like many other Buddhist *stupas*, a huge whitewashed dome surmounted by a golden towerlike structure. The four sides of the tower were painted with the eyes and nose of ever-watching Buddha, and around the base of the mound, at chest height, were brass cylinders inscribed with prayers. The faithful walked clockwise around the mound, spinning these "prayer wheels" as they went, each turn of the cylinder releasing the prayer into the air.

Around the *stupa* a crowd milled and mingled: monkeys, tourists both Western and Eastern, vendors, and occasional monks in crimson and gold. A shrine to a Hindu goddess shared space with the Buddhist statues, the two religions having found no ground for dispute.

Rachel took four photocopies out of her day

pack. Each one showed the face of the monk they were looking for, with the drawings of fornicating monkeys blocked out to avoid offending anyone to whom they showed the picture. She handed out the copies.

Min held his up, squinted at a monk walking past, and made a helpless face. "We'll never find him."

Rachel looked at the photocopy and then the monk, and saw the same thing Min had: With short hair and identical clothing, there was not a lot to distinguish one monk from another. Whether or not they found the one they wished depended entirely upon the skill of the unknown artist.

Alan pointed to a triad of speckles near the right eye of the drawing. "I think our monk has three freckles or moles by his right eye."

"Okay, then, that's what we'll look for. Got that, Wiles?" She spoke slowly, and tapped her finger near her own eye. "Three moles. Right eye."

Wiles gave her a look that promised punishment to come. It made her heart beat a little faster.

"Alan, you go with Min, since he's more familiar with the area and his Nepali is obviously a lot better than mine. I'll go with Wiles." Dividing the team based on language abilities would make asking questions easier.

At least, she told herself that was true. It wasn't as if she was inventing reasons she had to be close to Wiles, even if she *would* like to squeeze his butt. Just once. Maybe she could say one of the monkeys did it, if he complained.

Rachel smiled brightly and looked at her watch. "We'll meet back here in half an hour and compare notes. Okay? Okay. Let's go, then." She made a beeline through the milling crowd toward a monk, leaving Alan staring after her and Wiles to follow in her wake.

Wiles quickly caught up with her. "Eager to get out of Archer's company already?"

She cast a glance over her shoulder, checking that Alan and Min were proceeding with their task, then looked at Wiles. "No, I was getting so aroused by his presence, I had to get away before I embarrassed myself. I was *this* close to pinching his butt, I tell you," she said, holding up her thumb and forefinger. "Do you think he would have minded? Or maybe a gentle pat would go over better," she said, opening her eyes wide and putting on her best ditz look. "Or do you think a pat is a little too one-of-the-guys?"

He made a small, panicked sound and looked at her with wide eyes.

"Maybe I need something a little more erotic,

like a squeeze?" she asked. "If his butt is out of shape, though, I'll get a handful of flab."

"I don't think guys worry about things like that," he croaked.

"Sure they do. They flex their glutes if they know they're going to get grabbed. But maybe you don't have to, maybe everything is tight already?"

He gaped at her, and she grinned. He was *so* shy about sexual topics. She loved it. There was torture unbounded in store for him.

Then she wondered just how firm Wiles *would* feel if she grabbed him. "Maybe a fondle would be best," she said, imagining doing just that to Wiles. "The man can't be completely against having me touch his rear. I even think I could spank him and call him a naughty boy, and he'd still like it."

Wiles gazed at her long enough that she began to think *he* might like to be spanked. Maybe he wasn't quite as sexually shy as she'd been thinking, at least when it came to action as opposed to words.

What was going on here? Damn it all, she should have gone with Alan. She felt a high potential for self-humiliation in the air. She wasn't one to resist a temptation, though.

"Here's what I would really do," she said, stopping to face him, her pulse tripping in her veins.

"I'd stand close to him, almost but not quite touching, then put my hands gently to either side of his face." She held her hands beside his cheeks, close but not touching. "I'd slowly pull his mouth down to mine."

His eyes widened.

"I'd kiss him," she said softly, leaning toward him, still not laying a finger upon him. "Part my lips. Let his tongue inside.

"And when his tongue is in my mouth," she went on, caressing his skin with the words, "I'd slide my hands down his chest and around his back, and then down over his buttocks." She mimed the action, and they both stood caught in the imaginary seduction. The potential for a kiss hovered in the air, an electric presence waiting to be grounded in contact.

"*Then* I'd squeeze. I'd pull him toward me, until I felt him pressed against my belly. He'd know then that I wanted him."

"I suppose he would," Wiles whispered.

Rachel was aware of every nerve in her skin, eager to feel him, aching to close the distance. And yet, she was terrified that he *would* touch her, *would* kiss her. He'd know then that she wanted him, and her pride would be humbled. He could laugh at her, and she would have no retort to save her lost face.

She balanced precariously between desire and

135

fear, and swayed toward him. The broadness of his chest and shoulders protected her from the milling crowd, sheltering her, inviting her to touch, to nestle against him and feel the comfort of his arms around her.

He bent his head down, his lips lightly brushing her brow, his breath feathering over her skin. He lowered his mouth, his lips hovering above hers.

Warm desire poured through her, urging her to close that small distance. She felt the barest hint of touch, so light it hurt her with the desire for more.

And then her animal sense of self-preservation jerked her abruptly back.

This was Wiles, smart-ass Wiles, who wanted nothing more than to be the one in charge. She could not believe he sincerely wanted her. Could not believe this was not a game he played, toying with her even more than she toyed with him.

As she pulled away, his seductive look changed to a careless grin, and the tension of a possible kiss was broken. "Or you could just pinch him, if you'd rather," he said, and shrugged as if to say he couldn't care less. He turned his back to her, scanning the crowd. "I think that monk we were following is wandering off."

She felt his sudden distance as chill as if a wind

had blown off the Great Wilcs Glacier.

What had just happened? Had that been a serious bit of interest on his part, or just a joke, a manipulation? Thank God she'd pulled back before making an even bigger fool of herself. Thank God he didn't know she would have been willing to be kissed.

She forced back an impending sense of hurt and narrowed her eyes, staring at Wiles as he stood with his back to her. It was as if she was not worthy of his notice. As when she had stared at his school-days rugby photo, she tried now to force her way inside that too-beautiful head.

It was almost beyond belief that he had been making a genuine pass at her, unless making passes was as instinctive to him as a dog getting fresh with a human leg.

Either way, she had better take a care to protect her feelings. She might not deny herself the pleasure of a night in his company, if sincerely offered, but she would be a fool to ever expect anything more from him.

As the Buddhists said, in all of life there was suffering, and our miseries created from clinging too tightly to our desires.

To desire more than the physical from Wiles would be to desire the impossible. He was not the type of male that caring mates were made of, least of all a mate for her.

* * *

They talked to several monks, getting negative answers to their queries. Harrison's mind was barely on the task at hand, though. He was too busy giving himself mental kicks to the head.

What had he been thinking?

What had he been thinking?

He had almost kissed her—had let his lips brush her forehead. He had been certain that her words were a flirtation meant for him, and that she was inviting his advances. The friction between them had aroused him, creating an electricity unlike anything he had felt before. For those long moments when she had stood so close, saying what she would do to him, he'd wanted nothing more than to give in to the wild impulses of his hormones.

It was only when Rachel stepped abruptly back that he had remembered with whom he was dealing, and found the sense to stop himself. It was only then that he remembered she was talking about how to seduce Archer, not him.

He was embarrassed by his own behavior, both personally and professionally. He had been taught better than to make a pass at a fellow agent. This was what it led to: muddled thinking on his part, and poison glances and ill will on hers.

She'd probably file a sexual harassment complaint against him with B.L.I.S.S., and then he could say *so long* to his budding career.

Not to mention the sheer embarrassment of wanting a woman who barely tolerated your presence. When she'd stepped back, and he'd realized his mistake, he'd tried to pretend it had all been a joke. If there had ever been a woman less likely to welcome the advances of one Harrison Wiles, she was Rachel Calais. She looked ready to spit half the time she looked at him.

Which was how she looked at him now, after that near-kiss fiasco.

Why had he wanted to kiss her? He didn't even *like* her. Not really.

Well, maybe just a little.

They approached yet another monk, and showed him the photocopy. Harrison asked in Nepali if he knew the man in the drawing, and the monk shook his head, no. They moved on.

Rachel kept two steps in front of him, not deigning to allow him into her field of vision.

It was the other half of the time Rachel looked at him, the non-ill-will times, that was the problem. Sidelong glances full of mischief, that was what had gotten to him, and it had screwed up his thinking.

Then there were her secretive smiles hinting at private thoughts.

Her closeness, while they climbed the stairs,

and her faint, flowery, utterly feminine scent. It made him want to find the rose hidden among the thorns.

The way she walked, that got to him, too. He watched her gliding steps as she walked in front of him now, moving with the unconscious grace of a woman who could carry a jug of water on her head and never spill a drop. None of that shuffling, slouching gait common to young women, for Rachel. She moved like royalty.

And, damn it, if forced to admit it he'd say that he got a bit of a kick out of her sassiness and her never backing down. There was something about her confidence that drew him. She seemed to want him to challenge her, as if she thought herself more than an equal match for him. It was like a dare.

Fool that he was, he wanted to take her up on it. He might have even liked it if she'd spanked him and called him naughty.

Bloody hell, he was a mess, wasn't he?

She had him turned upside down, not knowing if he was going or coming. He didn't enjoy it—did he?—but he couldn't keep himself from coming back for more. Miss Calais had turned him into a masochist, begging for both mercy and punishment.

He dug his hands through his hair, tugging on the strands as if by doing so he could rein in his own emotions. Where was the man he thought he was, a man both restrained and honorable?

Blast. Y was right not to give him command of a mission, if this was how he behaved.

They had gone past the *stupa* and down some steps to the Peace Pond, a modern cement pond with a golden statue of the Buddha in the middle of green, algae-scummed water. A monk was going around the other side of it.

Harrison caught up to Rachel. "There's another."

She nodded, and they went around the other side of the pond to head off the monk.

"And I'm sorry," Harrison said. "About earlier. It was unprofessional of me to act that way. It won't happen again."

She glanced at him, her expression unreadable. She neither accepted nor declined the apology, letting the silence stand between them as they continued around the Peace Pond to the monk.

Brilliant. She was probably mentally composing her sexual harassment letter to B.L.I.S.S. at this very moment. That wasn't quite the type of punishment he was hoping for.

Good God. Get a hold of yourself, there, boy.

The monk had noticed their interest in him, and stood waiting as they approached.

"*Namaste,*" Rachel said as they reached him,

holding her hands together as if in prayer in front of her chest. It was the traditional greeting in Nepal.

Harrison followed suit, then felt a shock of surprise as he took in the monk's features. The man's skin was dotted with freckles and moles, including three large ones in a triangle beside his right eye.

Rachel took a pocket camera out of her pack and held it up with a smile.

"Excuse me," Harrison said in Nepali to the monk. "Would you mind if she had her picture taken with you?"

The monk nodded, and Rachel handed the camera to Harrison and went to stand beside the monk. She smiled like a tourist.

Harrison snapped a photo.

"Thank you," Rachel said in English to the monk.

The monk held out his hand and rubbed his thumb against his fingertips. "Rupiya?"

Rupees were the monetary unit of Nepal. Rachel looked annoyed, but rooted around in her day pack, pulling out small paper bills worth about three times what the usual panhandling monk was given for a photo—as a donation for the monastery, of course. She smiled at the monk as she handed them to him, and kept visible within her hand several more bills of higher denominations.

"You are from one of these monasteries, here, around the *stupa?*" she asked.

The monk didn't say anything. He must not speak English. Harrison translated Rachel's words, playing the part of guide for the curious, ignorant tourist.

"I live here, yes," the monk said in Nepali, and gestured toward a monastery partly hidden behind some trees.

"Is this where you trained?" Rachel asked, smiling and bright-eyed.

"No, no, far away. In the mountains, near the Ganesh Himal, close to Tibet."

"Really! How interesting. What's the name of your old monastery?" she asked through Harrison.

"Tangunboche Gompa."

Rachel frowned. "That's a mouthful, isn't it? Here, show me on my map where it is. Could you, please? I'm going trekking in a few days, in Langtang, but maybe I can talk my guide into taking me to your monastery, too."

The monk shook his head. "It is very hard to get to, and there are no tea houses for trekkers. Better to stay in Langtang."

Rachel set her wad of bills down on a cement ledge, and unfolded her map beside them. "I am curious, though, where you came from. If you tell me, then I can label my photo."

The monk stepped closer and studied the map, then stabbed his finger down. "Here. Maybe ten days from Usuna." Usuna was the nearest town on the trekking map to the end of the monk's fingertip. There was no road leading there, just a path.

Harrison met Rachel's eyes, the silent question going between them: Was it enough? Dared they push for more information?

Tentatively, Rachel said, "It's so far off the beaten path. Do you get many visitors?"

The monk smiled and shook his head. "It is very quiet, except for the wind. Not like Kathmandu. Maybe once, twice a year travelers will stop and spend a night, or a few days, if they are ill or in need."

Harrison felt his hopes sink. If Tangunboche Gompa got the occasional hiking visitor, then it was unlikely to be in the lost city of Yonam. There had to be a tie, though, if Archer was so intent upon finding this monk.

Rachel raised her eyebrows at him, and he gave an almost imperceptible nod.

"I've heard," Rachel said through Wiles, "that monasteries are good places for local people to go when they are sick. Does Tangunboche do much healing?"

The monk responded to the question with a frown of confusion. "Where did you hear this? We learn the basics of medicine, yes, but people in the hills usually go to a shaman when they are ill, rarely a monastery. Some even try to find Western medicine, if they can afford it or can get it for free."

"Oh," Rachel said. "Durga Acharya must have been wrong. I thought he was from the hills and knew what he was talking about."

Harrison flinched. Bloody hell, what did she think she was doing? He wasn't going to translate that! Talk about a lack of subtlety!

But the monk didn't need a translation to comprehend Durga's name. It took a few moments as he mentally traced down his sense of recognition, but then his face darkened, and he shook his head at Rachel and Harrison. Without saying another word, he started to walk away.

"Wait, wait!" Rachel said, grabbing her wad of bills and going after him.

The monk hurried his step, sandals slapping on the concrete.

"Rupiya! Rupiya!" Rachel cried.

Vendors selling Tiger Balm and wooden flutes immediately swarmed her at the shout of "money," trapping her in their midst.

Harrison darted around the throng, leaving Rachel to fend them off. The monk disappeared through an opening in a screen of planted bamboo. Harrison followed, coming through in time to catch sight of the monk rounding the corner of a monastery, his maroon skirts flapping around his ankles.

He sprinted after the man and came around the corner just as the monk stuck his head back to check for followers. They collided, Harrison grabbing the man's shoulders before he could either fall or flee.

"Wait, please!" Harrison said in Nepali. "I'm not going to hurt you." The monk struggled in his grip, so he applied just enough strength to let the man know he would not get away.

"Let me go!"

"Answer a couple questions."

"I will shout for help!"

Harrison tilted his head at the quiet lane where they stood. Monkeys and cicadas chirruped in the trees and brush, but all else was quiet. "People will hear, but will they do anything? I want nothing from you but information. I am no friend of Durga Acharya."

The monk tried to pull away again, and Harrison let him, holding up his own hands to show he meant no harm.

From the corner of his eye Harrison saw the bright pink of Rachel as she came past the corner. She slowed to a stop, staying out of the monk's line of sight.

The monk glared at him.

"A few questions," Harrison said. "The man is no friend. Tell me, what did he do to upset you so?"

The monk shook his head.

"I know he did harm to women," Harrison said softly.

"Durga?" the monk asked in surprise.

Harrison felt a moment of confusion. Were they speaking of the same man? He took the photocopied drawing out of his pocket, unfolded it, and showed it to the monk. "Did Durga draw this?"

The monk nodded, lips tight. Then, reluctantly, "There was more to the drawing." He pointed vaguely at the white paper surrounding the portrait.

"Monkeys," Harrison said.

The monk nodded.

"How did you know him?"

"We traveled together," the monk said. "From Tangunboche Gompa to here, Kathmandu. He drew the picture the last day I saw him, here, at Swayambhunath."

"Was Durga a monk at one time?"

The man laughed. "It would have been better if he were. He was escaping from something, I don't know what, but he had no interest in following a spiritual path."

"Do you know where he came from, where his home was?"

"He never said." The monk made a restless movement, as if ready to abandon this interview.

Harrison felt a rising sense of frustration. There was information here, if he just knew what the right question was. "What makes you say he was escaping from something?"

The monk gestured with his hands. "He had no balance. He was a bitter man who could not release the darkness in his heart. He poured his anger out upon the world, in words and in deeds, and it was visited back upon him."

"What happened?"

The monk shrugged. "The last time I saw him, he had been in a fight, and I fear it was with drug dealers. *That* is why I wanted nothing to do with you when you said his name. I know nothing of his harming women. Durga told me he was leaving Kathmandu, and that is the last I know of him."

Harrison nodded, believing the monk, and believing as well that he had gotten from him all that the man knew. "Thank you for talking to me. They were questions that needed answers. Can I make a donation to the monastery?"

The monk narrowed his eyes, and with a jerk

of his head indicated Rachel, behind him. "It is not as she thinks. We maintain balance, give and take. We are not greedy. You can repay me by telling me what you want of Durga."

Harrison sighed. "Nothing, of him. I'm sorry to have to tell you this, but he's dead."

The monk's eyes widened.

Harrison went on, "He left behind a web of trouble, and I'm trying to clear some of it up. If anyone else asks you about Durga, it might be better if you pled ignorance."

The monk shook his head, as if unwilling to believe such things, his expression sad.

Harrison thanked the monk, then watched as the man turned and went into the building. Rachel came forward to join him.

"What did you find out?" she asked as they both turned to walk back the way they had come.

"Our friend Durga was in trouble long before he found his way to Thailand." He told her everything the monk had said.

She shuddered. "Drug dealers. I do *not* like the sound of that."

"Drug dealers, or maybe the angry boyfriend of some girl he had abused. We know little, except that he was a first-class rotter."

"And we know he was at Tangunboche. We'll have to tell Alan the location of the monastery, won't we? I don't see how we can avoid it."

He glanced at her, taking in the frown of concentration between her eyebrows. He was surprised that she could be so professional with him, after his amorous blundering.

They came back in sight of the temple, and Archer saw them at once and came jogging over to them, holding his backpack with both arms, tight against his chest as if rescuing a baby from a fire.

"There you are! Someone tried to steal my pack! Holy place, my ass. They'd peel the gold off the statues, given the chance. Good thing Min here could chase the little scumbag down."

"Wait, wait, slow down! Someone tried to rob you, *here?*" Rachel asked.

"I put my bag down between my feet for a moment, and next thing I knew it was gone. Min chased the thief and got it back."

Min grinned and puffed up his chest. "I am a very fast runner. Good thing I was here to save him."

"Did you call the police?" Rachel asked.

Min shook his head. "I got the bag, and gave the boy a good shaking. Better than the police."

Harrison looked at Min and wondered. To grab a backpack from between a man's feet spoke of daring, stupidity, or desperation. Was someone else already on Archer's trail?

"I don't want the police," Archer said. "I have

the bag, and nothing is missing. We don't need the hassle."

"You are glad you have Min with you now," Min said, begging for more praise.

"I'll make Alan buy you dinner," Rachel said. "A 'Thank you, Min, and farewell to Kathmandu' dinner."

"Farewell?" Archer asked.

Rachel smiled. "We found your monk."

"You did? Where? When do I get to talk to him?"

"Um, you don't. It was hard enough to get him to talk to us once."

"You approached him without me?" Archer looked at Rachel with accusing eyes. "What were you thinking?"

"It's okay, Alan, don't worry. We got the information you needed. He told us where he came from—"

"I have to talk to him," Archer insisted.

"I don't think he wants to talk to anyone anymore. What did you want from him? If it's really important, maybe Wiles can go back and coax it out of him."

Archer said nothing, his lips pressed together, his face flushed with anger.

"We have what we need, don't we?" Rachel asked soothingly. "We can finally get this show on the road and get out of Kathmandu." She touched his arm and softened her voice yet further, looking up at him with wide eyes. "We were just trying to help."

It was Harrison's turn to frown, as a sick little twist of jealousy bit at his gut.

Archer's mouth relaxed a fraction, and he put his hand over Rachel's. He tried to smile. "I know. Just . . . next time, come get me. This is very important."

"You won't be left out in the cold. I promise."

Harrison silently vowed to see that happen, exactly. The colder, the better, and it wasn't just information he planned to keep Archer away from.

Chapter Eight

The foothills of the Himalayas

Sweat trickled down between Rachel's breasts. Her cotton money belt, worn under her clothes across the small of her back, was soaked with it. Her breath came heavy through her open mouth as she trudged with slow but sure steps up the rocky dirt path, her day pack with its two liters of water heavy on her back.

Thank God for porters. Ten dollars U.S. a day to have a man carry all one's clothes and equipment was ten dollars well spent.

This was their first day of actual hiking, and the group was spread out single file on the path, the strong porters out of sight somewhere ahead of them. For six hours they had been climbing steadily, the path leading through small villages of mud-brick houses and terraced fields growing millet, rice, and corn.

Alan was ahead of her, his safari shirt more wet than dry. The back of his neck was turning red where he had forgotten to apply sunscreen. He'd tried to make conversation with her when they started out this morning, but the exertion of the hike had quickly stolen his breath. She wondered if it was only her continuing presence behind him that kept him moving forward, afraid she'd think him an out-of-shape wimp.

Ahead of Alan, Min led the way. Wiles took up the rear. Before leaving Kathmandu, she and Wiles had privately tried to use the small computer to access satellite images of the hills around Usuna, hoping to find either Tangunboche Gompa or Yonam itself. There were no images on file that mapped the vicinity of Usuna with the type of detail they needed, and first clouds and then the darkness of night had interfered with the efforts to collect fresh images. At least B.L.I.S.S. now knew the direction they were headed, which was a comfort of sorts.

Rachel doubted that even if they *had* good images of the area, though, they would be able to tell if a village was or was not Yonam. The place had to look unremarkable not to have been noticed from a puddle-jumping airplane before now.

The last village they'd passed through had been an hour ago, the children running out to gawk at them and call the greeting *"Namaste,"* their hands together in the prayer position. They giggled when Rachel gave the greeting back.

They hiked now in a scrubby forest of oak, pine, and rhododendron. The canopy was too sparse to provide protection from the sun, making the sweat trickle down her temples.

The heat of the sun turned suddenly chill, the bright glare turning gray. She looked up from the path and saw clouds drifting down over them, from the great mountains that were hidden somewhere behind the hills. A minute later a fat drop of rain hit her on the shoulder.

Damn.

Another hit, and then another, and she pulled off her day pack and jerked out her plastic slicker, shaking it open with hurried movements. She was about to toss it over her head when she heard footsteps, and turned to see Harrison running toward her, his large pack no hindrance to his movements.

"Hey, I thought the rainy season was supposed to be over!" he said.

"A mountaineer should know better than to trust the weather."

"I should have known better than to put my rain gear at the bottom of my pack, too."

The sprinkling of rain suddenly became a deluge, and Rachel did the only thing she could: flung half her slicker above her own head, holding it over her like a tarpaulin, and held up the other half for Wiles.

He ducked under the offered cover, his side pressed up close to hers, and took hold of the slicker. "Cheers," he said in thanks.

His arm went lightly around her lower back, making it easier for them to walk in synch. She looped her own thumb through one of the belt loops at the back of his pants, the sudden contact between them making her feel almost faint for a moment.

Alan had disappeared around a curve up in the path ahead. She was alone with Wiles, and aware of their bodies next to each other beneath the slicker, aware of the warmth and solidness of him. She wondered if he was as aware as she, or if his only thoughts were to be out of the rain.

Even held loosely above them, the plastic slicker quickly turned into a greenhouse, capturing heat and moisture. The place where their sides touched became saturated, sticking them together.

The rain suddenly turned to hail the size of chick peas, pelting down with roaring violence.

"Under here," Wiles shouted over the roar of the hail. He pulled her into the boughs of a pine, wedging them between lower branches. He kept his back to the outside, his pack taking the worst of the hail, shielding her from the storm.

She was pinned up against him, her back to the tree trunk, her arms folded up against her breasts, her loosely fisted hands lying lightly against his chest. He had one arm braced against the trunk, to keep from falling on her.

"Can you reach into the pocket on the left side of my pack?" he asked.

She started reaching for the tag of a zipper.

"Sorry, my left, your right," he said.

She shifted to the other side, her breasts brushing against him as she tried to find the pocket then struggled to open it. She was flat up against him as she dug her hand deep inside, rooting around. "What am I looking for?"

"It should be smooth and firm, about the size of a banana, only straight."

She looked up at him. "Aren't I in the wrong pocket?"

It took him a moment, but then he started to pull away. "I'll find it—"

"No, here it is." She pulled something silvery out of his pack. "What is it?"

He took it from her. "A B.L.I.S.S. Standard Issue Indestructi-sheet." He unrolled and unfolded it, revealing something that looked like a silver emergency blanket.

"Standard-issue, huh? Then why don't I have one?"

"You would have, only conversation stopped after you threw the condoms at me."

"I've got good aim, don't I?"

"Mm." He pulled aside the slicker and used the Indestructi-sheet to make a tent over their heads, using the branches of the pine for supports.

"Excellent," Rachel said in approval. "This is my type of technology. No buttons, no batteries, no instruction manual. Just like a man." She waggled her eyebrows.

He made a little noise.

She poked at the silvery roof. "What else can it do?"

"Almost anything you want."

"Even better."

He cleared his throat and glanced down at her. "I'm sorry about the close quarters."

She shrugged, laying off the sexual teasing. "Better this than getting my head pounded by chunks of ice."

"I'm flattered," he said. "I must have gone up in your estimation. I'm better than gouges in your scalp."

She made a face and tried to be a good girl and not think about the delicious feeling of his hips pressed against her. They had been carefully formal and polite with one another since the near-kiss incident at the Monkey Temple. That didn't mean that the possibility of touching him hadn't been daily in her thoughts, though. "I didn't mean to stoke your ego. I'm trying to look at the bright side of being squished in a tree."

"A 'glass half-full' type, are you?"

A smile pulled at one side of her mouth. "Depends what's in the glass."

A look of devilment crossed his face and he parted his smiling lips to respond; then his cheeks tinged pink and he looked away.

Could he really have such a shy streak? "How many women have you slept with?" she asked.

He turned back to her with a jerk. *"What?"*

"I mean, look at you. You must be quite the lady's man."

"I'd rather be a gentleman, thank you."

"Oh, come on. Tell me."

"No."

She narrowed her eyes and made a contemplative moue. "Then tell me how old you were when you lost your virginity?" The moment she said it, she realized the question could be turned back on her, and she had no intention of giving him an answer. Dammit. Whenever she wanted to hide something, it had a way of pushing itself to the tip of her tongue.

He made a face. "Eighteen."

She laughed, surprised. "You're kidding! I'd have thought younger."

"I would rather it had been even later."

"Why? Did you embarrass yourself?"

He looked offended. "No. Of course not."

"Well, then?"

He shifted uncomfortably and hesitated. "It was with the mother of one of my friends. She seduced me."

Rachel choked on her own laughter. "Oh, my God. She did a Mrs. Robinson on you."

"It was bloody awful, and just about ruined my friendship. How can you look your chum in the face after you've been in his mum's knickers? I didn't talk to him for months."

Rachel stopped laughing just long enough to ask, "Did he ever find out?"

"He's never taken a cricket bat to my head, so I assume not."

"How long did you see her?"

"Just the once. She was recently divorced, but still. My friend's mum."

"I'll bet it was one helluva night, though."

"Could we possibly change the topic?"

"Sure." That got her off the hook for answering the question, herself.

After a moment he suddenly asked, "What makes you happy?"

160

"What do you mean?" she asked, surprised.

He shrugged. "What do you like in your half-full glass? What makes Rachel Calais get giddy with delight?"

She shifted, feeling now the vulnerability of being pressed so close to him. He was inside her personal space, trying to touch her where she rarely allowed herself to be touched by anyone.

"Why?" she asked.

"Curiosity."

"That's not much of a reason," she said, purely for argument's sake. God knew it was all that got her up, some mornings.

"Curiosity has probably prompted half the discoveries of history," he said.

"I'm not unknown territory, waiting to be explored."

"To me you are."

She frowned at him. What was that supposed to mean? "You have your file."

"It told me nothing. You are not what it led me to expect."

"Aren't I?" she asked, looking up at him. Curious. "How so?"

"I'd be a fool to say."

"I don't know if that means I'm better or worse than what you had in mind."

"Neither, really," he said. "You're beyond be-

161

ing qualified in such simple terms as 'good' or 'bad.' "

"Is that good?"

"There you go again."

She smiled and met his eyes. His face was only inches from hers, the world beyond shut out by the sheet and the pine boughs. She unfisted her hands, letting her palms lie against his chest.

In the quiet there was only the sound of the hail and of their own breathing. She felt the thump of his heart beneath her palms. Water trickled down her face and dripped onto her upper lip. She licked it off, his gaze following the movement.

They stared at each other, and then she ducked her head, suddenly shy, and suddenly not wanting to know if it was rejection or acceptance she would get from him. She lifted an edge of the sheet and peeked out, wanting to look anywhere than at him. "The hail is letting up. It's turning back to rain. We'd better catch up to the others."

"Aren't you going to press me to describe how you're different from my expectations?"

"No." She edged past him, pulling the sheet with her, forcing him to follow. She'd be too embarrassed to press and be suspected of fishing for compliments from him.

"Strange girl."

"I thought the pink hair had already clued you in to that."

"That's faux strange."

"Gee, thanks," she said, breaking free of the pine branches and getting soaked in a spray of water off the needles.

"Why do you want people to think you're strange?" he asked after a moment. He put his arm back around her as they came onto the path, their steps both hurried and careful on the newly formed mud. The rain slapped their bodies where the sheet left them exposed, water seeping up their clothes. "Why the hair?"

"Because it really doesn't matter." It was hard to think with his arm around her and with her body still tingling from being pressed up against his. "What cosmic significance does it have if I dye my hair or pierce my nose?"

"So you're thumbing your nose at the rules of society."

She shook her head. "I'm proving to myself that the world won't end if I break a rule. It's just hair. It doesn't matter." And then, almost to herself, the words hidden beneath the sound of the rain, "Nothing matters, really."

But he heard her and stopped walking, forcing her to stop, too. "That's a nihilistic attitude."

She looked at the rain, not at him. "I'd rather think of it as a vaguely Buddhist one. All is ephemeral. All passes away. I find it comforting."

"Why, Rachel?" he asked, distressed.

Because she could be a nobody and a failure, and think it the same as being a success. Because she could live or die, the people she loved could live or die, and the world would be no different. Because if nothing mattered, she didn't have to care. And if she didn't care, she could never be hurt.

She didn't say any of that, though. She shrugged. "Guess I'm strange."

He didn't respond. She kept her eyes averted, not wanting to know what he thought of her. Then, to her surprise, he pulled her briefly against him in a hug, releasing her before she could react.

She blinked up at him. What was that for? But he had his gaze directed ahead.

"I think I see Min up there. Come on," he said, and hurried her along with him.

They caught up to Alan, Min, and one of the porters where the trail dead-ended at a narrow, gushing river that was almost a waterfall. Alan had a yellow slicker covering him, and even from behind looked dejected and weary, his arms hanging loose at his sides. Before he turned around, Wiles folded up the silver Indestructi-sheet and stood unprotected in the rain, while Rachel donned her slicker.

"Where'd the trail go?" Rachel asked.

Alan turned at the sound of her voice, his face flushed and pouty under his hood. He pointed accusingly at the river and blew out an unhappy, affronted breath.

Rachel twisted her lips. "Damn. I was afraid of that." In dry weather, there would have been no river. When rain hit the foothills of the Himalayas, however, it had nowhere to go but down. It took the fastest route available, and Rachel didn't know which had originally come first: the human footpath or the rainwashed gully.

Min gestured to the porter, who no longer had his pack with him. "He says there's a tea house ten, fifteen minutes ahead. That's where the others are waiting."

"Good news, eh, Alan?" she asked cheerfully. "I for one am glad we won't be spending the night in tents."

A smile struggled to surface on his mouth, but sank before making it to the top. "That is not a path."

She squatted down and yanked a brown, wormlike creature off the laces of Alan's hiking boot. She held it up for him to see for a moment, then flicked it into the brush. "Land leech. Rain brings them out. There probably aren't any in that water, though."

Alan made a disgusted noise and scrambled

into the water. The porter had already started to climb straight up the rocky cataract.

The porter's "ten or fifteen minutes" turned out to be half an hour of slogging through water and mud, and stepping from one precarious rocky foothold to another. Rachel was wet to the skin, the slicker worse than useless.

Then, just as a first roll of deep-throated thunder rumbled through the air, the tea house appeared out of the mist. One by one they stepped out of the rushing water and stumbled up the bank to the muddy yard. Rachel and Alan took temporary shelter with the porters in a lean-to full of firewood, while Min and Wiles went to go find the landlord.

A huge pile of granite stones sat ten feet from the tea house.

"Is that some sort of burial cairn?" Alan asked.

Rachel shook her head. "Building materials." The tea house was a rough structure. Hand-hewn lumber made up the framing, and the walls had been filled in with small, sharp stones. There was no mortar visible, just rocks with empty spaces between them. One good earthquake, and the whole thing would shake to the ground.

The roof looked as new as the rest of it, though, and was made of corrugated metal, which promised a dry night if not a warm one. There was glass in the windows, and twenty feet from the side of the building was a newly constructed outhouse.

"Thank God, they have showers," Alan said.

"Don't count on it," Rachel warned, bending down to flick leeches off her boots.

"But it says they do!" A sign hanging above the door proclaimed in red paint: HOT SHOWER!

"Do you remember how the porter said 'ten minutes' to get here?" she asked, looking up. "Remember how steep stretches of path were called 'flatty-uppy'? You have to learn to translate the Nepali version of English. 'Hot shower' at a tea house means a bucket of hot water brought to you in the outhouse."

"Not these outhouses," Wiles said, joining them in the shelter, water dripping down his forehead. "They're not finished. They haven't installed the squat toilets yet, and they're still digging out the septic pits."

Archer looked ready to cry.

"It's not so bad," Rachel said, consolatory, and doing her best to subdue a hysterical mirth building in her throat. "At least the place is too new to have vermin. Well, many vermin. And they should have food, assuming they're open for business. Momos, for sure," she said, referring to the popular form of dumpling. She knew he hated momos.

Alan's face slackened. His miserable expression made her relent, and she added, "They probably have Snickers and Mars bars for sale. We won't let you starve."

He did not look comforted.

Ten minutes later and Rachel was alone in her new room, laying out her wet clothes to dry and unpacking her big bag, checking for places water might have gotten in. Her room had two narrow beds—cots, really—with a thin foam mattress on each, thin Indian-print spreads, and the usual damp-heavy pillows always found in tea houses.

Lightning flashed in the gathering gloom outside the lumber-framed window, but there was no worry about loss of electricity. There *was* no electricity. Thin, cheap candles were on the windowsill and in a wooden sconce near the door.

Rachel tucked her small flashlight and Zip-Loc bag of toilet paper under her pillow, for easy access in the night. Third-world travelers came prepared.

She found the satellite phone/computer in her bag, dry inside a larger Zip-Loc. She hadn't had a chance to check her e-mail before they left Kathmandu, and didn't know if Pamela had written back.

She went to the door and peeked into the hallway. It looked empty. She listened to make sure no one was around, then went to the window and opened it. She turned on the computer and unfolded the fat antenna, hoping that she was facing the right way for a satellite to pick up her signal, and that the storm wouldn't interfere. With only half a belief that it would actually work, she clicked on the icon for Internet access.

A few soft beeps and clicks later and she was in her Hotmail account, a little bubble of delight in her chest. It was working! Too cool. She hoped she didn't have to give the computer back to B.L.I.S.S. after all this was over.

She sorted through her mail. Junk, junk, junk . . . and a letter from her sister. She opened it, heart beating, wondering if B.L.I.S.S. was monitoring her. Probably. But what choice did she have? Besides, they must have guessed that she would ask people about the organization.

She scanned the e-mail, her eyes catching at "Archer."

Alan Archer is going trekking with you? No way! Now there's a blast from the past. Funny how things work, isn't it? I found myself talking about him a few months ago, don't know how I got on the topic. Hadn't thought about him in ages. And now you're off into the hills with him!

Yes, funny how things worked, wasn't it? She would very much like to know to whom Pamela had spoken, and how Archer had come up in conversation.

I always wondered if he had a thing for you. You seemed oblivious, though, or maybe just not interested.

Rachel had been secretive, was all. She hadn't wanted Pamela to offer her opinion on Rachel's losing her virginity to an older man.

Pamela's e-mail was food for thought, though. If Pamela was, however inadvertently, B.L.I.S.S.'s source of information about Rachel, then that would explain why Wiles did not know more about her history with Alan: Pamela didn't know, so B.L.I.S.S. didn't know. All B.L.I.S.S. knew was that Alan had once liked Rachel, and would likely trust her because of their shared history.

Pamela went on about her food wars for a while, about her new lover, and then:

Never heard of B.L.I.S.S. Sounds interesting, though. I'll ask around. Might be good for you to get involved with an organization like that, do something useful with that brain of yours.

Rachel let out a breath of disappointment. She'd been counting on Pamela to find out something useful already.

Or maybe B.L.I.S.S. had hacked into her e-mail and deleted any information about themselves, putting in this plea of ignorance, instead.

She checked her watch. Five-thirty P.M. Nepal time meant 6:45 A.M. on the East Coast of the U.S. Pamela would be awake. Her heart thumped as she closed the Internet connection and began to dial the phone, knowing that B.L.I.S.S. could eavesdrop, but also knowing that they would give themselves away if she was suddenly disconnected or there was too much "convenient" static.

A rapping came at her door just as her sister's phone began to ring. She hung up and shoved the unit under her pile of stuff on the other cot, the sweat of the guilty breaking out over her body. She plopped down on her bed.

"Rachel?" Alan asked from the other side of the door.

"Come in." She used her fingertips to brush her damp hair off her forehead, and hoped there was no flush on her cheeks to betray that she had been up to something.

He opened the door and poked his head in just as another roll of thunder rumbled over them. He was still wearing his coat and boots. "This place is filthy. There's a thin layer of dirt over *everything*. Lice and fleas can breed in dirt, you know."

She stifled a sigh. "We're probably the first trekkers to even stay here. I wouldn't worry about it."

He stepped more fully into the room, half closing the door behind him. She was suddenly aware of how small the room was and how much space he took up.

He came down the narrow aisle between the two beds, stumbling on her day pack and nearly falling on her. She steadied him with her hands. His legs brushed hers and then he was past, going to the window and leaning his hands against the sill, looking out. "Why do you have the window open? It's cold and damp enough in here already."

"You can close it. I like the sound of the rain and thunder, is all."

He pulled the window shut. "You've got a better view than I do."

She stood up and took a step toward the door, hoping to encourage him to follow her out. "Not for long. It's getting dark."

He turned around and looked at her stuff spread over the beds, touching one of her polar fleece sweatshirts and half lifting it off the pile. "It's like your pack exploded in here."

She took another step toward the door. The natural light was gray, dimming further every moment, and soon they would be in darkness.

She wasn't afraid of Alan, but something about having him move in her space without her permission was making her uncomfortable. She also didn't want him digging through her stuff and finding the computer.

"They'll be starting dinner," she said. "Come look at the menu, and I'll order for you. It usually takes them about an hour to prepare things in tea houses."

He sat on her bed. "I'm in no hurry."

"Do you want me to look at your room, check out the dirt?"

He shrugged. "I guess it's no dirtier than this one."

A long moment of silence stretched between them. She shifted and felt something under her stockinged foot. She looked down, and in the deepening shadows could just make out clods of dirt on the floor, from his boots. Her own boots were beside the front door, along with everyone else's. She wondered if his clothes were making a wet spot on her bed.

He patted the mattress beside him. "Sit. I haven't had a chance to talk to you all day."

Lightning flashed outside, and a fresh burst of rain drummed on the metal roof.

She hesitated, weighing options and consequences, then reluctantly went and sat on the edge of the bed beside him.

"You did a good job today," he said, leaning back on his hands, elbows locked.

"I should say that *you* did. This is old hat for me. It's not easy for the average person to make it through a day of trekking in the foothills of the Himalayas."

"Men are stronger than women."

"But women are known for endurance."

He sat forward and let his knee fall to the side until it touched hers. He lowered his voice, looking at her. "Still, if I put my arms around you and held tight, you wouldn't be able to get away."

She tried to smile, searching his face for seriousness. "Ah, but you wouldn't try to hold me against my will."

"No, of course not," he said, chuckling, then grinned. "Not unless you asked me to."

"I don't play games, Dr. Archer," she said primly.

He touched her hair, playing with the ends where they brushed her shoulders. He tugged, once. "I know you don't play games. That's why I like you. Why I always liked you. You have always been so to-the-point, so frank about how you felt and what you wanted. Those few nights we spent together . . . they have never left my mind, Rachel. Now, finding you here, just when I need you—it almost feels like fate, doesn't it?"

She flashed him a smile, hoping he couldn't

see the tremble to it, then slapped him on the knee with a little more force than was friendly. "You're not trying to talk your way into my bed tonight, are you?"

His face held a moment of surprised guilt, and then there was a rapping on the half-open door, and both of them turned to look as Wiles stuck his head in. Wiles's eyes widened at the sight of them sitting so close together on her bed. "Rachel?"

She jumped to her feet, Alan's hand falling away from her shoulder. "Wiles!"

"What do you want?" Alan demanded, as if speaking to a rude peasant.

"The landlord's wife wants to know your order, for dinner."

"Great!" Rachel said, thankful for the excuse to escape. "Come on, Alan, let's go! Up, up!" She gestured for him to get off the bed. "Food is waiting!"

She felt Wiles watching her, silent, his gaze intensely interested. He would never believe she hadn't invited Alan in.

She didn't pause to wonder why she cared.

Laughter and startled shouts went up from the group of Nepalis sitting on the floor of the dark kitchen, as flames from their paraffin lantern leaped four feet into the air, reaching for the wooden rafters above.

"God's sake, they're going to burn the place down," Harrison said.

"I'm going to close my eyes and trust they know what they're doing," Rachel said.

Harrison watched the group, made up of their four porters, Min, the landlord, and some of his local friends. They were drinking *rakshi*, the home-brewed rice liquor that could peel the enamel off your teeth, and talking in Nepali.

The kitchen was a wooden room, as new as the rest of the building, but its ceiling was already stained black with soot. The cookstove was a small iron box on the floor, one end open for shoving in thin strips of firewood, a stovepipe going out its back. It sat on a square of fireproof dried mud. He and Rachel sat as near to it as they dared, keeping their feet and hands warm in its heat, trying to ignore the damp and cold of the uninsulated tea house. The rain had slackened off, and the lightning had become distant flashes, the thunder out of hearing.

Archer had already gone to bed, after grouchily slurping down a bowl of ramen soup, plainly displeased to be sitting on the cramped kitchen floor amidst the peons while he ate his lowly fare. Harrison thought the man would have liked to stay in the kitchen to keep an eye on Rachel, despite the uncouth company, but exhaustion had won out over lust and possessiveness. Archer had nodded off, mouth hanging open and a line of drool dribbling from the corner of his lips. When Rachel nudged him he'd awoken with a snort, wiping the spittle off his chin with the back of his hand. He'd looked horrified when he realized what he'd just done in front of his la-dylove, and had slunk off to his cold and empty room shortly thereafter.

Good riddance. Harrison hoped the wanker stayed in his room, where he belonged.

Harrison was feeling the weight of exhaustion himself, not that he'd let anyone see it. First there'd been the flight on a propeller plane to the airstrip nearest to Usuna—which meant not near at all—then an overnight bus ride, and finally they'd hired a truck to take them as far as the roads would go. The group had been weary al-ready when they started out late this morning, but moving on had been more appealing than losing a day in the dusty village where the truck had let them out. Adrenaline had fueled their muscles during the hike, but they were all feeling its lack now.

The group of Nepalis roared again, as another burst of flame shot up.

"What are they *doing* to that thing?" Rachel asked.

"Probably pouring *rakshi* on it."

"We should give a bottle of it to Alan, to disinfect the bushes when he goes to take a . . . well, you know."

A grin pulled at his lips. "I wouldn't put it past him."

"That's what he was in my room about, you know. The dirt." She made a noise of disgust. "As if he were expecting to stay in a Holiday Inn."

"It didn't look like that was his real reason for paying you a visit," Harrison said, careful not to sound critical.

She shrugged one shoulder and stretched her stockinged feet closer to the warmth of the stove.

The landlord's wife moved a half-burned piece of wood deeper into the fire. A sullen-faced thing, she had sat cross-legged and silent in the shadows the whole evening.

Harrison held his counsel, waiting to hear if Rachel might say something more about Archer, but mostly enjoying sitting quietly beside her, looking at her.

The fire and the lantern light had turned her skin to golden velvet, her hair to dark red. She wore no makeup now. Without it, her eyes were young and innocent, her mouth gentle. She was wearing another *shalwar kameez,* this time of a dark green and blue floral print, similar to the fabrics many of the hill women wore. She had a polar fleece sweatshirt pulled over it for warmth.

He liked Rachel this way, her skin clear and clean, her clothes soft and casual. He'd always had a weakness for natural-looking women. There was something accessible about Rachel as she was tonight, as if she would invite being touched and would be honest and open if she spoke about herself. There were no veils of paint and silk to keep her hidden.

As he studied her, a hint of sadness dimmed her features, the gentle cast of her mouth turning vulnerable. "What are you thinking?" he asked.

She glanced at him. "You're supposed to offer money for an answer. The usual rate is a penny, but I don't speak for less than twenty bucks."

"I'm too poor. You're only paying me ten dollars a day as your mountaineering expert."

"A living wage, here. But I can't believe you don't come from money, back home."

He grimaced, wondering how she had guessed. "Why do you say that?"

She gestured vaguely at his hair and at his person. "You have the 'look.' You appear younger than you probably are, and well groomed even when you shouldn't. Inbred sense of style, even when in cheap clothes. Good teeth. Clear, smooth skin."

He felt himself blushing. "Lucky genetics."

"No, you come from money. I'm middle class,

and it's obvious. I'll never look effortlessly beautiful or well dressed, no matter how I try."

He raised a brow. The less she tried, the more beautiful she was.

"I do try. Or I *have* tried, in the past," she went on, misinterpreting his look. Her voice faded out. "But I decided it really didn't matter."

"So we're back to that topic."

She looked at him.

"What matters," he explained. "You wouldn't tell me, earlier today. What makes you happy?"

"Not being asked personal questions, for a start."

"It's a harmless question," he defended.

"Why don't you tell me about your family, instead? You already know enough about me, from that freaking file. Even up the score."

He thought of his screwed-up family, and the mess that had led him to work for B.L.I.S.S., and suddenly he had an inkling what Rachel had been feeling when he'd confronted her with even the small amount of private information he'd been given about her.

She was watching him, reading his thoughts clearly enough in his expression. "It's not so much fun to have your personal life spelled out for a stranger's perusal, is it?" she asked.

"I'd hoped we wouldn't be strangers. We'll be working closely together for weeks yet. Understanding each other might help that working relationship." Now there was a reasonable argument, unassailable by even her.

She stared at him, and he got the sense that he had just said something wrong. Very wrong. She shook her head, eyes closed as if in disgusted disbelief. "Good night, Wiles." She started to get to her feet.

He grabbed the hem of her sweatshirt and jerked her back down. "Christ, Rachel," he said under his breath, "stop behaving like a princess."

"I beg your pardon?" she gasped, yanking the hem of her shirt out of his hand.

"I can't say a thing without you taking it the wrong way. It gets bloody annoying, walking on eggshells! It's not going to kill you to be civil and engage in a conversation with someone who is genuinely interested in hearing your thoughts."

"But you're not interested. You just want to better our working relationship."

He rolled his eyes. So that was it. "Lord save me from oversensitive women."

She poked him in the arm with a sharp finger. "Hey! You're the one who is supposed to be helping the women of the world."

"Shhh!" He gestured with a tilt of the head toward the drunken locals and the cook still sitting silent in the shadows.

"Like they're listening."

"You never know who might be eavesdropping, and able to understand more English than they let on."

A peculiar snorting sound came out of her.

"What?"

The stifled giggles came out full force. "You! Me! All of this! We're huddled around a tiny woodstove, toilet paper in our pockets, no hope of a shower for weeks, and we're supposed to be"—she dropped her voice to an airy whisper and rounded her eyes—"spies!"

"No one said it would be glamorous."

"And our villain is a lonely doctor whose worst sin is probably jerking off to memories of pelvic exams."

Harrison shuddered. It was a bleak picture she painted. "Wouldn't that be bad enough?"

"This is all such a crock. Worse yet, it's a *silly* crock."

"Then why did you agree to it?" he asked.

"You really want to know?"

"Please!"

"Boredom. However implausible your tale of Yonam, searching for it beat the hell out of hauling another group of tourists to Pokhara and back."

"That's it? You don't care about what Archer plans to do, if he manages to find the drug? I thought you said your loyalty was to the women of the world."

"It is. If there really is such a threat. I'm more inclined to believe that we'll wander around the hills for a month, find nothing, then drag our sorry asses back to Kathmandu. Alan will be so eager to get back to flush toilets and sterile food, he'll forget about Yonam and take the first flight out of here. And that will be the end of our adventure."

"You take a dim view of our chances."

"A realistic view. There's not much point in doing otherwise."

"What happened to turn you into such a cynic?" he asked.

Her mouth twisted. "It's what makes me happy. There's my answer to your question! I don't need a cause, or a religion, or a 'spiritual' life to be happy. I don't need an ambitious career, or a husband, house, and three car garage. I don't need a baby, either, although that seems to be what everyone thinks will make a woman happy. Blech." She shuddered. "All I want is a clear, unbiased view of the world and enough novelty to keep me interested. Good food and good wine— which I admit I won't be getting on this trek— and sex now and then. I'm not getting any of that, either, unless you want to help me out there? It's been ages since I had any, and hey, you bought the condoms."

He gaped at her.

"What? You wanted honesty, didn't you? It's been so long, I'm probably tighter than a virgin."

His eyes widened.

"Oh, don't look so worried. I wasn't really offering, so you don't need to get all prissy over it."

"I do not want to think of the degree of tightness of your genitalia."

"Not at all?" she asked, with a peculiar, hopeful curiosity.

"No. What do you take me for?" he asked, appalled.

"What *don't* I take you for? Don't you think of naked women, like, a hundred times a day? I thought all guys did."

"It's disrespectful."

"What?"

"It's disrespectful to undress a woman in one's mind, especially if a man knows her."

She gaped at him. "But you must! Guys always do that. Don't you use acquaintances in your sexual fantasies?"

"You wouldn't want me to imagine having sex with you, would you?" he evaded.

She stared at him for a long moment. "I think I'd be a bit insulted if I didn't warrant so much as a quickie. I'd assumed standards were pretty low for mental sex."

How had he gotten himself into this conversation? He was far, far out of his depth. "You'd feel better if I fantasized about using your body?"

"Well, yeah. I used to be a bit of a porker, and I'd like to think slimming down has earned me a few points in sexual attractiveness."

"I'm sorry, I just can't do it," he lied. Sure he could do it, but he was trying his best not to.

She kicked his foot. "Oh, come on. Don't be rude!"

"Rude!"

"Tell me, where would you do it? In your mind, that is. Would you imagine us out on the trail, doing it real fast before anyone could catch us? Or are you more of a clean sheets and locked door kind of guy?"

"Stop it!" He could imagine a thing or two to call her bluff, but goddammit, he was going to be a gentleman and mind his thoughts! "*I'm* the one who's going to have to file a sexual harrassment suit!"

She stuck out her tongue at him. "You're no fun."

He dug his hands into his hair. "Christ."

"Now, I wonder, did *he* ever have sex? I heard a theory that Mary Magdalene was actually his wife, not a prostitute."

A choked sound gurgled in Harrison's throat.

"I thought it was an interesting idea, anyway," she said.

"Is nothing sacred to you?"

"No. That was my whole point. I'm a cynic, remember? A realist."

"A nihilist."

"Yes, that too," she said cheerily. "Will you answer a question for me, now that I've answered yours?"

He groaned, low and quiet. He felt beat up and abused by their conversation so far, and feared what she might have in mind. "As long as it has nothing to do with the tightness of virgins."

"From your reaction, one might think you had a fear of sex. But what I want to know is, why do you work for B.L.I.S.S.? I mean, a well-educated, good-looking guy from a rich family, shouldn't you be working for the British government or something? More official James Bond than this rinky-dink outfit you're with."

"It's not 'rinky-dink,' a phrase I assume to be one of your charming Americanisms."

"The point, Wiles."

He sighed.

Waited.

Considered.

If she was ever going to let down her walls and trust him, he'd have to give something away of his own, first. "You can't work for the government or be a police officer when you have a criminal record. I have one."

Her mouth and eyes went *O!* "No way!"

He grimaced. "Unfortunately, it's true."

She scooted closer to him and leaned forward, her eyes shining. "What'd you do? Did you kill someone?"

"Er . . . not exactly. But I tried to."

"No!" She stared at him in shock, then made a noise and shook her head. "I don't believe you."

"My father. I chased him down the street with a knife—one of those big Ghurka ones, a *khukri*. I was screaming, 'I'm going to kill you' the whole way, so he had plenty of witnesses when the police came. The neighbors thought it quite a show."

She gaped at him, wordless for long moments. "So, were you a kid or something?"

"Nineteen. Old enough for it to stick."

"But, your father . . . He didn't press charges, did he?"

"He's an ass of the first water, which was why I was chasing him to begin with. Of course he pressed charges. I'd frightened and embarrassed him, and he had to make me pay."

She pulled her knees up and wrapped her arms around them, her attention focused completely on him. She shivered, in what looked like delighted fascination. "Tell me everything."

"You're supposed to be inching away from me, looking scared."

"Are you kidding? This is the most interesting thing I've heard about you."

"Now, see, that's the problem with women," he griped. "I try to be a noble guy, and you barely speak to me. I say I tried to kill my own father, and you pay me more attention than the entire time I've known you. God save women from their own bad judgment."

"Stop whining and tell me why you tried to kill your dad."

He took a deep breath, considering where to begin. "My father . . . is a cad and a scoundrel."

"So that's where you get it from," she said.

"Do you want to hear this or not?"

"Oh, yes!" She shivered again.

He frowned at her. "My mother was only seventeen when she met him at an art museum. Mom was a stunner, the type of woman you can't look away from. Still is, really. But she's unsure of herself even now, and I can only imagine what she was like back then.

"Dad was a few years older, and from a different class. His family has money, and a pedigree going back five hundred years. Mum thought she'd met Prince Charming. Dad was young

188

enough that he convinced himself he was in love with her, too.

"Neither of their families approved of the match, so they did what any young idiots would do and eloped."

Rachel lay her cheek on her arm as she watched him. "I would say that that sounds terribly romantic, but I know there's a knife at the end of the story."

He snorted. "Sure that doesn't turn you on?"

"Show me yours, and maybe it will."

He felt his cheeks heating in embarrassment. "Have you no shame?"

"Not really. So they eloped?"

"Eloped, struggled to get by, and then I came along and the romance ended. By the time I was a year old, he had moved out and started living with an underwear model. He didn't divorce Mum, though, I think because being married saved him having to promise to wed anyone else."

"Did he keep in contact with you?"

"Only because of Mum. He'd come back to her for a few weeks between girlfriends, and he paid for my schooling."

"Your mother kept taking him back?"

"Every time. You'd think she'd learn that he was never going to be the husband she wanted.

189

It tore her up every time he left, and she'd cry for weeks."

"Maybe she liked the drama."

"Maybe," he admitted. The thought was a new one to him, and not particularly welcome. "But I didn't. It got too much for me to stand, seeing her destroyed like that every six months. She obviously couldn't send him away on her own, so I decided to do it for her."

She started to laugh. "Oh, Lord! She won't have thanked you for that!"

"No," he grumbled. "But that's the story of why I chased my father down the street with a knife, threatening to kill him. Did it twice, actually," he added with a half smile.

"You were just trying to scare him, though, right? You wouldn't have actually done anything?"

He shrugged, uneasy with the question, as he had been uneasy with it for years now. "At the time, who knows? I was young and stupid, and saw him as someone who was hurting my mother. There wasn't a lot of thought that went into it."

She grinned and playfully pushed his arm with her fingertips. "Savage! So where's your father now? Are you still in contact with him?"

"He's back home in England. I never hear from him, and if my mother does, she doesn't tell me.

I think I scared her more than I did him."

"You fiend, you," she said, laughter in her voice.

"Yeah, just what I wanted, to frighten my own mother." He rubbed his face and stared into the shadows, new worries mixing with those old feelings. His growing emotional involvement in this mission concerned him. He was not certain that inside him there didn't still lurk the same impassioned, stupid boy who had chased his father with a knife. He could remember the feeling of rage, and the complete loss of rationality that went with it. There were moments he almost felt that same way, when Archer was near Rachel. It didn't help that Rachel showed every sign of thinking Archer was still the boy she had loved as a teenager.

It was better, though, that Rachel took him only half seriously, as she did now, than that she should ever look at him with the shocked terror his mother had.

Rachel yawned and stretched, her arms above her head, her back arching, thrusting her small breasts into prominence even through the polar fleece. He forced his eyes away.

"That was as good a bedtime story as I've had in years. Thank you, Wiles." She stood. "Since you've shown no inclination to join me, I fear I must retire alone to my boudoir."

"Lock your door."

"To keep you out? Never."

"Rachel . . ."

She wrinkled her nose at him, kissed her fingertips, and touched them lightly to his forehead. "G'night, Oedipus."

He muttered, and watched her go. And wished he knew if there was anything sincere beneath her teasing.

Rachel woke from her doze to darkness and the pressure of her bladder. She brought her wrist in front of her face and lit the Indiglo of her Timex watch: 2:10 A.M.

She lay still, trying to force the discomfort of her bladder away from her thoughts and fall back asleep. She heard the wind gently rattling her windows and whispering through the gaps in wood and stones. Muted snores came from another room.

Her bladder ached.

Damn it.

She groaned and rolled to her side, reaching under her pillow for her flashlight and toilet paper. The round side of the flashlight bumped against her fingertips, then was gone as she accidentally nudged it past the edge of the bed. There was a loud thunk and then a moment of rolling, plastic on wood.

"Crap!" She leaned over the side of the bed, staring into the utter darkness beneath her cot. She gingerly brushed her hand over the floor within reach, with no success. "Piss."

She climbed out of bed, the chill air making her bladder contract another few degrees. She hunkered down on the floor, patting around under the cot, thinking of spiders. "Damn, damn, damn. Oh, screw it!"

She stood and rooted through her pack on the other cot, fingers searching her gear until she found the night-vision goggles. Ha! There was a use for them, after all! She put them on and flipped the switch, the room turning from black to contoured green.

Her bladder demanded she *go,* now, without stopping to look again for the flashlight. She slipped on her coat, undid the simple hasp lock on her door, and padded in stockinged feet down the hall, slipping on her boots at the entryway.

She would not think of wild animals and yeti, no, no. No leopards, no bears. She hurried across the yard toward the dark and unfinished outhouse, the night wind making her pull her coat closed over her chest.

Behind the outhouse was a newly dug septic pit. She scanned the area with her goggles for any sign of lurking wildlife, then jerked down her pants and squatted over the edge. *Don't let me fall in, please don't let me fall in,* she prayed.

Guys had it so easy. No hanging *their* butts into the air five times a day.

Maybe this dead-of-night outing was cosmic punishment for her behavior tonight. She recalled some of the things she'd said to Wiles and moaned in embarrassment, hiding her face in her hands. What was wrong with her?

She had to get a grip. She had to put aside this silly crush and start acting like a normal human being. Her attraction was leaving her so afraid of him, she could barely be civil.

She shook her head. Some days, it was a lesson in humiliation to be Rachel Calais.

Her business finished, if not her self-scolding, she came back around the outhouse. The scent of wood smoke hit her nose, and she raised her gaze to the tea house.

Someone ran along its side, then disappeared behind it, the figure unrecognizable. She stopped and stared, surprised. Then the wood smoke came to her even stronger, and the goggles glared with greenish white light from one of the windows.

A flush of panic rushing through her, Rachel lifted the goggles off her head, suspecting and dreading. The greenish white light immediately turned orange.

Fire!

"Fire! Fire!" she screamed, running toward the

tea house. "Wiles! Alan! Min! Wake up, fire! Fire!"

Panic sent her heart thumping hard enough to make her ill. Her companions could not fall victim to the flames, *No!*

"Wiles!" she screamed. "Wiles! Get out! Wake up, damn you!" He could not burn, could not!

She used the goggles to bang on windows just above her head, going down the side of the building, shrieking, trying to remember who was in which room, and where the rooms faced.

"Fire!"

Male voices shouted from inside, then all was confusion as windows were kicked open, flames licked up into the rafters, and people started coming out of the building like weevils from old bread, yelling and shouting. Searing heat came off in a constant blast.

She didn't see Wiles. Damn it, where was he? Her muscles went loose and weak with the terror that he might die in there. She put the goggles back on, forced her jellied legs to move, and ran around the building, screaming his name over the roars and crackles of the fire. A window on the front side crashed as a backpack was thrown through it, the bag landing right in front of her. She yelped.

"Rachel? Is that you?"

A silver blob was perched in the fractured window frame, glowing with the reflected light of flames. Wiles, and his Indestructi-sheet.

"Get out of there, you idiot! Don't you know enough to leave a burning building? Jump, damn it, jump!"

He leaped nimbly to the ground, sheet streaming behind him like a cape, then straightened and grabbed her by the shoulders. "Are you all right?" His face was concerned in the green light of the goggles.

"Of course I am, you idiot. What were you doing in there, packing? It's a fire, damn it! You're supposed to get *out*."

"I was looking for you."

"Wha . . . ?" she started, then looked at the backpack. It was hers. "Oh." Warmth washed over her, pooling in a queer little quiver in her belly. That was her room he'd jumped out of. He'd come looking for her, instead of saving himself, the moron.

He pulled the goggles off her head, pulled her into his arms, and held her tight. She remained stiff against him, her cheek against the hardness of his sternum, smelling the acrid smoke in his clothes. Safe in the comfort of his arms, though, some recess of her mind allowed a delayed attack of nerves. Shivering, she closed her eyes and relaxed against him, letting herself be held. She would let him be the strong one for this one moment, and thank God that he seemed to have no care for her bad behavior earlier in the evening.

There was a popping roar from the fire, the heat burning their skin and driving them away from the tea house. They separated, and she was alone again in her own skin, the few inches between them feeling like miles. It had been so long since she had been held and comforted, she had forgotten the peace to be found in it. She missed it already.

Wiles pulled the night goggles on over his own head and scanned the undergrowth and trees at the edge of the yard. "I'd like to know who set this," he said.

"It was an accident, wasn't it? Those drunk idiots with the paraffin lantern."

"Perhaps."

"Who else could it have been?" she asked, but before he could answer she remembered the figure she'd seen running by the tea house. She told Wiles what she'd seen, and added, "The only person I could say it wasn't, was Alan. Alan is too tall."

Wiles lifted the goggles off his head and turned to look at the burning building. "Someone knows where we're going and doesn't want us to get there."

A cold fear slithered into Rachel's belly, squirming and twisting like a snake.

The trek wasn't just for fun anymore.

Chapter Nine

Rachel sat on a rough bench outside the army checkpoint, savoring the chance to rest. The checkpoint was a two-room shack in the middle of nowhere, and the guard on duty was taking his time about giving the group the stamps and permits to continue their journey into the next district, despite Alan's bribe-bought "go anywhere" pass. She could hear the murmur of the men's voices inside, but paid little attention. She was too beat.

The group that had continued the trek after the tea house fire was smaller and more subdued than the one that started it. A week had passed since the disaster, but they had yet to regain their enthusiasm or high spirits. Rachel was as unsettled as the others, every face but Wiles's and Alan's one to distrust.

Min would be a possibility for the culprit behind the fire, except she had been intimate with the man and was convinced there wasn't a villainous bone in his body. Not every man from her sexual past could turn out to be a bad guy—it would be too depressing a comment on her taste in men, if so.

Besides, how could Min have plotted ahead of time to be on this journey? He couldn't. She had gone to him. She could imagine no motivation he would have to stop them, anyway.

Had it been one of the porters? Again, why? And how would one of them have known the group's real destination?

She had ruled out the tea house landlord: He would never have burned down his own building. All that remained of it was a smoking jumble of rocks and blackened timbers, and she sincerely doubted he had fire insurance.

Maybe someone had paid one of their porters to sabotage their efforts after the man was hired. It was the only thing that made sense.

She took a sip of water from her bottle and sighed in frustration. Such a conclusion brought her no nearer to the answer to the question "who?" Her thoughts were going in circles, suspecting everyone in general but unable to narrow down to anyone in particular.

Maybe it *had* been the drunkards, with their paraffin and *rakshi*, and the person she'd seen running by the tea house had been one of the drunken locals, going to take a piss and still too drunk to have noticed the fire. She didn't know.

The expedition's supplies and personnel had not gone unharmed. The fancy phone/computer/gps unit had not made it out of Rachel's room, having been left behind on the cot along with the damp clothes she had spread out to dry. Two of the bags with supplies and gear had gone up in flames.

One of the porters had inhaled smoke and received second-degree burns. He would not be continuing on with them, and one of the others had insisted on accompanying his colleague back to civilization. Archer's group was left with two porters to carry what remained of their gear: young brothers named Krishna and Porna.

Maybe one of the departing porters had been the arsonist. Wishful thinking, but not impossible.

Rachel and the others had passed through the small village of Usuna five days past, and received directions to Tangunboche Gompa, the monastery where the monk in Durga's drawing had once lived. The only thing she knew for cer-

tain about their heading was that it was uphill. Up, up, always up.

"Well, that slices it," Wiles said, coming out and plopping down beside her. His arm brushed against hers with easy familiarity. "We'll just have to turn back."

"Why? What's going on in there?" She leaned back against the sun-warmed wall of the checkpoint and closed her eyes. Wiles wanted to be the leader, so she'd be nice today and let him worry about the permits. She'd rather doze anyway, and savor the accidental touches of his arm against hers. She was too tired to care what he thought of her, which perversely made her able to relax in his presence.

"Your boyfriend got impatient and decided on self-service. Tore a permit right out of the soldier's book."

She winced, eyes still closed. "Oh, Lord." She was embarrassed for Alan, and embarrassed as well that he really was an ex-boyfriend.

"I've never seen a soldier's eyes bug out in quite that way."

"Is Alan going to prison?"

"Min's hope is that he's going to his wallet. Archer, however, doesn't quite see the necessity."

She reluctantly opened her eyes and sat forward. The bench was high enough that her feet dangled, and she didn't want to put them back down on the hard ground. "Maybe I can explain it to him," she said, but made no move to get up.

Wiles leaned forward and frowned at her. "Rachel? Are you feeling all right?"

"Just tired."

"Are you sure that's it? You didn't eat much at breakfast."

"The fried potatoes had cumin on them. I hate cumin."

"And you've been walking slowly. Are you sure the altitude isn't getting to you? We're at about fourteen thousand feet."

She closed her eyes, listening to the rapid thumping of her heart. It hadn't slowed much since she'd begun resting, nor had she fully caught her breath. Her muscles held a peculiar sort of exhaustion, unrelated to the familiar pain of overexertion; they were, instead, dully devoid of strength. It might indeed be oxygen that she was lacking.

"Damn it," she muttered, embarrassed by the display of weakness. "I never get altitude sickness."

"You know it can't be predicted. We're going to have to stop here until you adjust."

She mustered the energy for a frown. "No." She dug around in her day pack and brought out the terrain map. She traced her finger along the trail route that a villager had uncertainly sketched in for them. It seemed to skirt along the edge of the mountain they were on, crossing only a couple contour lines. "We should only gain another two to three hundred feet in the next five miles."

"If the map is accurate, which it probably isn't. You don't want this to get worse."

"Nor do I want to camp next to an army checkpoint. We can go until the trail really begins to climb, then stop."

"You're too stubborn for your own good," he said, a touch of anger in his tone.

"And you're overprotective," she said. She liked the feeling of his watching out for her, though. "No one dies at fourteen thousand feet. I'll be fine. Just slow."

She looked past him as Alan was shoved out the door by a red-faced Min. "Assuming, that is, that we're allowed to move on."

"I paid good money for that permit!" Alan complained.

Rachel sighed and pushed to her feet, wishing she could dissociate herself entirely from the man. Why hadn't she seen what an ass he was when she was a teenager? Wiles stood as well, laying his hand on her arm. "You should rest."

She gave him a weak smile. "Altitude sickness has its advantages. I think that soldier is ready for a display of feminine helplessness."

She saw that Alan was staring at them, silent now. His gaze was fixed on Wiles's hand on her arm. "Alan," she said, stepping away from Wiles's warm touch, "you stay out here."

Alan snarled, "That idiot in there is wasting our time. You can't reason with people like that."

"Sit." She pointed to the bench.

"But—"

She pointed her finger at him, motioned to the bench again, and glared a warning.

"I am not a child," he sulked, and shuffled over to the bench.

Inside, the middle-aged soldier sat tight-lipped across a rough wooden table, his expression greeting her with the same pleasure he'd meet a pile of dog waste with on his clean floor.

Rachel sank slowly onto the bench opposite, letting exhaustion and humility show in her every move. She pried open a corner of the lid on the sadness within her, just enough to bring a sheen of tears to her eyes.

The soldier's own eyes widened, the line of his mouth softening.

Female tears. Would men never grow a defense against them?

God willing, no.

Five minutes later, she and Min emerged from the shack with both the permits and an earnest caution from the soldier that there were Maoist rebels in the area. Twice in the past week there had been skirmishes with soldiers—which was the reason he had been so reluctant to issue the permits in the first place. He'd been concerned for their safety.

The news of rebels in the area unsettled Rachel. They hadn't been known to harm foreigners, but robbery was a strong possibility. A Nepalese girl had been raped by a rogue Maoist a few years ago, too. There was nothing comforting about armed outlaws roaming the hills.

Min seemed even less pleased than she, his normal energetic exuberance transformed to tense jumpiness.

"Miss Rachel, this is not good. If Dr. Archer meets with the Maoists, he will get us all shot."

"Probably." How could she argue?

"The soldier may be right, and we should not continue."

"I'll talk to Alan," she said, but hadn't the energy for it right then.

Min made a noise.

"I'll *talk* to him, I said. Besides, we've never had trouble before, no matter the warnings or alerts. We've never seen a single Maoist."

Min didn't protest further, but the look on his face said he was not reassured. Neither was she.

They gathered the group together and got back

on the trail. They walked for three more hours, Rachel growing increasingly slow, her legs not wishing to obey the fuzzy orders of her brain. Her lungs were starved of air, her heart thumping too rapidly in her chest as it tried to pump enough oxygen-thin blood to her muscles.

"We're stopping here," Wiles said, pulling them all to a halt. It was a flat area, within earshot of a river.

"There's plenty of daylight left," Alan said.

"We're stopping." Wiles unshouldered his pack, and Min did the same. Rachel sank to a rock and sat, unprotesting, her brain filled with no thoughts other than a vague thankfulness for being motionless.

"I'm the one paying for this expedition, and I think I should be consulted about how many hours we waste out of a day. I—"

The rest of Alan's words were cut off as Wiles strode up to him and got in his face, whispering words low and harsh that Rachel could not make out. She closed her eyes.

A moment later she opened them to Alan bending over her, looking into her face, touching her forehead, taking her pulse. His petulant expression of before was replaced by concern, his examination of her efficient, his tone professional as he asked her questions about her breathing, her appetite, and whether or not her head hurt. She realized with surprise that he was probably an excellent doctor, and was even more surprised to realize that she trusted him with her physical care.

"I'm going to give you some Diamox," he said. "It should help with the symptoms. I'm going to make you drink water, too. I don't think you've had enough."

"So what's the prognosis? Is my brain going to swell out my ears?" she joked, half serious. "Lungs going to turn into swamps?"

His mouth quirked at the corner, but he didn't respond with jokes in kind. "You're going to be fine. You should have told me sooner about your symptoms, but no harm done. Rest, Diamox, water. You should feel better by morning."

She met his eyes and saw there a genuine concern. There was no lust or pleading yearning in his gaze now: just a human, caring consideration for her well-being. She suddenly remembered the gentle treatment he had given the porter who had been burned in the tea house fire—a porter he had no reason to care two figs about.

In a moment of need, the real man showed himself.

Guilt hit her, for all the unkind thoughts she'd had about him. Had she let Wiles's dislike of this man color her judgment? There was kindness in Alan, but she had let herself forget it and focus on the negatives in hopes that Wiles would find her more attractive that way.

Her cheeks heated in shame. What a self-serving coward she was.

She accepted the Diamox tablets from Alan and drank the water he prescribed, as well as downing a mild sleeping pill he gave her. By the time she was finished her tiny tent had been set up, and the lure of curling up in the warmth of her sleeping bag was too great to resist. Too tired to feel guilt for not helping set up camp, she climbed inside her tent, pulled off her boots, and burrowed into the down bag.

She awoke to darkness, and male voices arguing in hushed tones.

"She needs to eat," Wiles said.

"Let her sleep. Leave her alone. She doesn't need you pestering her." That was Alan.

"She's hardly eaten anything all day. She needs to keep up her strength."

"Which she'll best do by rest. Don't you think I know what I'm talking about?"

"Oh, for God's sake," Rachel said, loud enough for them both to hear. "I'm certainly not going to sleep with the two of you yapping outside my tent flap."

Silence greeted her words, then furious, accusatory whispering, the words of which she could not make out.

She sighed loudly, lay still for a moment to savor the dregs of sleep, then scrambled up and pushed back the flap of her tent.

Wiles and Alan were both standing there, watching her, looking simultaneously annoyed and embarrassed.

She slipped on her boots, leaving them unlaced, and stood, striving all the while to pretend that neither Wiles nor Alan existed. She looked instead to the sky: It was a clear blue green on the horizon, but overhead the stars were out, and the mountainside itself was black with night.

A small campfire burned a few yards away, and farther on the porters fussed with pots over the low glow of their kerosene cookstove.

"Min!" Rachel called, and trudged in her loose boots to the campfire, where Min had just stuck another piece of wood into the flames. "Min! We can't burn wood! You *know* that!"

He looked up at her and grinned. "I did not cut anything. It was on the ground."

Rachel glared at the cheery little fire and at the pile of broken branches—some suspiciously fresh—that Min had set to one side. Deforestation was a major problem in Nepal, and Rachel only allowed gas or kerosene stoves for cooking on her treks. "It's a bad precedent."

"Sit," Min said, unrepentant. "I will bring you *dhal bhaat*."

The fire was already burning, the wood already gathered. She sighed and sat on the ground, and tried not to enjoy the leaping flames and crackling warmth of the contraband fire.

Alan sat down beside her, while from the corner of her eye she saw Wiles go to help the porters and Min with dinner.

"Are you feeling any better?" Alan asked.

"Enough to be easily annoyed, apparently."

"Let me rub your shoulders," he said.

"No—"

But he wasn't listening. He scooted around behind her and put his hands on her shoulders, kneading at the tight muscles below her neck. It should have felt good, but despite herself she found her eyes going to Wiles, nervous that he would see what was going on.

"You're tense," Alan said.

She closed her eyes and tried not to care if Wiles saw her letting Alan touch her. It was a back rub, that was all, and what did it matter what Wiles thought? Alan was her friend. "The tension is just from not feeling well." She paused. "And maybe it's this weird trek we're on."

His hands slowed their movement; then he lightly dug his thumbs around the edges of her shoulder blades. She shivered. That really *did* feel good.

"What do you mean? What's weird about this trek?" he asked.

"That soldier at the checkpoint, warning us about the rebels. It makes me wonder why we're so determined to get to Tangunboche Gompa. Any other monastery might do as well, and there are plenty in safer districts. Chasing down that monk by a drawing—it's like we're on a treasure hunt, only I'm not sure there's the treasure you want at the end, and even if there is, the danger might not be worth it."

"What we're doing isn't worth possibly finding a cure for an incurable disease?" he asked.

"You know I can't argue with that," she said, turning to look at him over her shoulder. "But I *can* argue that you'd likely find the same plants in other districts that cross the same elevations."

He used his palms to massage down her spine, dwelling on the small of her back. She relaxed, enjoying it. *Wiles* hadn't offered to rub her back for her, after all.

Alan bent close to her ear. "What if I told you that I have more information than I've let on? Would that make you feel any better?"

She looked at him again, their faces so close they almost touched. "What type of information?"

He kissed her softly on the cheek, letting his lips lie against her skin long enough to make it feel like a mark of possession. She was suddenly uncomfortable with him again. She could feel no more than friendship toward Alan, but he wasn't satisfied with that.

When he finally broke away he whispered, "Trust me. We do need to get to that monastery. It will all be worth it in the end, I promise. You have no idea."

He was right. She had no idea what she was doing.

Harrison saw Archer kiss Rachel's cheek, and wanted to strangle him. The man hadn't even noticed Rachel wasn't feeling well until it was pointed out to him, but all he had to do was pull a couple of Diamox out of his bag, and suddenly he was a beloved hero.

Even after Archer's childish behavior at the army checkpoint, Rachel still couldn't see what a wanker the man was.

Archer resumed rubbing her back, and Harrison ground his teeth. He took the plate of *dhal bhaat* from Min that was intended for Rachel, and carried it and his own dinner over to the fire. Min and the porters Porna and Krishna followed, the campfire too cozy a lure to resist. Harrison sat down on the opposite side of Rachel from Archer, and handed her the plate of rice and stewed lentils.

Archer stopped his massaging when Rachel thanked Harrison and started to eat; then Archer looked at the second plate Harrison was holding. Harrison smiled and started eating.

Archer's eyes narrowed. He went to his pack, dug out a couple of candy bars, then sat back down and noisily opened one up, drawing Rachel's attention.

"Alan, don't you want some rice?"

"I've had about as much as I can take," he said. Harrison was sure he had. The man's pride couldn't even handle getting up to fetch his own meal.

"But Snickers bars? Really. That's no dinner. Go get yourself a plate."

"I'm content with this. Would you like one?" he asked, holding out a bar.

"You need to take better care of yourself," she chided, sounding too concerned and mothering for Harrison's taste.

"I'll take one!" Harrison said, and reached around Rachel, grabbing the candy bar from Archer. "Thanks!"

Archer gaped at him.

Rachel made a noise suspiciously like a giggle. "Wiles, go get Alan a plate of *dhal bhaat*. If you take his dinner, the least you can do is get him something nutritious to replace it."

"It's not necessary—" Archer started.

Lisa Cach

"Hey, no problem," Harrison said, then rubbed his nose with the back of his hand, coughed into his palm, held his hand away from him for a moment as if to examine something on it, then wiped it on his pants. "Glad to serve you."

Rachel made another of the suspicious noises, and devoted herself to deep study of her food. With a cheerful whistle, Harrison jumped up and went to get Archer his food. The lentils were flavorless and watery tonight. He'd be sure to give Archer an extra-large helping.

"You should not be whistling so," Min said when Harrison and he returned to the fire. Harrison handed the plate of *dhal bhaat* to Archer, and enjoyed the wrinkling of the man's nose.

"Why not?" Harrison asked.

"It is like the sound of the yeti."

"The yeti whistles pop tunes?"

"We're high enough, and far enough from villages. We may see one." Min's face was devilish in the firelight. Porna and Krishna were silent, listening. Harrison knew they could understand much more English than they could speak. "Before you see one, first you hear a high-pitched whistle," Min said. Krishna and Porna nodded.

Despite himself, Harrison felt the hairs go up along the back of his neck. Rachel gave an exagerrated shudder.

"You don't really believe they exist, do you?" she asked Min.

"There are too many stories. *Some*-thing is out here."

Rachel put her food aside and drew up her knees, taking on that same rapt listening expression she had given Harrison when he told her about chasing his father with a knife. The girl had a ghoulish heart.

"Tell me," she said.

Harrison sat close beside her, and saw that Archer scooted even closer to her other side. Harrison inched a little closer still, until his arm was pressed against her side. Her attention only on Min, Rachel seemed not to notice that she was being sandwiched between them.

"The yeti's paw can break the neck of a yak with one hit. A mountain woman tending her animals, she heard the whistle. Something hit the back of her head and shoved her face into a stream, holding her under, like it was trying to drown her. When she woke up, there was lots of blood from a rip in her head, and four of her animals were dead. Big footprints all around. It was a yeti."

"She didn't see it?" Rachel asked.

"Other people have. Long arms, flat face. It smells bad. People see it at sunset, mostly, but it can attack in the night."

215

"But you've never seen one?" Rachel asked.

"Only leopards. They come at night, too."

"But they're not around *here*, are they?" Archer asked.

"You go to the stream at night and be quiet, and maybe you will see one come to drink."

"They won't come into camp, though, right?" Archer asked.

Min shrugged. "Maybe. Maybe the cat is curious. Bring your torch if you go out to pee, and shine it around. If you see green eyes, you will know it is a leopard."

Rachel put her hand on Archer's knee. "He's just trying to scare you."

"I read in the *Kathmandu Post* that an early morning jogger was killed by a leopard a few weeks ago," Harrison said.

"Mauled, not killed," Rachel corrected. She patted Archer's knee. "And really, Alan, that was a freak event. The scariest thing I've ever seen in the hills is a bear. You've got nothing to worry about."

Harrison had forgotten about bears. Maybe *he* wouldn't be going out in the woods to relieve himself, either.

"At least up here, we don't have to worry about the Man with the Hook," Archer said, making Rachel laugh.

"What?" Harrison asked, leaning forward to

see past Rachel to Archer. "Who's the Man with the Hook?"

"Hook?" Min asked.

Krishna and Porna frowned.

"It's an urban legend in the U.S.," Archer explained. "About a man with a hook for a hand. Teenagers in a parked car, scraping noises—I can't remember. Rachel, do you know how it goes?"

"Well . . ." she started, and launched into a dramatic telling of the story, complete with sound effects. When the hook story was done, she went on to a variation where the teenage boyfriend ended up hanging in a tree, his blood dripping on the roof of the car where his girlfriend sat all night in terror. That tale was followed by one about a vanishing hitchhiker, and then one about a girl in a party dress, walking alongside the road, who turned out to be a ghost wanting to go to one last dance.

By the time she was done, they were all sprawled on the ground, heads propped on hands, like children listening to a storyteller. Harrison had listened with only half an ear to the stories, his attention focused instead on her mobile expressions and the gestures of her hands.

She almost seemed a stranger as she spoke, and he wondered at the oddity of that until he realized: She was showing a wide range of emotion. In her private conversations with him, it was a battle to get her to show anything but a shell of annoyance, or an equally impenetrable one of biting humor.

Her storytelling was acting, not real, but it hinted at what was beneath that pink hair and tough-girl exterior. He had an insight about her, and his heart almost stopped with the shock of it: She was shy. Like many actors, she could only show herself when hiding behind the mask of a character.

Remembering the racy, suggestive way she had talked to him that night at the tea house, and her belligerence on other occasions, he almost couldn't believe it. But it made sense, didn't it? It fit with her reluctance to tell him anything personal about herself.

He had to accept it: Rachel Calais was painfully shy.

Following close on that shocker, he realized something else: She probably liked Archer because he wasn't threatening. He was a clumsy guy she knew from her youth, who openly adored her. She had nothing to fear from him.

Did it follow that he himself scared her, given the way she usually treated him?

Maybe. But why? Why would she fear him?

Maybe she thought he didn't like her. That

wouldn't be too surprising, given the bad start they'd gotten.

He should do something about that. He loved her hard, sassy shell that took no flak from anyone, and was even turned on by it in a rough, contentious sort of way. The thought that she might be tender and vulnerable deep inside, though, made his heart melt, and brought out all his protective instincts.

Just because she was shy didn't mean she should be wasting herself on that idiot Archer. She ought to know she could do better.

What had she told him, that day at the Monkey Temple? Something about it being basic human nature to like people whom you knew to like you back.

With the end of Rachel's stories, the group around the fire began to break up. Archer leaned over Rachel, kissing her cheek, stroking her hair, and whispering "Good night" with more portentous meaning than Harrison cared to hear.

Flabby-assed wanker.

Rachel went into her tent before he could talk to her, but then emerged a few minutes later carrying her torch and toilet paper. She disappeared into the woods, apparently unworried about yeti, bears, or the Man with the Hook.

When Archer's back was turned, Harrison set off after her.

A branch poked him under the eye, and he twisted his ankle on a rock. Cursing under his breath, he stumbled on, searching for the light of Rachel's torch. The sound of the river grew louder, drowning out his ability to hear movement in the forest around him.

He was beginning to wonder just how far he'd wandered from camp, and to berate himself for not pausing to get his own torch, when he saw the white, erratic glow of hers shining on the ground as she walked.

He stumbled toward the light, still some twenty feet away through the brush and trees. She was getting ahead of him, and he hurried through the undergrowth, half afraid now of not being able to find his way back if he lost her.

He had almost reached her when she suddenly lifted the light from the ground and aimed it full-force into his face. She shrieked. He shrieked too, putting up his hands to shield his eyes from the light.

Then suddenly she was beating him on the chest with her torch.

"You idiot! What are you doing, barging through the woods like that in the dark? You scared me out of my wits, you frickin' moron! Christ!" She beat him on the head. "If I hadn't just peed, I'd have to change my underwear. What's *wrong* with you?"

He lowered his arms as the beating lessened. "I'm protecting you from bears?"

"Aaa!"

"I'm sorry, I'm sorry! I wanted to talk to you, away from Archer. This seemed like a good opportunity."

"While I go to make use of the bushes. Yeah, great timing."

"Hey, I said I was sorry."

He couldn't see her face, what with the torch pointed now at the ground, but he heard her give an exaggerated sigh and could imagine her expression of exasperation.

"Okay," she said. "So now that you've hunted me down, what did you want to talk to me about?"

"I wanted to tell you, I think you're hot."

"*What?*"

Had he just said that? Bloody hell. "Hot?" He sounded like an American teenager. "What I meant was, I wanted you to know . . ."

"Yes?" She sounded more than a little testy.

"To know that I think you're hot." Damn it to hell! How had that word come out again? "I mean, you've got a great figure, from what I can see. Not many slender women have breasts as nice as yours, not unless they're fake."

"Gee, thanks. I'm so glad you noticed."

"No, I mean, you've got beautiful eyes. And

you're funny, really funny when you want to be."
Why hadn't he stopped to think before charging
off into the woods? Why? Why?

"A comedian with good breasts. No wonder
B.L.I.S.S. wanted me."

"You're smart, and tough, and tender."

"Are you describing grades of meat?"

He tried to grab her shoulders, missing slightly
and thumping her in the cheek. "Rachel. What I
mean is, you've got a great personality. Don't
waste yourself on Archer."

" 'She's got a great personality' is what people
say about ugly girls." She was silent a long moment, and he could almost hear the gears churning in her head. "Ohhh, now I get it! You chased
me down because you're still afraid I might fall
under Alan's spell."

"I want you to know that you can do better.
You don't need to sink down to his level. You're
better than he is."

"All these compliments—if they can be *called*
compliments—are about keeping me from Alan.
What's wrong with you, Wiles? Why is it so
damned impossible for you to believe that I have
a rational head on my shoulders and I'm not falling in love with Alan?"

"Aren't you? He was looking awfully affec-
tionate toward you, and I didn't see you pushing
him away."

"What did you expect? What did you damn well expect? This is what I was hired for, isn't it? And it makes me sick. I hate having to lead a friend on like that. It's cruel and it makes me feel dirty."

"He can't be your friend. You can't think of him that way, Rachel."

"Damn it, Wiles! I've said time and again that my loyalty is not to Alan, but you still don't trust me!"

"Your loyalty is not what this is about."

"It is too!"

"It is *not!*" He jammed his fingers through his hair and made a pained noise of exasperation. "This isn't what I meant to be fighting with you about."

"Pray tell, what *did* you mean to fight about?"

He took her face in his hands and kissed her, hard.

The torch dropped, bouncing off his foot. She was stiff with surprise. He gentled his lips on hers and pulled her close, one arm going down around her back, his other hand into her hair to cup the back of her head. She began to relax within his hold, her mouth softening, and then tentatively responding. A fresh spurt of desire went through him at her acceptance.

He slipped his hand under her shirt, stroking the silky skin of her back, then reaching down into her panties to cup and massage her buttocks, pulling her up against him as he did so. The softness of her belly cradled his erection, and he coaxed her mouth open to thrust his tongue inside.

She made a yearning, moaning sound in the back of her throat, and he took it for invitation. His questing hand went lower, his fingertips finding the opening to her sex and resting there just within the parting, feeling the first drops of moisture as they arrived. Her arms came up around his neck as she pulled her mouth away from his, burying her face in the space below his jaw.

For a moment he thought she was embarrassed, but then he felt the touch of her tongue and the gentle scraping of her teeth along his neck. She made that moaning sound again, as if starving for more. His blood pounding in his ears, he lowered her to the ground, trying to find a space clear of rocks and roots.

Her hands tore at his shirt, yanking it upward. He pulled it off over his head, flinging it into the darkness, and then went to work on her own double layer of tunic and polar fleece, fighting to free her from them and from the manacles of her bra. The moment she was bare, she pulled him down on top of her, and he felt the pillowing of her breasts against his chest, and the nubs of nipples made hard by the cold. She wrapped her legs around his hips, urging him against her, their bodies still divided by chinos and her flimsy trousers.

He found her mouth again, gaining entrance, and rolled her over on top of him. She arched away from him enough that he could fondle her breasts, their mouths still together, her sex against his as she rocked atop him. She took her lips from his and slid her mouth to his ear, panting softly as she moved against him. She took his earlobe into her mouth and sucked. He groaned.

"Rachel! Rachel, are you out there?" Archer called.

She made a mewling noise of frustration and nipped his ear, then sat fully upright atop him. He turned his head and saw the moving blade of light from Archer's torch.

"I'm here, Alan," Rachel called out. "But give a girl some privacy, will you? Jeez! You're embarrassing me!"

"Oh! Sorry! You were gone so long, I just worried. . . . All that talk of wild animals . . ."

"Please, I'm fine. Trust me, right now no leopard is going to want to get anywhere near me."

"Do you need some Imodium?"

Harrison felt the quiver through her body as she stifled a laugh. He reached up and held a breast in each hand, squeezing gently. "No, it's not that bad," she called back to Archer. "Better to let these things run their course, anyway."

"I don't want you to get dehydrated."

"Alan. Please. This really isn't the time to carry on a conversation." Harrison moved his hands down to her hips, holding her hard against him as he thrust. Her fingernails curled into his chest, and she softly moaned.

"Are you sure you don't want the Imodium?"

"Alan!"

"I'll wait for you back at camp."

"Thank you!"

As soon as Archer's light was out of sight, though, she crawled off Harrison and started searching for her clothes. He reached for her in the dark, finding the warm smoothness of her arm and gently tugging her back toward him. "Wait, don't go yet."

"Don't go? Are you kidding?"

He traced his hand up her arm, her neck, and pulled her close, kissing her gently on the cheek in the same place Archer had, wanting her to remember *his* kiss. "Don't let Archer kiss you good night again."

She jerked away from him, out of his hold. "You're back to *that* again? Is that what all this was about? Making sure I stayed on your team?"

"I trust you."

"No, you don't. You just spent ten minutes trying to persuade me that you were better than Alan."

"*Archer's* the one I don't trust, not you. I don't want him touching you."

He could feel her movements as she jerked on her clothes. "Why do I suddenly feel like a fire hydrant, peed on by two competing dogs?"

"That's nice talk, when—"

"You just can't stand that someone might like Alan, can you?" she asked. "You not only have to be alpha dog, you have to wipe out all trace of the competition."

"That's not what—"

"I must have been out of my mind," she muttered, and got off him, crawling over to fetch her torch where it lay on the ground.

He wrapped his arms around her waist and pulled her back into his embrace, planting a kiss firmly atop her head. "We'll talk about this later. You have it wrong."

She struggled in his grip, and he let her go, watching her hurry away through the trees. His body ached with promises unfulfilled, and it was all he could do not to run after her, pull her back into the dark woods, and finish what they had started.

He didn't know how she had managed to twist the meaning of their impassioned tumbling, didn't know how she could take it to mean anything other than what it was: a blatant display of his attraction to her. He found his own shirt and pulled it on, and then sat with his head in his hands, alone in the dark, wondering what the hell had just happened.

Rachel had no idea what the hell had just happened in the woods with Wiles. It was worthy of a full night's pondering, but there was Alan, waiting with his medical kit beside her tent. She stepped out of the woods and into the faint light of the dying campfire. Min and the porters were nowhere to be seen.

"I think it's run its course," Rachel said, placing her hand over her stomach and smiling.

"You're sure?"

"Relatively. I've been through it before, and know the signs." She yawned, fist to her mouth. "I think those sleeping pills you gave me before are still in my system. God, I'm tired."

She started to step by him, but he caught her in his arms and held her. She let her arms hang at her side, not returning the hug, and irritably thought that she was getting quite enough unsolicited embraces this night.

"I worry about you," Alan said into her ear. "This is no type of life for you. I hate the thought of something happening to you out here, of you getting hurt."

She relented and patted him on the back. "But I know you'd take care of me, if I did."

"I would take care of you forever, if you'd let me."

She caught her breath. "Alan . . ."

He kissed her forehead and released her. "Go to bed."

She met his eyes and was pained by what she saw there. It was going to be horrible to have to disappoint him, and the coward in her was grateful that it could be put off for some little while yet, until this quest was over. She touched his cheek, smiled, and said, "Good night."

In her tent, her restless thoughts would not leave her at ease, and she scattered her backpack's contents over the small space in an effort at reorganizing both it and her mind. Worries about Alan's unreciprocated feelings for her were soon washed away by the more vivid recollections of her encounter with Wiles.

She didn't know what he had been thinking, but in the privacy of her own tent she could admit that what they'd been doing had felt awfully good. She gave up organizing her stuff and switched off her flashlight, lying inside her unzipped sleeping bag and mentally replaying again and again the feel of Wiles's hands and lips, and the hardness of his erection as she straddled his hips.

Her body reawoke, aroused by the memories. She felt the heat in her sex, the tingling desire that asked for a finish to what had been started. She pressed the palm of her hand tight over herself, eyes shut, willing Wiles to come back and take up where he had left off. Who cared why he had done it? She wanted more.

As if on cue, she heard the zipper on her tent flap. She let out her breath, her heart thumping wildly in her chest. He'd said they'd talk about it later; she remembered that now.

The moment the tent flap was open, she said, "I was hoping you'd come," and pulled him inside, finding his mouth and taking it with her own.

And just as quickly, she realized it was not Wiles. She jerked her mouth away.

"Rachel . . ." Alan whispered.

Crap!

He used his weight to push her back, until she was lying under him, her mind frantically running through options. She'd already welcomed him, already kissed him—damn it, how was she supposed to get rid of him now?

He nuzzled her neck, kissing it. "I came to make sure you were all right. I brought some pills with me, in case you weren't."

Yes! She could say she was still sick!

But pills . . . she didn't want to take pills, not

now, not when there were no witnesses. Friend or no, he shouldn't have tried to come into her tent so quietly, without so much as whispering her name in warning. What if whatever pills he gave her were tainted with the Yes drug? She couldn't believe it, and yet . . .

She shuddered, as he lowered his mouth to her breast and nibbled her nipple through the cloth.

"Yes," he said against her breast. "Shiver for me."

She made a face in the dark. Her hands patted through her things, searching for tactile inspiration. Damn that Wiles, where was he when she needed him?

Something hard was under her thigh. She squirmed until she could reach it, but then his leg came down over the back of her hand and she was caught.

Her fingers could just barely move over the thing under her thigh. She tried to figure out what it was, Archer gnawing away on her nipple all the while.

She was pretty sure . . . Yes, she thought it might be . . .

Ah, hell. This was going to hurt.

Before she could think twice about it, she pressed the trigger and sent three hundred thousand volts into her body.

Chapter Ten

The pain made her cry out, Alan's own holler of agony loud in her ear, as the shock transferred from her to him.

Confused electrical signals wrought chaos in her muscles, turning them to helpless, quivery jelly. For long moments she was incapable even of getting her finger off the trigger of the stun gun where it remained trapped beneath her. It felt as if someone had ripped out her skeleton, leaving her muscles to flail along on their own, accomplishing nothing.

As the shock died away her dazed mind began to make out the hubbub of voices, and then she saw the flashing of lights as Wiles, Min, and the porters lifted away the tent flap and gaped inside at the chaos.

Rachel lay helpless, Alan in no better shape beside her, moaning. The shock had exhausted their muscles, leaving them too weak to move.

"What is it? What happened?" Wiles asked.

"Christ . . ." Alan groaned.

"My fault," Rachel managed to whisper, and from somewhere found the strength to slowly force herself into a sitting position. With a shaking hand she found the stun gun. She held it up. "I accidentally lay on the trigger and set it off."

Alan pushed himself up, as weak as she, and stared at the stun gun. "Why the hell do you have one of those?"

"Protection. Maoists. Thieves," she said.

"It's goddamned dangerous," he said, the last syllable coming on a puff of breath as if saying it had taken all his strength.

"I know. But no harm done, really, right?"

She looked at Wiles, but his expression was unreadable. Whether that was for her benefit or Alan's, she didn't know. Then his gaze met hers, and his eyebrows raised for just an instant, enough to ask her, "Didn't I warn you about him?"

She tossed the gun into a corner of her little tent, then fell back onto her sleeping bag and wrapped herself inside its safe, nonsexual comfort, pulling the soft edge up to hide most of her face. "I'm going to sleep."

Refusing to explain anything further to anyone, or even to see them out of her tent, she shut her eyes.

She opened them to the pale light of morning and irate voices. One of them was Alan's, whining as usual.

Of all the . . . Could she never get any rest around here? Traveling with these guys was worse than traveling with a pack of teenage girls. Jealous, petulant, secretive, vindictive: They had it all.

As for what she felt about either of them after the high-jinks of last night . . . She was going to need a whole lot of caffeine in her system before she was in any shape to handle that question. Even *thinking* about thinking about last night made her cross and gave her the throbbing start of a headache.

She scratched her scalp and grabbed her toothbrush, toothpaste, and a bottle of water. Squinting against the bright morning light, she crawled out of the tent and stood up.

The tumult of voices went up a notch, and at the same moment she heard Wiles, his voice low and close by. "Don't move."

She squinted at him, a dark, motionless figure, then looked out at the rest of the camp. Half a dozen men in fatigues, assault weapons at the ready, were scattered around and looking testy. Her eyes widened.

Maoist rebels.

Goooood morning, Nepal! She should have stayed in bed. "What do they want?" she asked under her breath, her fist clenched tight around her Colgate and toothbrush.

"That's not quite clear yet. They appeared just a minute ago."

A rebel barked at them in Nepali to shut up.

"Yes, sorry!" she returned in their language.

Min, Porna, and Krishna were sitting on the ground together, their hands behind their heads, their faces bent down toward their knees. They plainly wanted to give the rebels no reason to use their weapons.

Half the rebels remained standing at the ready, their guns in their hands, while the other half slung their weapons over their shoulders and started a rough search through their captives' things. Rachel's tension relaxed a bare half notch as she realized their intentions were probably limited to robbery. As long as no one did anything stupid, they might get out of this unharmed.

"Those are my medical supplies!" Alan complained, watching a rebel unzip his red canvas kit. "Don't touch those!"

Her heart skipped a beat as the soldier looked up at Alan, then belted him across the face, knocking him down. Alan sprawled, stunned, and watched with wide eyes as the man held up vials and examined packets. The rebel glared at Alan, then zipped the kit back together and threw it on the small pile of supplies his compatriots had already gathered.

A rebel gestured at Wiles and Rachel to take several steps away from her tent, then crawled inside. Rachel grimaced as she realized that she hadn't yet put on her money belt. It was lying beside her sleeping bag. She had the equivalent of about five hundred dollars U.S. in there: a small fortune, by Nepalese standards. It was meant for travel emergencies.

Perhaps this qualified. The rebels would be in a good mood when they finished robbing her, which she considered worth the money.

The rebel holding a gun on Min and the porters suddenly ordered those three men to raise their faces. Rachel watched as Porna and Krishna obeyed. Min kept his face down, then slowly lifted it, but turned to the side, as if trying not to look at the man.

The rebel stepped to the right, to see Min's

face better, then shouted to his leader to come quick.

Min bolted up and dashed for the woods. Shouts erupted, and a spray of gunfire. The rebel troupe disintegrated into a mass of noise and disorganization, everyone wanting a shot at the fleeing Min. The rebel inside Rachel's tent was no exception, coming out with gun at the ready, finger already pulling the trigger.

Something punched her in the leg. Rachel took a startled step, then dropped to the ground. She lay there in confusion, trying to figure out what had happened, and then tried to sit up, pulling her legs under her. An excruciating burn erupted in her outer thigh, as if a lit firecracker had been shoved under her skin.

Wiles was on his knees beside her, his expression frantic. "Rachel! Where? Where?"

She could only gape at him, not able to believe it. Had she been shot? *Shot?* Her?

The rebel who had done it was suddenly looking down on her as well, a look of horror on his face. He started apologizing in quick and earnest Nepali, and pressed his hand hard over the wound on her thigh.

She screamed.

Wiles punched the man in the face, dropping him unconscious beside her. "Archer! Get over here, man!" Wiles shouted.

There was no answer, and Wiles shouted again. "Get *up!* Get *over* here!"

"They'll shoot me!" Alan screamed back.

The rebel leader was shouting orders, and then he, too, was beside Rachel, Alan's red medical kit in his hands. He spoke to them in halting English. "I am being so sorry. This, this was not to happen."

"He's a doctor," Wiles said, gesturing with his head towards Alan. "Get him over here."

The leader barked an order to his men, and two went and fetched Alan, pulling him over to her. It finally went through Alan's head that they weren't going to hurt him, and he shook off their hold and grabbed the medical kit from the leader. He gestured them all back, but Rachel grabbed Wiles's hand and didn't let him go. He positioned himself behind her, her head resting in his lap.

"We have to cut open your pants, Rachel," Alan said. "I have to see what's going on."

"Pull them down," she ordered, her mind trying desperately to maintain a hold on rationality. She reached with her free hand for the tie under her tunic top. "Don't ruin my pants. They're good pants."

Wiles squeezed her hand. "They're already ruined. Don't make Alan jostle you any more than he has to. The pants don't matter."

"Spoken like a man," Rachel said, but let her hand fall away.

The rebel leader gestured his men away. The man who had shot her moaned and stirred, and the leader, a disgusted look on his face, dragged him away by his foot.

"Wait!" Rachel called in Nepali. She was trying not to listen to the tearing of her trousers, or to think about what her leg looked like underneath—or to let herself notice the frickin' burn of agony that was making her jaw clench and clammy sweat break out over her body. Alan used gauze pads and applied steady pressure to her wounds.

The leader turned and looked at her, the question on his face.

"What happened to Min?" she asked.

"The man who ran? He is gone. We did not catch him."

She let out a breath, relieved beyond speaking.

Alan shoved up the sleeve of her shirt. He wiped a spot on the meaty part of her arm with an alcohol-soaked gauze, and readied a syringe. "I'm going to give you some Demerol," he said. She flinched as he plunged in the needle.

"Why did you chase him?" Wiles asked the leader. "He was just a trekking guide."

"He was a traitor. He used to be one of us. He belonged to a different troupe, the same one Kumar used to be part of," the leader said, gesturing to the rebel who had recognized Min. "Your guide, he betrayed the troupe before a planned attack on an army outpost. For money." He spat on the ground. "Many lost their lives that day."

"Have you had a tetanus shot within the last few years?" Alan asked Rachel.

"A little over a year ago."

"Good, we don't have to worry about that, then. I'm going to have to irrigate the wound with saline, though."

Rachel's thoughts were getting fuzzy, the pain in her leg receding. She glanced down at her thigh and saw a mess of blood and purple skin. Alan held up an oversize syringe of saline, a monstrous needle sticking out its end. He lowered it toward her leg.

"This sucks," she said, and passed out.

Chapter Eleven

When she woke, she was in a bed.

What the . . . ?

She stared uncomprehendingly at the small, clean room, lit by brass butter lamps, and by the fading light of day from a window over the middle of her bed. The air smelled of old dark wood and incense, and the twin hums of silence and of the wind outdoors thrummed in her ears.

She tried very hard to remember where she was, and how she had gotten here. She remembered waking up in her tent and crawling out . . . to see the Maoists in their camp. Min running.

Then what?

Deuced if she knew.

Vague, fuzzy dreams meandered through her

thoughts, and a few images of being on the trail. Carried? Night, and distant lights. A Nepalese woman holding a cup to her mouth and helping her to the toilet. Or had she dreamed that?

She pushed herself upright and felt a clench of pain in her thigh. She pulled back the sheet and blanket and saw her leg swathed in bandages. How . . . ? She slid a finger under the edge of the gauze and felt the prickle of a suture. Stitches! She yanked her hand away, appalled, and looked in horror at the bandage on her thigh.

Then she noticed what she was wearing: a man's T-shirt, and nothing else. She pulled the neck of it up to her nose, sniffing. Wiles. Thank God for small favors.

Trying to ignore the ache in her leg, she slid over to the deep windowsill and looked out. The high peaks of the Himalayas stretched upward in jagged teeth, their snows painted by the twilight in shades of pink and gold. Gray veined their sides, where winds had blown them bare, and above them the sky was a deep, pure, endless blue. The beauty of it stunned her, and for a moment she felt the world falling away from her, no space left in consciousness for anything but the landscape before her.

Putting her weight on her good leg, she rose to her knees and unfastened the window, pulling it open. A gust of air blew back her hair, cold and startling. She leaned through the opening and looked down.

She was several stories above the ground, and that ground itself sloped steeply away, disappearing into timbered darkness. Off to the left, on a rocky promontory, stood a *chorten*—a type of Buddhist shrine that looked like a large stone bell—and from the eaves of her building to surrounding trees stretched string after string of multicolored prayer flags, snapping in the wind.

A single-file line of maroon-clad monks walked slowly up a narrow path, toward the building.

Tangunboche Gompa. That must be where she was. They had made it the monastery, obviously with no help from her.

The door opened behind her, and she heard a surprised intake of breath. She turned, seeing the middle-aged Nepalese woman of her dim memories. The woman had a broad, friendly face.

"Namaste," Rachel said in greeting, her hands before her in the prayer position.

"Namaste," the woman replied, and continued in Nepali, "You are feeling better?"

"Yes, thank you," Rachel said, and closed the window before returning to the warmth and modesty of her bed covers.

"Maybe you would like to wash and eat?"

"Oh, yes, please. Washing would be wonderful. And my friends, the four men? They are here?"

"Yes, your friends are here. They are eating dinner with the monks. They have been worried over you." She set a tin cup and a pill on the same dark chest where the lamps burned. "The doctor, he sent medicine for pain. You drink this tea, and I will be back with water for washing, and food. My name is Chini."

"Chini—" Rachel called to her, as the woman was heading out the door.

"Yes?"

"What happened to my leg?"

The woman looked at her in surprise. "You were shot by Maoists."

"Oh." Cripes. She hoped to God she hadn't done something stupid to precipitate it. How embarrassing.

Exciting, too. Shot. She'd been shot! What a great story that scar was going to tell. She reached under her bandage to feel the tip of a suture a second time, to make sure it was really there. She didn't know anyone who had been shot before.

Rachel thanked the woman, and took up the pill and the cup of tea, almost feeling it was the mentally soothing tea she needed more than the pain pill. A small sip from the cup revealed it as Tibetan salt-butter tea—tea churned with yak butter and salt. A lot of foreigners couldn't stomach it, but Rachel had long grown accustomed to—almost fond of—the fatty, salty flavor.

Later, with Chini's unembarrassed help, she was able to wash her hair and clean her body, all while sitting in a shallow, round tub just big enough to catch the water poured over her. Chini managed to keep both the bandage and most of the floor dry, too.

The activity tired her more than she had expected, and she was ready for a nap by the time she had pulled one of her own tunics on over her bare skin and eaten a bit of the millet porridge called *tsampa*. Chini left her lying clean and contented, under the covers of her cozy bed. It was full dark by now, and the small flames of the lamps cast the room in flickering, golden tones.

Maybe getting shot wasn't half so bad, if it meant getting this kind of care. It sure beat sleeping on the ground.

The touch of a hand on her forehead woke her from her doze. Alan smiled at her. "How's your leg feel?"

She shifted it, testing. "Hurts."

"That's the bruising, mostly. The bullet went right through the fatty part of your thigh. I think it nicked your muscle, but nothing severe. No arteries damaged. I put stitches in to cut down on the chance of infection, in this environment."

"The bullet went through the fat? First time I've ever been grateful for chubby thighs."

"They have their uses," he agreed, with a light in his eye.

She knew he meant wrapping them around his waist, and the thought brought a mental shudder of revulsion. She looked past him, and saw Wiles waiting patiently in the shadows. She smiled at him. "So we made it to Tangunboche. Would you two believe, I don't remember a thing past Min running off?"

Wiles came forward and beat Alan to the edge of her bed to sit, leaving Alan to make do with the floor. "Dr. Archer kept you drugged up for the pain. You've been awake several times, but never completely 'here.' But quite so much medication isn't needed anymore, right, Dr. Archer?" he asked with meaning.

"We'll see if she needs it. But, Rachel, I want you to know it's not unusual to forget the time surrounding a trauma. You shouldn't worry about that, or try to force it." He sounded like he'd rather she *not* remember. Had he done something stupid or cowardly?

"To fill in the blanks for you, though . . ." Wiles began, and then recapped for her the shooting. He was curiously terse when describing it, and she wondered if there were elements he left out.

After the shooting, the rebel leader had felt guilty enough to assign two of his men to help carry her to Tangunboche Gompa on a stretcher made of the Indestructi-sheet. He'd also left them the medical supplies, camping gear, and food, although they'd still taken Archer's group's money and electronics. "Honor has its practical limits," Wiles said dryly.

No more stun gun or night goggles, then, Rachel realized. They'd done her precious little good, but she was sure Wiles must be sorry for the loss of his toys.

"Wiles and I have been talking," Alan said, "and we both agree that Min might have been up to something on this trek. If he informed on his fellow rebels for money, it seems possible he might have been paid to spy on my expedition."

Rachel blinked at both him and Wiles—as much surprised by the accusation against Min as by them speaking civilly to each other. "Why would he spy? And paid by whom?" she asked.

Alan shrugged. "The government, maybe. The official from whom I bought the travel permit might have been suspicious. He knew I was a doctor; if he thought there might be a pharmaceutical issue involved, he may have wanted a share of the profits."

Rachel shook her head. "I can't believe it, not

of Min. I've worked with him before, and he has always been trustworthy."

"You didn't know he was a former Maoist, though," Wiles said. "You can't let personal feelings determine whom you trust."

"I wasn't," Rachel snapped. "I was basing my trust on my past dealings with him." She tightened her lips, angry now because there was too great a possibility that Wiles was right: She may very well have misjudged Min. Did that mean he might have burned the tea house? And had he faked that stealing of Alan's day pack at the Monkey Temple?

"At any rate, he's gone now, and good riddance," Alan said.

"And then there were five," Rachel said.

"Hmm?" Wiles asked.

"Like the Agatha Christie mystery *Ten Little Indians*. The characters are killed one by one."

"Only no one has died," Wiles said.

"No. But first the two porters, then Min . . ."

They were all three quiet for a moment, and then Rachel spoke. "So. While I've been sleeping the sleep of the drugged, have you found out anything about the healing that the monks supposedly do here?"

Alan looked at her stupidly for a minute, as if trying to figure out what she was talking about. It was the best indication she'd had yet that he had been lying to her about their destination. He couldn't remember the implausible story he'd told about Durga's drawing.

"Er, well, it turns out that the monastery is known for something completely different than healing," Alan finally said.

"Oh?"

"Yeti," Wiles said, with a grin.

"What?"

"Yeti. They have a scalp and a hand, preserved in a dark, locked room. Supposedly actual relics of the actual creature."

"Oh, Lord."

Alan made a face. "They won't let us see it. I offered to take a sample back to the U.S. for analysis, but they refused. Probably because it'll be so obviously fake."

"Or maybe they don't want you pointing out what they already know," Rachel said. "You'll destroy the magic."

"But if it's fake, it's not magic."

"For whatever reason, they need to leave open the possibility of its being real," she said, recalling the ethnology courses she had taken. "A story can be both true and a myth. Dragons might not exist, but crocodiles do, and are likely the starting place for many dragon tales."

She realized that the same could be said of Yonam. She might be expecting to find a dragon of a kingdom, when the reality might be a small lizard of a village. The city need not be either entirely mythical or entirely real, at least not in the ways she had been expecting.

With a shiver she recalled what Beti had said about finding Yonam: Searchers encountered a wall of fire, a river of ice, and a yeti. They already had two out of three, if you were willing to stretch your interpretation.

"Whatever," Alan said. "I just wish they'd let us see the scalp."

"You seem more disappointed about that than about there being no new medicines to investigate here at the monastery," Rachel ventured. "This was a long way to come for nothing."

"Oh, I don't know. I think the monks may be able to point us in the right direction."

She raised her eyebrows in question.

Alan's own eyebrows twisted in distress, and he glanced at Wiles, obviously not wanting to speak in front of him. Wiles was apparently in no mood to humor Alan's desire for privacy, though, mission or no. He stayed planted firmly on the side of Rachel's bed.

Rachel gave Alan a facial shrug, implying it would have to wait. "How long until I'm fit for duty?" she asked, instead.

"You can use the leg now—it's just going to hurt a lot, especially going up or down stairs or

250

a hill. Any time you use that muscle, it will hurt. I think we'd do well to give you another four or five days, at least, to let the worst of it pass."

"That should be enough time to figure out where we're going next," she said. "Don't you think, Wiles?"

He shrugged, retreating into his dumb-ox persona.

Rachel sighed and yanked her covers up to her neck, her pulling forcing Wiles to get up and release the blanket caught beneath him. "Thank you for the visit," she told them both, and shut her eyes.

If Alan was going to hold his secrets and Wiles was going to play the mute, then she would rather sleep. Let them go chat with each other, the stubborn blockheads.

Three days later, Rachel was desperate for their company. Chini was sweet and friendly, but obviously had been hired by the monks as a sort of chaperone for the time Rachel was in their monastery. She got the subtle impression that the monks felt they were doing her a favor by providing her with female companionship and limiting her time with Alan and Wiles.

Not that either Alan or Wiles trusted each other enough to allow private visits, anyway.

She spent most of her time alone in her room.

The few times she had tried to limp her way down a dark corridor, she had passed monks who seemed uncomfortable with her presence. No one said anything specific, but she got the feeling that she was a disruption by her very presence. The polite thing seemed to be to stay out of sight.

Which she did. She spent long hours leaning on her windowsill, gazing out at the mountains, trying to recapture that stunning sense of awe she'd felt upon first viewing them. The mountains were still as beautiful, only now they reflected back to her a cold barrenness, a jagged, unfeeling blankness that had neither thoughts nor care for her. There was nothing upon which a human soul could grasp.

She needed that sense of awe, from the first night. She needed *something* to fill her mind and her heart, because isolated in her room as she was, without distraction or activity, she was coming much too close to the grief she had kept buried for a year and a half. The bare mountains told her only that there was no comfort to be had in the world outside herself.

At first, she thought it was the painkillers that were making her moody and had sneakily cut down the dose Alan sent her.

It didn't make a difference.

As hour grew on hour, alone with herself and

her memories, cracks appeared in the plaster she had sealed over her grief for her parents. She tried to paste them over with thoughts about Alan and Wiles: the revulsion she felt whenever Alan made a sexual innuendo, and the disturbing after effect of perverse arousal such suggestions left with her. She didn't want to sleep with Alan, but suggestive words—from whatever source—made her think about sex, and her body knew it.

Her thoughts about Wiles were even less coherent. That brief, hungry, frantic encounter in the woods felt as if it had happened five years ago, not five days. Electrocution, a gun shot, and mind-fogging painkillers had battered their way to precedence over any lingering thrills that might have zipped along her synapses. It had happened in darkness, giving her no images to recall but darker shadows upon shadows, and the white beam of her flashlight on the ground. There were moments she wondered if it had happened at all.

Finally, late on the fourth night, while a single lamp flickered against the utter blackness of night, the grief broke through her seals, and she wept.

It was as if it were only a week that stood between her and the day they died, not eighteen months. The grief was as fresh, the tears as hot, her sobs clenching her belly and making her bury her face in her pillow to drown the gasping sounds she made.

Absurdly, the most pain came from remembering a summer evening at home—no one evening particular, but rather a blending of many that had passed in similar style: her parents sitting in white iron chairs on their back deck, cups of tepid coffee forgotten on the rail, watching the sun go down and swallows swooping through the air for their dinner. There had been a quiet perfection to those evenings, a peace that Rachel was afraid had gone from her life forever.

A keening moan strained the back of her throat, and she started punching the wound on her thigh, as if that physical pain could somehow free her of the one ripping her apart inside.

In the midst of her agony, a strong hand grasped her wrist, stopping her self-beating.

"Hush, Rachel. Hush," Wiles said, and lay down behind her, pulling her up against him and wrapping his arms around her body, holding her arms motionless like a swaddled baby.

And like that swaddled child, some ancient instinct gradually quieted her cries. He stroked the hair back from her forehead, whispering soft shushing sounds against the back of her ear, and rocked her gently in his embrace.

When she finished crying, there was an emptiness inside, a blessed vacancy of feeling. She stared at the wall beside her bed, a creature of physical sensation and no thought.

Wiles eased her down onto her back, and lay on his side next to her, tucking her hair behind her ear and tracing the tracks of drying tears with his fingers. "Tell me what it is."

She met his eyes, and at the thought of giving voice to her sorrow felt a new upwelling of grief. She didn't want that, not again, not so soon.

Instead of speaking, she took his face between her hands and brought his mouth down to hers. She would lose herself in sensation, and drive away the sadness that could not be changed.

He kissed her back, his lips gentle where hers were hungry. She slowed down, matching her touch to his, wanting to coax him to it, not frighten him away.

His hand moved down over her breast, fondling it through the T-shirt she wore. She wore no bra, and only panties below. His hand moved in a slow circle, gently pinching her nipple between thumb and hand. She opened her mouth to him, and he rose up on one elbow to come down on her from above, his tongue accepting her invitation.

She ran her fingers into his hair, then trailed them down over his strong shoulders. Relaxing beneath him, she gave herself up to him, and would go wherever he wished to take her. She wanted to disappear into pleasure, escaping from herself and the world.

His hand moved down her rib cage, over the soft plane of her stomach, and to her thigh, where the feel of the bandage made him pause. "Your leg. I don't want to hurt you."

"It only hurts when I use it. There are ways around that."

He met her eyes, uncertainty in his, not sure yet that she meant to give what she implied.

"There's nothing to stop us," she said. "I'm protected, and healthy." She had an IUD, one of the new ones with hormones that kept her from having a period.

"I am, too. Healthy." He seemed embarrassed, as if the practicalities somehow had no place in this.

She smiled and tugged on his T-shirt, as she remembered now she had done that other night. He helped her strip it off, and when his chest was bare she felt a ripple of desire go through her. He was achingly beautiful, his skin gold and smooth in the lamplight as if he were a gilded statue.

Only this statue was warm and alive, and using both broad hands to move her own shirt up her body. She rose up to help him peel it off, and then lay back, exposed to him, deriving an erotic thrill from being bare to his eyes.

This invitation, too, he accepted, using mouth and hands to explore her body. Then one hand found its way lower, and slid within the stretchy confines of her panties. His fingers ran through the curls covering her mound, then gently delved into the dampened folds beneath. Her lips parted, her breath expelling in a sigh of rewarded want.

He used her own wetness to glide his touch over her flesh, in strokes that started slow, then grew quick, until Rachel thought she heard her own heart thumping in time with the strokes. She grabbed his shoulders, urging him on, but then he suddenly stopped. She gave a soft cry of frustration, and he released a sound that was almost a laugh.

"Patience, my darling," he said softly.

He pulled at her panties, and she lifted her hips to help him. They were gone a moment later, and she watched the muscles move under his skin as he undid his own pants and kicked them to the floor.

When he lay back down against her, she felt the thickness of his erection pressed against her hip. The muscles deep inside her sex clenched in desire, and she reached down to touch the silky head where it was caught between their bodies. He jerked at her touch, even as a wave of yet more powerful hunger moved through her body.

She started to roll onto her side, to give her hand more space to grasp him.

"No," he said, and held her down. "Let me."

For a moment she wasn't sure what he meant, but then he slid down the bed, between her legs, and lifted her uninjured one over his arm. His mouth came down on her, hot and wet and all-enveloping. She dropped her hands to the bed and arched, a soft cry traveling up the back of her throat.

His tongue played at her very opening, dipping in, teasing her with its hint of what was to come, and then moving back up with his lips to play with the center of her sensation. He suckled at her while his fingertip took the place of tongue and traced over her entrance, then slid deep inside only to retreat as quickly. He kept it poised at her opening, drawing small circles in her flesh.

She moaned and felt the start of her orgasm coming, brought on as much by pleasure as by the hunger to feel more of it.

He came back up her body, and did not stop her this time when she took his sex in her hand. It was surprisingly thick, deliciously firm with a texture like sand-washed silk. She wondered whether it would hurt, taking one so large inside her, but did not care. She almost *wanted* it to hurt, the small fear adding to her excitement. He lifted her good leg up to his hip, and followed her guidance to her entrance.

He did not enter all at once. As her hand fell away, he eased the head inside, then out again, coating himself with her moisture, and parting her hidden lips so that they retained no resistance against him. He braced himself, his arms pillars on either side of her. He looked down into her eyes, capturing her gaze as he went deeper with each thrust, and then plunged fully inside in one strong, fluid movement. Her body stretched to accept him, the sense of fullness agonizingly sweet.

The intimacy of his gaze unnerved her, and she closed her eyes, giving herself over to her body. Her passage had given way to his entry, aroused flesh molding itself to his sex until she did not know where she ended and he began, except that with his every move new sensations flashed through her like sparkles of phosphoresence in the dark ocean. It was only a moment more before she found her release.

"Rachel," he cried hoarsely, as her muscles contracted around him, and then he was shuddering, thrusting quickly in her, then lowering himself down atop her and holding her tight within his arms as his hips continued to move. For a moment he became rigid and motionless against her, and she knew he had reached his own peak. She felt both satisfaction and a sense of greedy possession, to know that he was spending himself within her.

She felt the pulse of his orgasm die away, and he relaxed. His weight was heavy and welcome, and she held him tight, his smooth skin sticking to hers, the both of them damp with the sweat of exertion.

He carefully disengaged his hips from hers, and eased himself onto his side, careful not to jostle her hurt leg. He slid his arm under her pillow, and with his other arm pulled her up against him, she still on her back but now cradled within the long curl of his body, one of her legs resting atop his thigh. His hand on her rib cage felt as if it covered half her chest, so broad and protective it was.

He kissed her on the temple, then again, gentle as a butterfly, at the corner of her eye. She shut her lids, the cherishing tenderness of his kiss touching something deep within her.

"Tell me why you were crying," he said softly.

She opened her eyes and looked into his own. They were dark pools reflecting the warm golden flame of the lamp, and she could not look into them and answer. Instead, she shifted her gaze to the shadows of the ceiling, and found with concentration that she could speak without emotion.

"My parents were killed in a car crash a year and a half ago. It was over the Christmas holidays. They'd gone to visit friends, but on the way home . . . A young man behind the wheel of an SUV. He'd fallen asleep and crossed the center line. They were killed instantly."

She was quiet, remembering that long wait at the house, worry setting in as the hours crept by and her parents still did not return home. She'd been alone in the house, waiting, going to the window at each sound of a car, until finally a car *did* come, but with the roof lights of a police cruiser.

Irrational as it was, she blamed Pamela for not being there that night, for not being with her when she got the news. Her sister had been living in a tree at the time, and it had taken two days to get word to her of what had happened.

"After the funeral, after the critical things were taken care of and the house sold, I went back to the university. But it all seemed meaningless. What did my dissertation have to do with life? It wouldn't change anything, not in my life or in anyone else's. I didn't see the point.

"All my life, I'd been one of those overachieving 'smart' kids, getting near-perfect scores on the SAT and GRE, graduating not only early, but magna cum laude from undergrad. Academics had been everything to me.

"When my parents died, I realized school meant nothing.

"Between insurance and investments from my parents, my sister and I both have enough money that we won't ever have to work, not if we're frugal. So I left school. Why not?

"Most of the time I'm fine," she said, trying to sound as if that were true. "But sometimes the grief sneaks up on me. Takes me by surprise." She glanced at him. "I keep thinking it should have gone away by now. A year and a half. But it stays, just as strong. The only thing to do is avoid it."

He didn't say anything, just gazed at her with a sympathy she could not stand. She looked away, out into the dark corners of the room.

His hand moved up to her chin, and he gently turned her face to him. He kissed her lips.

She turned into his body, rolling onto her side so that she could feel him against her length. She ignored the pain in her thigh and lifted her leg over his, scissoring his own muscled leg between hers. She kissed his throat and hid her face in the space between his shoulder and neck, grateful that he had remained silent. She had had enough of people saying they were sorry, and wanted now only what he gave her: his arm strong on her back, holding her close and safe.

After long minutes they pulled apart, Rachel

again on her back while he propped himself up on one elbow, looking down on her. His fingertips played idly with her nipple and traced circles on her breasts. With his fingertip he ran a line down the bridge of her nose, then dropped it lightly onto her lips. He left it resting there. She looked at him in question, a half smile on her mouth beneath his finger.

"I've fallen in love with you, Rachel Calais," he said.

Her smile faded, surprise feeling like fear in her chest. "You can't have."

He raised his brows in question.

"You hardly know me," she said, feeling a panic building in her heart. "It's too soon."

"I can't help its having happened. I tried long enough, believe me," he said, a crooked smile on his mouth.

"I—I can't say the same back," she said, the panic blooming full within her now. She had given thoughts to lust, not love, believing her heart too battered to risk giving itself to another. "I'm not ready yet. It's too soon—Why did you tell me?" she cried.

"Love is not something to hide. I swore to myself, long ago, that when I finally fell in love I would tell the woman."

Her eyes widened. *"Finally?* Have you never been in love before?"

His smile was small, almost vulnerable. He shook his head no.

A weight came down on her, the pressure of being the beloved. "I love you" demanded "I love you, too," but whatever she might feel for him was lost in the maelstrom of panic.

"You're not in love with me," he said, reading her thoughts on her face. His smile wavered, and she knew that he was hurt, however much he might wish to be fearless in his declaration.

"I feel something near to it, I think," she admitted. "In time, maybe . . ."

"I put you on the spot, spoke too soon," he said.

She felt a painful embarrassment, for him or for herself, she didn't know. "No, you were right, it is not something to be hidden."

"But you wish maybe that I *had* hidden it, at least for a while yet."

"I don't know what I wish," she said, and meant it. "I'm glad you're here, though." She lay her fingertips against his lips.

"I'll take that, for now."

He kissed her and trailed his mouth down to her breasts. She raised her arms above her head, opening her body to him, willing to give him this if nothing more. He moved lower yet, coaxing open her thighs, his tongue finding her. She reveled in the sensation, happy to give up her body's secrets a second time.

With bliss suffusing her flesh and making her languid, she turned her head to the side, her eyes half closed. Even as the first soft moan left her throat, she saw that the door to her room was ajar.

In the dark space between door and frame, the pale face of Alan looked in, his gaze meeting hers. His expression gave away nothing. A moment later he silently retreated, pulling the door shut behind him.

The next day, Chini told her that her group was meeting in a room with several monks, and she was asked to attend. She limped down thc hall in the direction Chini sent her, a dread in her heart.

She was embarrassed and ashamed that Alan had seen her with Wiles. Embarrassed, as anyone would be to have been observed engaged in intimacy with another. Ashamed, because he now knew her to be a liar for having accepted affection from him. Ashamed, too, at the pain she'd caused.

Wiles had, of course, been worried most over the effect Alan's knowledge of their affair might have on the mission. Even more, he cursed the effect Alan's spying had had on her ardor, for she had been unable to continue what they had started.

She opened the door to the room and found it empty yet of people. There was little furniture on the bare, dark wood floors: just a few flat cushions and a low table, set before a row of lattice windows. The mountains glowed beyond, their snows and the clear blue sky almost blinding.

She found a cushion and eased down on it, facing the mountains. Still, she sought an answer from them that would not come; sought even the question itself, for she did not know what it was she wanted that might repair the wounds in her heart.

Someone settled onto a cushion next to her. She turned, expecting to see Wiles or Alan, but instead it was Gelu Rinpoche, the most holy and learned man in the monastery. He had come by her room, once, to meet her and offer his welcome to Tangunboche.

He didn't say anything, instead gazing out the windows at the same mountains that had captured so much of her attention. She didn't know how old he was—maybe fifty, maybe sixty. His hair was salt-and-pepper, a bare quarter of an inch long. His maroon and gold garments left his arms bare, but there were no goose bumps on his smooth brown skin, despite the chill of the room.

His silence was a white page, upon which she found voice to write.

"I wish I were the mountains and felt nothing," she said.

He was quiet for some moments, as she had guessed he might be, before he answered her. "It is not in running from your feelings that you will be free of suffering."

She faced him. "Yet if I remain with them, I suffer."

"Remain with them, and then you will understand them. When you understand them, you can release them. *Then* you will be free."

"They are like a great lake of water, and swallow me," she said softly. "I drown in them."

"Then I will teach you to breathe."

To her surprise, he literally did exactly that. It was not just the in and out of air that he showed her, but the attention she could pay to it. With that attention, she was able, briefly, to break free of the utter hold of emotion. It reminded her that she was composed of a body and a mind in addition to her feelings. It let her experience those feelings from a safe distance.

The sadness was still there, but for a moment, at least, she did not mind its presence. She did not need to run.

Voices and footsteps broke the quiet. Wiles, Alan, Krishna, Porna, and several monks trickled into the room, finding places to sit on the floor. Rachel concentrated on her breathing, tried not to mind the confusion of emotions at being in the same room with both Alan and Wiles.

She could not resist glancing at Wiles. He moved as if to come sit beside her, but she warned him off with a bare shake of her head. She did not want to flaunt their connection in front of Alan, for all that they were past hiding it.

Despite that, her body ached with yearning when Wiles found a seat several feet away. She wanted the comfort of his closeness, and the warmth of his presence at her side.

When they had all settled, Alan found a place where they could all see him, and stood. He met Rachel's eyes, but as last night there was nothing she could read in his expression. His gaze swept over his small audience, and he began to speak, one of the monks translating for him.

"Two years ago, while in Thailand, I met a man who said he was from the mountains of Nepal. His name was Durga, and he was dying. There was nothing I could do to save him.

"Durga told me that he would never have fallen ill if he had stayed in his village, for there grew there a plant that kept sickness at bay. He didn't tell me why he left, or the name of his village, but he did show me *this*."

Alan reached into his shirt collar and pulled out a silver medallion on a chain. He lifted it over his head and passed it around.

"He said it showed the way to his village.

"Then, sadly, Durga died."

Alan paused, letting that fact soak in. "He had no friends, no family there. There was no one to take care of his body, or his things. So I did. And amidst his things I found a notebook, full of drawings. There was no writing, nothing to explain the pictures: He must have been illiterate. But I eventually figured out that the drawings were a journal, of sorts, showing the route Durga had taken from his home in the mountains to where he eventually ended up, in Thailand."

Rachel sat stunned, all breathing forgotten. A drawn record of Durga's travels: *That's* what they'd been following all this time.

"Which is why I am here now: This monastery was one of Durga's drawings. He was here, and his home village cannot be far away. It is my hope to find that village, return the medallion and notebook to his family, and perhaps, if I'm lucky, discover a new drug that will bring better health to millions of people throughout the world.

"We've come this far, thanks to the help of my crew," he said, nodding toward her, Wiles, and the porters. Then he looked to the monks. "But we need your help to decipher the next drawing, so that we may take the next step in our journey."

Alan took a piece of paper out of his day pack, and held it up. It was a tumble of lines and shadows, filling the page from edge to edge. He gave it to the nearest monk to examine.

Rachel looked at Alan, and knew she had forgotten for weeks the reason she was here. The Yes drug had been in the back of her mind, and Alan's supposed plot to find it, but it hadn't been as real to her as the daily dramas of the trek.

Alan's version of events with Durga did not match what Wiles and Beti had told her; but neither was it too dissimilar.

A shiver went down Rachel's neck as she realized: Yonam was real.

They were almost there.

She was packing up the last of her things the next morning when both Wiles and Alan came to her room, out of breath, their faces flushed. Surprise at seeing them together made her mute.

"The porters," Alan said.

"Krishna and Porna," Wiles said. "They're gone. One of the monks saw them early this morning, heading back down the trail the way we came."

"Not northwest, as the monks said we need to go?" Rachel asked.

"No," Alan said, his face twisted with anger,

"but they were probably in on it from the beginning, with Min. They've got what they wanted, now."

"Maybe they just didn't want to continue. The route we'll have to take . . ." she said, but both Alan and Wiles were shaking their heads.

Wiles explained. "They stole the drawings."

"The fire in the tea house . . ." Rachel said.

"Was probably deliberately set," Wiles said. "They hoped to steal Dr. Archer's things in the chaos, and didn't care who died in the process."

Chapter Twelve

Alan felt his thoughts growing cold and hard, like the serrated mass of ice that made up the glacier beside them. They had been hiking along its edge all day, watching the line of mountains on its opposite shore, seeking the silhouette of peaks that would match the image on Durga's silver medallion.

Before today he had never seen a glacier; had only had a vague idea of what one was. It was a vast river of packed ice and snow, flowing down out of the mountains just as would water after the rains. It was a frozen runoff, moving in slow motion, making great cracking booms and groans as it eased itself downhill.

Three days it had taken them to get here from

the monastery, and thank God for the monks, who had figured out that Durga's drawing was of this glacier. Alan himself had thought the lines and shadows depicted a rock-fall.

The monks had also found two local men willing to act as porters, although it was made clear that the men could spare only a few days from their farms.

Damn Krypton and Porsche, or whatever their names were. Damn Wiles and Rachel, too, for having left his mind in such disarray that he grew careless. For the first time in weeks, he'd not kept the journal taped to his stomach. Voilà, stolen. The thieves had been waiting for their chance.

Fortunately, the drawing of the ice was the only drawing left between that of the monastery, and that of the entrance to Yonam. Beyond that entrance, according to the journal, should lie the village from whence Durga had come.

Durga. The little bastard. He hadn't been able to get Durga to tell any of his secrets, even by dangling pharmaceutical morphine in front of his drugged little eyes. Shooting him up with an overdose had been a kindness, really. What better could Durga hope to get from life, than such a peaceful end? God knew that Alan had felt like doing violence to the man's corpse, when he'd been unable to find any trace of the sex drug in Durga's things.

Corrupt, thieving liars, that's what all the Nepalis were. He'd yet to meet one—except maybe the monks, but they were probably more Tibetan than Nepalese—worth the rice and lentils he ate. Wiles was tarred with the same foul brush, of course, no matter the English accent.

He slipped his hand into his jacket pocket and felt the ridged handle of the stun gun. Rachel and Wiles thought the Maoists had taken it. In all the confusion after Rachel was shot, it had been easy to hide the gun in his medical supplies.

When he got the chance, he would make Wiles pay for befouling his Rachel.

Rachel would need to be taught a lesson, too, but there were better ways than a stun gun to turn her back to him. He thought less of her for opening her legs to a stupid pig like Wiles, but he was scientist enough to understand that crude biological mechanisms sometimes won out over one's better sense.

The image of Rachel, spread naked in the soft light like an offering, filled his mind. A faint stir of voyeuristic excitement tingled in his loins.

Disgusting that it had been Wiles with his face in her crotch, of course, but maybe she'd been using him solely for sexual pleasure, and he meant no more to her than a vibrator. Still, he'd rather it had been the shaved head of a monk he'd seen between her thighs. Someone he didn't know.

Rachel needed punishment to show her the error of her ways, and education in where she was to seek her sexual pleasures from now on.

He would see that she got both.

Harrison shaded his eyes and gazed across the expanse of the glacier, trying to catch again the flash of light he'd seen from the corner of his eye. The day was partly cloudy, the glacier alternately glaring white and lying in chunks of gray and dirty ice as the sun was hidden or revealed.

"What is it?" Rachel asked, panting to a stop beside him. These three days had been difficult for her, her face chalk-white with pain as she forced her injured leg to do its work. She refused to stop, just as she refused all but minimal amounts of painkillers, complaining they clouded her thinking.

"I'm not sure. I thought I saw—There!" he said, pointing. "Archer!" he called back down the trail. "Show me that medallion again!" Slow as Rachel was, the good doctor was even slower, and was only now trudging up to join them.

"What, what is it?" Archer asked.

"See, straight across, those two small peaks with a flash of white between them, near their bases?"

Archer stood panting and red-faced, staring out across the glacier. "Where?"

"I think I see it," Rachel said. "Alan, give me the medallion."

Archer reached into his shirt and lifted the chain over his head, handing it to her.

Harrison watched Archer, wondering as he had for days what was going through the man's head. If it had been he who'd seen what Archer saw, he would be thinking about killing the man who'd had his mouth on his beloved's sex. Archer had shown no sign of such thoughts, though, and had avoided any reference to the scene he had stumbled upon. The only change was that Archer no longer touched Rachel, or sought her out privately.

Maybe Archer had mentally discarded Rachel, deeming her unworthy of his adoration. Harrison hoped that was true, but he wasn't going to put money on it.

Rachel held up the medallion, comparing it to the distant feature on the landscape. "It matches, as near as I can tell. What I wouldn't give for a pair of binoculars."

"It doesn't look *exactly* the same," Archer whined, taking the medallion back from her.

Harrison shrugged, faking nonchalance. If that *was* the entrance to Yonam they had spotted, then months of preparation and weeks of subterfuge were about to come to their culmination. The thought made the adrenaline surge in his blood. "It's up to you, Dr. Archer. Is it similar enough to make it worth checking out?"

Archer looked again at the medallion, then shrugged, his nonchalance as false as Harrison's. "There's been nothing else even close. We might as well take a look."

Rachel spoke to the porters, and when they shook their heads no, she nodded her understanding. They were not willing to risk crossing the glacier. Harrison couldn't blame them.

As stable as the ice and snow looked, it was a living thing, for the most part moving too slowly for the human eye to detect, but also prone to sudden, catastrophic alteration. Experienced mountaineers had been killed crossing similar terrain, when a sudden shift caused a boulder of ice to fall upon them, or an ice bridge to collapse beneath.

"Where are they going?" Archer asked stupidly, as the porters headed back down the trail, their backs free now of the weight of packs.

"Home," Rachel said. "We'll have to carry our own gear from here on in. If there's anything you think you can get by without, you might want to leave it here."

She was in no condition to carry a full pack. Before Archer could respond, Harrison cut in, addressing Rachel. "Archer and I will carry your things. You'll be straining your leg enough as it is, trying to stay upright on that ice. You don't need the weight of a pack unbalancing you."

He expected a battle to get her to agree, but instead she was quiet, then looked at Archer. Harrison did, too, wondering if self-interest would win out over whatever was left of his feelings for Rachel.

Archer looked back at them, and then at the packs of gear the porters had left. A flicker of despair moved through his features. "We can't have you falling and reinjuring yourself," he said without conviction.

"Thank you," she said quietly.

Rachel's acceptance of the offer unsettled Harrison far more than any fight would have done. She was probably in more pain, and closer to exhaustion, than she was letting on.

The wise thing to do would be to camp here overnight, and not tackle the glacier until tomorrow. Rachel needed the rest, Archer needed the rest—they all needed it. With Krishna and Porna running back to their masters with the journal, however, time was critical. An army helicopter could cover in an hour the same distance it had taken them days to conquer, and then this would have all been for naught.

Their climbing ropes had burned with the tea

house, and only one pair of crampons had survived fire, Maoists, and the fleeing porters. Harrison gave the crampons to Rachel, and she put them on while he redistributed the loads in the packs.

"Are we ready, then?" he asked, as he shouldered his pack and fastened the hip belt.

Two tired faces looked back at him and nodded. Misgiving fluttered in his gut: They were neither of them in condition for this. Even the excitement of being almost at their destination had not stirred their energy levels.

"Rachel?" he asked.

"Let's do it," she said. "Now or never."

Still, he hesitated. "I could go, myself, then report back to you two."

Archer made a noise of protest, and Rachel shook her head. "We all go. There's no point in your going alone."

He knew what she was implying: They had long ago lost their means of communicating with B.L.I.S.S. There would be no airborne cavalry arriving to save the day and wipe out the drug. It was up to them, and they had a better chance together than apart.

He remembered how Rachel had reacted the first time they talked about finding Yonam: She'd said it was a place she should "stay the hell away from." The hard, determined look in her eyes now, though, said that the devil himself couldn't keep her from it.

He nodded. "Follow my footsteps, and if you need help, ask for it."

Rachel was so tired, her leg so sore, she wanted to cry. She wanted to sit down and weep, and make everything go away.

Her thoughts bounced off the confines of reality, though, and she knew that the only thing that was going to get her across this damn glacier were her own two legs. She tried the breathing technique that Gelu Rinpoche had taught her, and the frustrated tightness in her chest eased slightly.

It wasn't the distance across the glacier that was problem; it was the slick, irregular surface. The crevasses, the tumbles of ice boulders. It was slow, careful going, because a misstep could mean a broken bone. Or worse.

Ahead of her, Wiles surmounted a rise and stopped. She forced herself up the slope, and when she saw the other side she felt her heart drop into her gut.

She really should just sit down and cry, breathing exercises or no.

A canyon was before them, extending off to right and left as far as she could see. It was only

twenty or so feet across, but that was enough.
More than enough.

"Rachel, you sit," Wiles said.

"Really?" She was so grateful, a tear slipped
out the corner of her eye.

"Lend me the crampons. I'm going to see if we
can get across on that ice bridge down there."

"Ice bridge?" She could see no ice bridge.

He pointed.

She saw, and wanted to throw up. Ten feet
down the side of the canyon, a narrow catwalk
of ice stretched like spun sugar across the void.

Wiles took off his pack, put on the crampons,
got his ice ax, and without further ado chipped
and inched his way down the side of the canyon.

Alan sat down beside her, the both of them
silent as they watched Wiles's progress. They had
gotten good at pretending nothing had happened, these last few days. Their exchanges were
friendly and shallow. She was afraid to ask him
what he really felt, and was too tired to care what
the answer might be.

"He's going to make it," Alan said.

Was that disappointment in his voice?

"Looks like it. That'll mean our turn, next."

"I've always been afraid of heights. Did you
know that?" Alan asked.

She looked at him in surprise. "No."

He pressed his lips together, his eyebrows in a

frown of worry as he gazed down at the bridge.

"Wiles can help you," she said. "I'll need help, myself. I wouldn't like to lose my balance on that."

"Funny, how much we need each other, isn't it? I would never have made it this far without you and Wiles. Things may not have worked out like I hoped, but there's a bond that builds between people in a situation like this, don't you think? I mean, between all of us."

She nodded, stunned. She wouldn't have guessed he could be so forgiving, so mature. So much a true friend.

"You don't think Wiles is mad at me, for having made a pass at you, do you?" Alan asked. "He's seemed kind of closed off, lately."

Alan was the shy puppy again, wanting to be liked. Or was it all a bit too much?

"He's just being a guy," Rachel said, and struggled to her feet. Wiles was emerging over the rim of the canyon, and she had no desire to continue this strange conversation. "Come on. Let's cross that bridge."

The ice bridge was wider than it had looked from above: about ten inches. Wide enough to walk across with ease, but narrow enough to disconcert, and leaving little room for stumbles. Wiles kept the crampons on and brought all their packs across, then led Rachel over the bridge, she clinging tight to the back of his jacket to ensure her balance.

"It's not so bad," she called back across to Alan. He waved weakly.

"We should just leave him there," Wiles muttered.

She told Wiles about Alan's fear of heights. However much Wiles might dislike Alan, she knew he wouldn't make the man struggle alone across that thin strip of ice. Nor would he leave him to freeze, starve, or wander lost in the wilderness. Wiles might be capable of violence in a passionate moment, but cold-blooded murder was beyond him.

She sat at the rim of the canyon and watched as Wiles and Alan started across the bridge, Alan holding on to Wiles's shoulders and moving slowly.

Suddenly, Alan slipped. He gripped hard at Wiles, throwing him off balance. Rachel felt a shriek rise into her throat, and trapped it behind her lips.

They fought for balance. Wiles's agility and the crampons saved them. He secured his footing, and acted as an anchor until Alan found his.

They took a couple more steps, and then she saw Alan turn his head and look down, into the abyss beneath them. He swayed, and as if mesmerized he took his hands off Wiles's shoulders.

"Don't! Don't!" she urged beneath her breath. What was wrong with him?

Wiles turned, and reached out to Alan. Or she thought he did—his body blocked her view.

Alan said something, she couldn't hear what, and then seemed to reach forward, as if to take Wiles's help.

Then suddenly *Wiles* lost his balance, his arms jerking for a hold that was not there, his body twisting, and then—

Then—

He fell.

A shriek vibrated up her vocal cords like a high note on the violin, breaking forth in a wail that could shatter glass.

He fell smoothly, quickly. She rose up, screaming, following with her eyes his descent until the angle of an ice outcropping blocked her view.

She scrambled back down over the edge of the canyon, to the end of the ice bridge, her own screams ringing in her ears. She couldn't stop them. On hands and knees she peered into the chasm. Where was he? Where *was* he?

Alan pulled her back.

"We have to help him! We have to get down there, and help him!" she cried, struggling against his hold.

"It's too late. Too late."

"He might still be alive!"

284

"I saw him land. His neck broke. Rachel, I'm sorry, I'm sorry. His neck broke. He's dead."

"You don't know!"

"I know. I saw it. Don't try to look. You don't want that image in your head."

"He's not dead. He can't be dead."

Alan hugged her against him, forcing her face against his jacket. She stared wide-eyed at the red fabric, at the black plastic zipper in front of her.

He wasn't dead. He couldn't be dead.

Just like her parents couldn't be dead. Not so sudden, so quick. With no warning.

No warning at all.

Something inside her that had begun to heal broke apart again, into a thousand shards as cold and sharp as glass.

Harrison groaned and opened his eyes. Min grinned down at him, barely visible beyond the bulge of Harrison's coat.

"Ha! I knew you did not die. But your coat, something funny has happened."

Harrison blinked. "Min? What are you doing here?" he croaked out.

"Saving you. What do you think?"

"But . . ."

"You think I can leave my lovely Rachel with you and dumb Archer? I have followed you since the monastery. I knew something bad would happen. Since Kathmandu, I have known there are secrets. You, Archer, Krishna and Porna. Everyone had secrets."

"Even you."

Min shrugged. "Maybe not so much a secret. More something too embarrassing to say."

Min helped him into a sitting position, air going "phhht" from holes in Harrison's bloated coat. Harrison groaned, his whole body hurting, but nothing seemed seriously damaged. He had landed on a drift of snow, blown into the canyon by some long-finished storm. "Were you really a rebel, or were you a government spy?"

"I was young and scared. A rebel, yes, until they asked me to kill soldiers. It did not sound like a good time, so I ran. But I did not give away the ambush. That was not my fault."

Harrison nodded, satisfied with the explanation and Min's look of indignation. He said, "Archer zapped me with the stun gun. Knocked me off that bridge."

"I saw. But I did not see what happened to your coat."

Harrison turned over his wrist, showing Min a black button. "The coat has gas cylinders embedded in it that turn it into an airbag when you hit this button."

Min gaped at him, started to ask another question, but Harrison had no time. "Is Rachel okay?"

Min shrugged. "Archer dragged her away. She tried to get down here, but he made her go. Told her you were dead."

"Bastard," he cursed. Did the man have no idea what that would do to her?

"Archer—he said something to you, before he zapped you," Min said. "I could not hear. What was it?"

Harrison shook his head. He was not going to repeat it. He didn't even want to think about it, but it sat in the center of his mind like a pile of rotting garbage, unmoving and unavoidable.

Archer had looked at him with cold eyes and a smirk on his lips. "I'm the one who popped her cherry. I screwed her a dozen times before you ever met her." Then he'd shoved the prongs of the stun gun against Harrison's extended hand.

Between words and stun gun, the words had given the greater shock.

Worse even than that revelation, though, was knowing that Rachel was now alone and in Archer's power, at the very doorstep to Yonam.

"How do we get out of here?" he asked Min.

Min grinned and pointed straight up the wall.

Chapter Thirteen

The passage through the rock was no more than fifteen feet long. It was more of a wide chute than anything else, spilling forth a tongue of snow from the slope on the other side. The passage bore a similarity to a female birth canal, what with the two small peaks rising to either side of the snowy tunnel like a pair of bent knees.

Rachel barely knew how she had crossed the rest of the glacier, or how she now found herself crawling up the snow, Alan urging her on from behind.

Her emotions were somewhere far away from her. She had become the mountains. Become soulless granite and snow. Even thought and memory were fractured, glinting in scattered pieces, like the bright fragments of a broken mirror.

Still, Alan urged her onward. He'd made her shoulder one of the packs, too.

They crested the slope behind the passage, then followed the only way open: a winding path that edged the base of cliffs and slipped through fractures in the rock.

It might have been a mere creek bed they followed; she didn't know. She didn't know if she cared. Alan had given her more drugs for the pain in her leg, and they had laid a welcome haze over her mind.

The sun was lowering toward the horizon when they came around a last wall of rock, and saw a village wedged tight in the bottom of a narrow valley. She stopped and stared.

Was this Yonam? It looked like no paradise she had ever imagined. It looked, instead, like every other Himalayan village she had ever seen. There were no more than twenty houses through its length. Narrow terraces inched up the slopes of the valley, green with some growing grain, perhaps barley. A figure moved here or there, but otherwise all was quiet.

The only element that was unusual was a dark gray-green swathe of granite mountainside above the terraces, on the north side of the valley. From this distance it looked as if the rock had been painted. Either that, or it was covered in some sort of lichen or low-growing plant. It must be the green skin of the mountain, of which the legends of Yonam spoke: It was the source of the Yes drug.

At a prod from Alan, she started down the faint trail to the valley. He babbled behind her.

"This is it! Rachel, we've found it! You have no idea what this means, how the world is going to change. And you're here for it! Do you know how lucky you are? How very lucky? You have no idea, no idea at all." Then he giggled.

The giggle stirred her from her stupor. How could he giggle? Harrison had fallen to his death, and Alan was giggling.

How *had* Harrison fallen, anyway? He'd been the more agile of the two, and he was wearing the crampons. She hadn't seen Alan do anything wrong . . . but that didn't mean he hadn't. She hadn't been able to see everything.

How dare he giggle!

How dare he, when Harrison had died trying to help him!

How *dare* he, the scum-sucking bag of shit! The numbness in her heart was seared away by anger. All-consuming, irrational, black-as-the-heart-of-Satan fury.

All thought subsumed by rage, she turned around and charged into him, taking him by surprise and knocking him to the ground. "You bastard, you selfish bloody bastard!" she screeched, and pounced on him, the pack on her back giving her extra weight. The air left him in a woof.

"Murderer! Frickin' murderer! Mother-f—" She pounded at his face with her closed fists, and felt the crunch of his nose breaking. He cried out, and blood poured from his nose.

Her advantage of surprise lasted no longer. He bucked her off his chest, knocking her to the ground. She struggled like a turtle on its back, trying to free herself of the pack's straps, using her legs to kick at him.

A bolt of pain shot into her leg and traveled through her body. She lost control of her muscles and lay there, twitching, as Alan got up onto his feet and came to stand near her head. As the convulsions died away, she focused on what he held in his hand. The stun gun.

"Cock-sucking—"

He zapped her again. "Careful, my darling Rachel," he said as she twitched. He unshouldered his own pack and opened it, digging out his red medical kit. Her eyes widened as he took out a syringe and an ampule of something unknown.

He paused, looking past her, down the valley. "I do believe we're attracting attention. I think we'll have company soon. You don't want them to see how bad-tempered you are, now, do you?"

"Fu—"

A short zap cut off her words, and while she lay there, helpless, Alan stuck the needle into her arm.

"You're going to feel so much better after this. Nothing is ever going to be the same again for you, Rachel. You'll wake up in a whole new world."

She felt as if she were being slowly dipped in warm honey, the golden sweetness of it seeping into her anger, immobilizing it. She fought against it, struggling to keep her eyes open and her mind awake.

"Are you feeling better, my love?" Alan asked, leaning down close.

She summoned all the will she had, and spat in his face.

Harrison and Min crouched low as they sneaked through the terraced fields, using the tall stalks of grain to hide them. He had told Min everything about the Yes drug and Archer's plans.

Nothing about the village spoke of a paradise, for either the men or the women. What women Harrison did see trudged about their duties with a dull, glassy stare in their eyes. Their hair was unkempt, their clothes hanging off their wiry, half-starved frames in a slovenly manner that other hill women would never permit.

The men were no cleaner, but they, at least, had flesh on their bones and a paunch to their guts. Several seemed the worse for drink.

The children were the worst of it all. They were too quiet, their big eyes constantly watching their elders, the littlest ones clinging to their mothers' skirts, seeking some shred of attention or affection that the women were too exhausted to give.

Yonam was a village of slaves.

"We have to find Rachel," Harrison said.

"We should wait until dark?" Min asked.

Harrison grimaced, knowing it was the best course, but not liking it.

"We have no weapons," Min reminded him.

"I wouldn't want to take on a whole village, even if we did. We're not here for a blood bath."

But there was one man he would love the chance to kill.

The next thing Rachel was aware of, her mouth was being forced open and something bitter and dry dumped in. She tried to spit it out, but hands held her mouth closed. They released her just long enough to pour water in, forcing her to swallow unless she wished to choke.

She opened her eyes to a crowd of unfamiliar male faces, looking frightened in the dim light. Frightened by her? They spoke in a dialect she could not understand, except for a word here or there.

"More," they said. She understood that. Then Alan was in front of her, forcing open her mouth again and dumping in more of the vile powder. His nose and the hollows around his eyes were brilliant purple red, and a dried crust of blood edged his nostrils.

"Puss—" she slurred.

He slapped his hand over her mouth, then leaned close and kissed her, hard, on the cheek. His other hand squeezed her breast.

He released her and then backed away, the others already filing out behind him. She realized she was in a small room, the walls covered in a stucco of mud. She was lying on a straw mat, on a wooden bed of sorts.

"Wait here for me. I'll be back," Alan said. "You'll be happy to see me, then." He closed a wood plank door behind him, and she was alone.

She lay still for a moment, but felt whatever drug he had given her trying to pull her back into a groggy, blissful dreamworld. She forced herself to roll onto her side and then sit up.

It was almost more than she could do.

She stuck out her tongue and tried to wipe the bitter taste from it. What had that been? What had that bastard given her?

A soft tingling ran through her body. When

would the bastard be coming back? He really was kind of cute. He should touch her. Squeeze her breast again. Give her a real kiss.

She jerked her head back, startled by her own muddled thoughts. She wanted to kiss Alan?

Something was wrong. She didn't want Alan, a part of her mind still knew that. Her body, though, was telling her something different, the feeling growing stronger by the second.

That powder he'd given her. Good Mother Mary in heaven, he'd given her the Yes drug. As soon as he came back, she'd be on her knees, begging him to let her suck him off.

The part of her that was still herself gagged.

She had to get out of here. But no, he'd told her to wait. She had to wait for him.

No! She had to escape!

He wanted her to wait. She must do what he said. Maybe he'd be kind, and have sex with her, if she did.

No!

The small light of her self-control was dimming. She looked frantically around the room, seeking she knew not what.

Her gaze lit on the backpacks, thrown against a wall. Harrison's backpack.

She thumped onto her knees, the hurt of doing so penetrating the thickening fog of her mind, and crawled to Harrison's bag. She opened the top, dragged out a handful of clothes, stuck her face in them, and breathed.

God, please, let it work. Beti had said the theory was that pheromones determined the master of the drugged woman. Let there be enough of Harrison's scent in his clothes to save her. Let it override Alan's foul self. Please, God. Please.

She dragged the pack over to the pallet, and unloaded its contents. She made a nest of them, and crawled in, surrounded by the scent of her lost lover.

She closed her eyes, and breathed.

Ten, twenty, thirty minutes later—she could not tell for sure—a hand brushed the hair away from the back of her neck, and then she felt the dampness of a tongue on her skin.

"Rachel," Alan said. "Undress for me."

She turned to look at him, and smiled seductively. "Only if you go to hell, first, you sick bastard."

His mouth tightened, his face reddening. He shoved her violently away from him. She turned her face back into Harrison's clothes, and smiled.

"It's the painkillers. They must be interfering with the drug," Alan said, as much to himself as to her. "I have to give them more time to wear off. More time. That's all it needs."

She heard the door shut behind him.

For the moment, she had won.

Chapter Fourteen

"There's Archer!" Min said.

"Wanker."

Archer had just come out of one of the small houses, accompanied by a group of village men, all talking excitedly. Rachel was nowhere to be seen, and Harrison guessed that she had been left inside the house.

"What's wrong with his face?"

Harrison narrowed his eyes, trying to make out the details in the distance. "It looks like someone gave him a beating."

The men led Archer along a path toward the edge of the village, then pointed across the fields, toward a swath of mountainside that was green in the low light of the sun. Some of the men were making motions with their hands that mimed scraping or wiping.

Harrison and Min crept closer to the group. "Can you understand what they're saying?"

Min frowned. "It's a dialect, but—I can catch some of it. They're talking about that green place, and how to take something off of it."

"You know there's only one thing Archer would be asking about. Go see if you can get a better look at that mountainside, without being seen yourself."

"And you?"

"I'm going to get Rachel."

Rachel opened her eyes at the feel of gentle hands on her face and hair. There was a gasp and shuffle, and as her eyes focused she saw two young girls, no more than eight or ten, looking at her wide-eyed.

"*Namaste,*" she said, sitting up. She felt groggy, but some of her strength was returning.

The girls stared, too frightened to respond.

"*Namaste,*" Rachel repeated, holding her hands in the prayer position.

"*Nama . . .*" the girls said so softly they could almost not be heard. They looked at each other, and seemed to find their courage. They nodded, and one went to peek out the door to the room while the other came forward and, with extreme timidity, took Rachel's hand.

"What is it?" Rachel asked in Nepali. "What do you want?"

The girl tugged on her hand, urging her up off the bed, and gestured that they should go.

"You're trying to help me?" Rachel asked. "You want me to escape?"

Both the girls started gesturing. *Go, go,* they were saying.

The girl at the door turned back to her vigil, then gasped, closing the door and turning to them with a panicked look on her face.

A moment later, the door burst open behind her, and all three of them screeched.

Wiles stood there, looking like a fury from the dead.

Rachel screeched anew, to see her dead lover standing before her. Her knees went weak, and she began to sink.

"Rachel!" He swept her up into his arms before she could fall, and held her close, her face pressed into the bend of his neck.

More even than the feel of him, the scent of him brought her back to her senses. He was real, he was here, he wasn't dead!

"It's you? It's truly you?" she asked hoarsely.

"Of course it is."

"You've come back from the dead."

"Come back from a great crack in the ice, is all. Min found me, helped me out."

"Min? He's here?"

"He's outside, spying on Archer. Turns out Min wasn't a bad guy, after all."

"I knew he wasn't. I knew it!"

"Are you okay? Did Archer hurt you?"

"I hurt him worse," she said darkly. "Broke his nose, I think."

At that, Wiles hugged her even tighter. "God, Rachel. You are amazing. Do you know that?" He kissed her on the mouth, hard, waking all her animal impulses.

She reached for his belt, tugging at the buckle.

He broke off the kiss. "Not now, my sweet," he said with some surprise, putting his hand over hers. "We have an audience," he said, gesturing with his head toward the staring girls, "not to mention a lack of time."

"Not now?" She looked at him in slack-mouthed disappointment.

"No, we can't."

She tried to kiss him again.

"Rachel? I love you, darling, but—"

"Just a quickie?"

He put his hands on her shoulders and held her away from him, looking into her eyes. "What's the matter with you?"

She blinked at him, struggling to find the part

of her brain that still functioned. "He drugged me. Morphine, I think. But the Yes drug, too."

Wiles's eyes widened, and he sucked in a breath. "Did he—"

"I outwitted him," she said. "I put my face in your clothes and breathed in your scent. I bonded myself to you, not to him." She closed her eyes for a long moment, concentrating, then opened them again. "You know this means I'll do anything you ask of me, for as long as it is in my system."

"Oh, Rachel," he said, and took her gently back into his arms, holding her like the precious creature she was. "I won't ask a thing."

Rachel felt a tug on her clothes. It was one of the girls, worry in her eyes. She gestured again for Rachel to *go*.

"Your little friends have the right idea," Wiles said. "It looks like the children are the only ones in this village with both the wit and the desire to try to save you."

"They would likely save their mothers, if they could," she said.

Wiles looked at her. "They would, wouldn't they? What kid wouldn't?"

"What are you thinking?" she asked.

"I'm thinking it might be time to work out a few childhood issues of my own."

* * *

Under cover of darkness Rachel, Min, Harrison, and every child in the village past the age of three sneaked their way through the grain terraces, toward the green mountainside. They carried oils and grease, and pitchers of the hard rice liquor *rakshi*.

Archer was in one of the small houses, drinking *rakshi* himself, along with a loud group of men. Rachel guessed he was scared to go back and face her.

Min was better able to communicate with the children than either she or Harrison. Some of the kids told him that their mothers seemed to know something was up, but had done nothing to stop them, not even when they stole their fathers' *rakshi*. Their fathers paid them no heed whatsoever.

It was a steep climb up the mountainside, but the children were more than able, springing ahead with nimbleness and energy. There was just enough moonlight to show them their footing, but the children probably could have found their way even in utter darkness. This was their home.

"We'll start at the top and work our way down," Wiles said, for Min to translate. "Be sparing, but cover as much as you can."

The children needed no further prompting, and like wraiths flitted out over the mountainside with their jugs and jars and pitchers. They dribbled oil, smeared grease, and poured *rakshi* over every inch of rock within their reach.

It was lichen that grew on the granite: a thin layer of some unique combination of algae and fungi, which grew nowhere else in the world.

After tonight, it would grow nowhere at all.

When the children were finished, they all fled back down the mountainside to their homes. This was only half the task they had to accomplish this night, and they needed to be in place for when the signal came.

Min produced a book of matches.

"Rachel? The honors?" Wiles asked.

She took the matches, and with a grin of delight struck the first one. The flame was small against the darkness, but the moment she laid it against a *rakshi*-soaked patch of lichen, it became a blue-yellow flash of heat and light.

They backed away, the blast of heat growing as the flames spread up the mountainside, leaping from soaked patch to soaked patch.

"Beti said there was a wall of fire," Rachel said. "Maybe the legends of Yonam were as much a prophecy as a history."

"Let it go back to being a myth," Wiles said.

"We will be stories only, too, like the Man with the Hook, unless we go," Min said. "Go *now*."

From the village, a male roar of horror was rising up. In minutes, the mountainside would be flooded with angry, fearful men trying to save the source of their power.

They would be too late.

"Then let's go!" Rachel said, and laughed at the destruction they had wrought. "Let them fight the fire, but let us go!"

They skirted the path back, hiding in the fields as the village men ran by. Archer was in their midst, stumbling as he ran, his voice reaching their ears above the others. "No! No, no, no!"

In the village itself, a new chaos was erupting as the children threw crockery and smashed containers, green-gray powder spilling into the dirt. They trod upon it, threw water on it, even peed upon it, as their mothers stood by and watched.

The women were helpless at the moment, but within a day, maybe two, they would awake from their trance of years, and a new world order would come to Yonam.

They stopped at the house where Rachel had been held, stepping over broken pottery and muddy smears of powder, and snatched up their packs. They didn't want to be here when the men came back from their burnt mountainside.

"What about Alan? Do we just leave him?" Rachel asked.

"If he's smart, he'll flee before the village men turn on him," Wiles said. "We can get him then.

He has nowhere to go but out of Yonam. Are you up to traveling?"

"Are you kidding? I could run all the way back to Kathmandu, I'm so glad to be leaving this place!"

"That's not just the Yes drug talking, trying to please me?"

"I've got a dozen better ways in mind to please you, good sir."

"I was hoping you'd say that."

"Can we *go?*" Min pleaded. "You can be boy-friend and girlfriend later."

"He has a point," Wiles said.

"Sad, but true." Rachel smiled, and they headed for the hills.

It was morning by the time the three of them came to the passage down out of Yonam. They were exhausted, and the climb down the snowy slope looked far more difficult than going up had been.

"I wish I had a sled," Rachel said. "Whoosh! We'd be down."

"We don't have a sled," Harrison said, "but we do have . . ."

"An Indestructi-sheet!" Rachel finished.

"An indi-what?" Min asked.

Instead of answering, Rachel dug the sheet out

of the pack and spread it on the ground. "No way am I sitting in front."

Min understood immediately and hopped on. Rachel got behind him. Harrison shoved their packs down the slope ahead of them, then found a place behind Rachel, his strong legs cradling hers.

"Grab an edge!" Harrison said, and then they were barreling down the chute, screaming in terrified glee. They bumped and thumped, chunks of ice bruising their butts, and then just as they came to the bottom then all slowly lost their balance, tipping over and rolling like a human car wreck.

Rachel shouted with laughter as she rolled to a stop, her heart thumping with exhilaration. It wasn't only the sled ride, but the destruction of the Yes drug, the escape from Alan, and the glorious feeling that, for the first time in a year and a half, all was right in the world.

The only thing unfinished was the capture of Alan, but all they needed to do was wait for him to come bolting out of the passage like a rabbit from a hole. There was no other exit from the valley of Yonam.

She flung her arms around Harrison's neck, laughing in joy. She heard and felt his own joyful heart thudding against her ear, but then as the sound grew louder she raised her head and looked out over the glacier.

That wasn't Harrison's heart she heard: it was a pair of helicopters.

"The army?" Rachel asked in trepidation.

Min answered. "Wrong type of helicopter."

Harrison wrapped his arm around Rachel's waist and grinned. "It's not the army, my darling. It's B.L.I.S.S. Grab that sheet!"

She did, and they all three held its edge, catching the clear, bright light of a Himalayan morning on its surface, sending a signal that could not be missed to the helicopters flying low over the glacier.

A few minutes later the chopper settled on a smooth patch of ice, and the door of the first one slid open. To Rachel's utter astonishment, a trio of women in tight white jumpsuits climbed down, then Beti . . . and right behind her, Pamela.

"Rachel!" her sister screamed, and ran toward her with such panicked desperation that Rachel found herself checking over her own shoulder to see if someone was about to jump her.

"Rachel! You had me scared half to death," Pamela said, and threw herself on her, holding Rachel so tight she could barely breathe.

"Pam. What are you doing here?" she asked, stunned.

"Are you okay? You're okay, aren't you? Are you hurt? Those monks at the monastery, they said you'd been shot. Were you shot?"

"Pam, I'm fine," Rachel said, beginning to laugh. Her sister's hair had come out of its braid in tufts, and her shirt was on inside out. She looked like she had been, literally, frantic with worry. Rachel's laughter softened, and she felt a start of tears in her eyes. "What are you doing here?" she asked again.

"That e-mail you sent me, about Alan Archer and B.L.I.S.S. I didn't think anything strange about it at the time I answered, but then it started to eat at me. Something was not quite right. Alan, reappearing in our lives so soon after I'd been talking about him, to someone who seemed unusually curious. You, asking about a nongovernmental organization, about which I could find out absolutely nothing.

"You're the only real family I have left," Pamela continued. "If there was any chance you were getting yourself into trouble, I wasn't going to sit by and let it happen."

"Your sister is a woman of unusual cleverness and perseverance," Beti said, and did not make it sound like a compliment.

"How did you find us?" Harrison asked.

"The last information we had from you, you were going to look for Tangunboche Gompa,"

Beti said, still looking as if she'd eaten something sour. "When Pamela infiltrated B.L.I.S.S. looking for Rachel, she insisted that we fly to the monastery and try to pick up Rachel's tracks."

"And you gave in to her?" Rachel asked in disbelief.

"I threatened them with full exposure," Pamela said with pride. *"New York Times. Washington Post.* I know reporters, I could make a stink."

"You won't do that now, will you?"

"Me? Of course not. I'd rather join."

Beti whimpered.

"We'll send you an application packet," Harrison said, and Rachel wasn't sure if he was joking or serious. "First, though, there's the matter of Archer to take care of. Beti, is that helicopter equipped with the usual B.L.I.S.S. assortment of arms?"

The Nepali nodded.

"I'll need an X3-7, fully loaded."

One of the jumpsuit-clad women dashed back to the helicopter to fetch it, whatever "it" was.

"What are you going to do?" Rachel asked, a sick fluttering in her heart. She couldn't bear the sight of Alan again, but neither did she think she could watch the man she loved gun someone down in cold blood.

The man she loved.

Yes, she knew it now. The fullness in her heart, the wholeness, told her it was so. There was no fear left in her, and the pain of loss had subsided to a minor ache.

"I'm going to administer justice," Harrison said. He saw the look on her face, and kissed her on the forehead. "Don't worry. You'll like this."

When she saw the massive tranquilizer gun that was the X3-7, she got an inkling that she would. She put her hand behind Harrison's neck, pulled his face down to hers, and kissed him.

"What was that for?" he asked, when it was over.

"It was because I love you. Past fear and pain, loss and sorrow, I love you, Harrison Wiles."

He smiled crookedly, and took her into his arms. "I'm really going to have to work on making you more of a 'glass-half-full' type of woman."

"Do your best, my love. I'm willing."

Epilogue

"I'm going to appeal!" Alan screamed, as he was shoved into the common area of the prison. "I have the right to appeal! You wait until I talk to the U.S. embassy. You'll see, you can't do this to me! I'm an American citizen, a *doctor,* and this is cruel and unusual punishment!"

The guards locked the door and walked away.

He'd been convicted of Durga's murder in a speedy Thai trial. He had no idea how he'd gotten from Nepal to Thailand, and even less idea where the Thai prosecution had obtained their damning evidence.

The last thing he remembered, he'd been sliding down out of the snowy passage from Yonam, and then been hit in the thigh with a tranquilizer dart. Right before he blacked out, he'd seen that loathsome Harrison Wiles, grinning down at him like a madman. Beside Wiles, Rachel had stood with her head cocked to one side and eyebrows raised, looking down at him as if at a curious animal bagged on safari. She looked no more concerned than if debating between having him skinned and having him stuffed.

Where the hell could Wiles have gotten a tranquilizer gun, anyway? It was driving him insane, not knowing what had happened, what forces had been at work to land him in a Thai prison.

At the sound of voices Alan turned around, taking his first look at his new home. He knew at once that there would be no Snickers bars here, no hot showers, not even any toilet paper. Instead, there was bare concrete. Water and filth trickling across the floor. A stench of feces, urine, and the worst of human effluvia.

Men were staring at him. Dark foreign men, in ragged clothes, who had been convicted of crimes as bad as his . . . or worse.

"Pretty boy," one of the men said, his words thickly accented. "Pretty, pretty boy."

Alan spun back to the locked door, grabbed the bars, and screamed.

* * *

B.L.I.S.S. Headquarters

"I'm nervous," Rachel said, and smoothed a strand of white-blonde, spiky hair behind her ear.

"You've no need to be," Harrison said, leading her to the broad double doors that were the entrance to Y's sanctum.

"What if she doesn't want me? What if I don't fit her idea of a B.L.I.S.S. agent?" Her gold nose disk had been replaced by a diamond stud, her *shalwar kameez* with a watery blue-green sarong and T-shirt. She'd bought the sarong at the diving resort in Malaysia where she and Harrison had spent the last two weeks.

A blissful two weeks they had been, too, spent as much in bed as in the warm ocean water.

"You've already proven yourself. *Y's* the one who's going to be nervous, not knowing if she can persuade you to join B.L.I.S.S. permanently."

Rachel stopped, and wrapping her arms around Harrison's waist, laid her cheek on his broad chest. She slid her hands down over his butt. "Won't she frown on fraternization between her agents?"

"Maybe. She'll just have to get over it, though, won't she?" He lifted her face in his hands and kissed her.

Lisa Cach

It felt as good as it had the very first time.

Rachel sighed when they at last drew apart. "I can still hardly believe the story about Durga."

"A tragic love story was the last thing I would have expected," Harrison agreed.

Min had learned Durga's history from the villagers of Yonam, and later told it to her and Wiles.

Durga had fallen in love with a girl who was to be the wife of another. They'd tried to run away together, but been caught. The girl had been given the Yes drug and handed over to her fiancé, and from then on had been lost to Durga.

Unable to bear seeing his beloved as the wife of another, Durga had taken a stash of the Yes drug and fled the village. No one in Yonam had ever heard from him again.

The girl Durga had loved had sought Min out, and shown him a portrait Durga had drawn of her, and that she had saved, secretly, throughout the long days of her unwanted marriage. The drug may have controlled her body, but it never touched her heart. She wept when she learned of Durga's death, and was convinced that it had always been his intention to come back and free her.

Indirectly, he had.

It was a mystery, where the heart would take one. The path might not look anything like what you expected, but the destination would be exactly what you needed.

Rachel faced the door to Y's office. "You know, there's just one thing I really want from Y, before I sign on with B.L.I.S.S."

Harrison raised his brow, as he reached forward and turned the knob. "Besides permission to fondle me whenever you wish?"

She rolled her eyes, then gave his tush a pat for good measure. "I'll do that with or without her permission. No, what she's got to do is finally tell me: *What* on God's green earth does 'B.L.I.S.S.' stand for!"

Harrison laughed and opened the door.

B.L.I.S.S.

*Looking for more action, adventure and, of
course, romance? Dive into this sneak peek of*

LYNSAY SANDS'

THE LOVING DAYLIGHTS

Shy Jane Spyrus loves gadgets. She can build anything B.L.I.S.S. needs in its international fight
against crime—although agents aren't exactly
queuing up at her door. It will take the dark and
sexy Abel Andretti to prove to Jane just how valu-
able she really is, and to show her how to love the
daylights out of something without batteries.

AVAILABLE APRIL 2003.

Chapter One

1:40 p.m., Thursday

"D & C meeting in twenty minutes, Jane."

"Yep." Jane Spyrus straightened from her worktable and smiled at the tall blonde standing in the doorway of her office. "I'll be ready. Thanks for reminding me though, Lizzy."

"No problem. Want me to stop and grab you on my way? Just in case you get too involved in what you're doing?"

Jane didn't take offense at the offer. She was famous for getting involved in projects and being late for meetings. "No, that's okay. I just have a couple more adjustments to make, then I'll head right over."

319

Lizzy Hubert nodded then moved slowly into the room. "What *are* you working on?"

Jane immediately shifted to block her worktable, aware that her face was flushing with embarrassment. "Nuh-uh. You'll see soon enough."

"Can't blame a girl for trying." The blonde laughed and gave a shrug. "See you in twenty minutes. I'll save you a seat."

Jane waited until the door closed behind the other woman before relaxing, then she turned to peer down at the items on her worktable. She shook her head.

It was silly to be embarrassed about this latest project. It was a brilliant idea. At least, *she* thought so. And she wasn't embarrassed by the B T Trackers she was also going to reveal today. Well, not as much. Yet, somehow these minimissile launchers made her blush and want to squirm every time she thought of presenting them. Of course, this was one aspect of her job that she truly disliked anyway. Jane loved creating new weapons and spy technology for B.L.I.S.S. but loathed presenting them at the monthly Development and Creation meetings. She was a very poor public speaker. Stammering and stumbling over her words, she knew she often sounded like a fool. It was amazing to her that Y approved any of her inventions for production.

Jane made a face at the thought of the head of B.L.I.S.S. Y was a hard-as-nails ex-agent who came across as all-knowing and all-seeing. She was the most intimidating woman Jane had ever encountered. Jane supposed it was the woman's lack of expression, which left one uncertain as to what she was thinking. That was also probably part of the reason it was so hard to gauge Y's age. Her face was remarkably unlined, yet she'd been at B.L.I.S.S. forever—or so said Jane's Gran.

Gran would know, too. All of Jane's family was involved in the intelligence industry in one way or another, most of them field operatives. Gran herself was an ex-agent and contemporary of Y's.

Field work wasn't Jane's area, however. She wasn't the risk-taking type. She preferred dusty old books and tinkering with technology to the adrenaline-pumping, life-threatening derring-do of being an operative. She liked to think that her job developing innovative new weapons and gizmos was just as important, though.

Picking up a tiny Phillips screwdriver, Jane made the last of several necessary adjustments to one of the prototypes of the BMML. It only took a couple of seconds; then she straightened, removed her glasses, and stared down at her creation with a pleased sigh. To the unknowing observer, this BMML—B.L.I.S.S. Mini-Missile Launcher—looked like nothing more threatening than a neon pink vibrator. Which was the idea, of course. That was its "cover." No one would ever dare to investigate, either.

Grinning, Jane began to pack everything away into her briefcase, then reached across the table to turn on the radio. She kept it tuned to an '80s hits station, and *"Whip It"* by *Devo* filled the room. The opening beats made her pause and bob her head. There was just something about the song: Jane didn't particularly care for it, but darned if every time it played she didn't find herself stopping what she was doing, cranking up the volume, and moving to the beat. As she did now. With the vibrator-like BMML still in hand, Jane began be-bopping around her office. When the chorus started—the only words she knew— she began singing into her creation.

"Am I interrupting something?"

Jane froze with the neon pink BMML still raised to her open mouth. Staring down, she wished the floor would split open and swallow her whole. It *would* have to be none other than Richard Hedde, standing in the door to her workroom. His smirk was so wide that Jane's own face ached in sympathy. She would never, *ever* hear the end of this.

Trying to pretend her face had not just gone

as red as a tomato, Jane lowered her makeshift microphone, turned off the radio with feigned calm, and faced the one person in D & C that she absolutely loathed. "Not at all, I was just t-testing my latest invention."

It was possibly the stupidest thing Jane had said in her life, and something Dick did not have the grace to let pass. "Truly Jane, I've always known you were socially backward, but if you don't even know the proper way to test that thing, you're more hopeless than I thought."

Jane hadn't considered it possible, but she actually flushed deeper. Mouth tightening, she put the BMML into her briefcase along with one she'd adjusted earlier. "Is there something you wanted, Dick?"

"Just to remind you that the D & C meeting is in"—he checked his wrist watch—"five minutes. We wouldn't want you to be late. Again."

Jane's teeth ground together in irritation, but she merely closed her briefcase, picked it up and crossed the room, walking with all the dignity she could muster. "I was just heading that way."

"Sure you were. After you finished testing your invention, right?" He laughed as she grabbed her jacket off the hook by the door and stepped into the hall. Following her out of the room, Dick pulled the door closed behind them. "By the way, Jane. I hate to burst another bubble, but your little prototype there was invented by someone else years ago. It even has a name. I believe they call it a vibrator."

"Ha ha." Jane picked up speed in an effort to escape her coworker. "Thank you for the newsbreak."

"Anytime," he called after her. Though she couldn't see his face and refused to turn and look, she could tell he was enjoying this immensely. Dick seemed to enjoy nothing better than humiliating her. "Always happy to be of help."

Muttering some unpleasant descriptive words under her breath, Jane continued along the hall to the conference room. She was relieved to find it almost full. That meant Dick would shut up. Temporarily at least.

"Jane!" Lizzy was seated halfway up the left side of the table. Jane moved in her friend's direction.

Other than Dick, Lizzy was the only member of the D & C department who was near Jane's age. All the rest of the members were older and had been recruited when B.L.I.S.S. was first put into operation. A job in D & C at B.L.I.S.S. was a lifetime job; the secrets were too big for anything else. Anyone who was thinking about signing on there had that explained quite plainly before they did. No one joined D & C at

B.L.I.S.S., then quit. Jane didn't know what would happen if anyone tried such a thing, but she suspected it wouldn't be good. As far as she knew, it hadn't come up. No one had been foolish enough to try or even wanted to. This was a great place to work, with unlimited funds and almost unlimited freedom.

"I can't believe you made it on time for a change," Lizzy teased gently as Jane hung her jacket over the back of the saved chair.

Jane gave a somewhat forced smile and sat down, very aware that Dick had followed her. Much to her relief, he didn't comment, just kept on walking, taking one of the two seats at the far end of the table so that he sat with his back to the windows.

"Y will be impressed to find you here and not stumbling in after she starts the meeting," Lizzy continued.

Jane grunted. Y never seemed upset by her tardiness, instead was almost expectant of it. Jane half-suspected that leniency was part of the reason Richard was so obnoxious to her. Where Y seemed to like her and was very patient with her lateness, Dick didn't get the same treatment. He wasn't particularly well-liked by anyone.

As if summoned by her thoughts, the door suddenly opened to admit Y and Jane's supervisor. Y was the head of B.L.I.S.S., but Ira Manetrue was the head of D & C. The gentleman, an old flame of her grandmother's, had taken Jane under his wing the moment she'd started here, and he considered himself something of a mentor to her. All of which made Dick all the more furious. Jane almost understood that part of his unhappiness, but Richard brought his trouble on himself. If he were just respectful and less of a greasy brown-noser he'd get further, but he made himself so unpleasant she couldn't bring herself to tell him. For the most part, she ignored him like everyone else. Or tried to.

"Good day, everyone," Mr. Manetrue greeted the room as he and Y took their seats at the far end of the table. Settling in with notepad and pen at the ready he asked, "Who's going to start the presentations today?"

His gaze zeroed in on Jane, but she glanced down at the pen she was twiddling. She would have to make her presentation eventually, but she didn't have the courage to actually *volunteer* to do it . . . or be first. Fortunately, the others weren't so shy and several raised their hands. Jane felt relief seep through her as Mr. Manetrue gestured for one of them to start.

Time passed swiftly as the others' prototypes were presented and displayed, but Jane had a terrible time paying attention. She was all too aware that as each person finished his presentation, she herself grew that much closer to giving her own. She started trying to remember what she would say. She always memorized a sort of speech for these meetings . . . and always forgot every word the moment she stood up. This time, the words appeared to have fled sooner than usual. Her mind was a complete blank.

"Jane?" Mr. Manetrue's voice pierced her panicked thoughts. She glanced up to find all eyes turned expectantly on her, and immediately she felt her heart sink. It was her turn.

Swallowing nervously, Jane picked up her briefcase, set it on the table, then stood and opened it. She started to retrieve items, noting with a sort of detached interest that her hands were shaking. Wishing once again that she weren't such a poor speaker, Jane closed the case and held up two small silver boxes.

"I . . . um . . ." She stopped and cleared her throat, then tried again. "Last month we lost one of our agents when she was forced to remove all her c-clothes and jewelry—including the wristwatch tracker which is standard issue to all field operatives. She was later found dead." Jane paused and took a nervous drink of water. Forcing a sickly smile, she continued, "That incident got me thinking about a t-tracker that would never be discovered."

"And you came up with a cigarette case?" Richard asked, snickering.

"It isn't a cigarette case." Jane rotated it so that he could see the box's thickness. "Besides, it isn't the case itself that is the tracker." She opened the object so that everyone could see the long white items inside. "I came up with BTT's— B.L.I.S.S. Tampon Trackers."

Taking in the expressions around her, Jane felt her stomach roll over. It was Y who finally asked, "Am I to understand that those are actual tampons?"

Jane bit her lip. While Y didn't sound upset, she also didn't sound overly impressed. "Well, yes. They can function as actual tampons as well. But they also hold tracking devices that have a range of—"

"But what if the agent isn't menstruating?" Y asked calmly. Richard was staring in horror, but B.L.I.S.S.'s leader seemed unrattled by the invention. Her matter-of-fact attitude had a settling effect on Jane.

"Oh, well, I thought of that. There are lubricated and unlubricated." She held up a second case and opened it. Inside were several more tampons, distinguishable from the others only in that they were an off-white. "The lubricated are easily inserted and easily removed, and only serve the purpose of tracking, while the non-lubricated are absorbent and—"

"The tracking device is waterproof, I presume?" Y interrupted again.

"Yes. It's at the very center of the tampon and tightly sealed. The circuitry has an estimated life of two years."

Y nodded, then sat back without comment. Everyone was silent. Most of the older members of D & C were eyeing the BTT's speculatively and nodding. Lizzy was grinning encouragingly. Dick—well, he was sneering nastily, obviously just waiting for an opportunity to tear at her.

Deciding not to give him that chance, and that she'd said enough on this subject for now, Jane replaced the two silver cases in her briefcase. Taking a deep breath, she then removed two more items. One was a four-inch square flat piece of wood with a spike sticking out of it; the other was a banana. She set the wood, spike up, on the tabletop, then impaled the banana peel and all. Next she retrieved several foil packets from her briefcase, wondering all the while what on earth she had been thinking. These next inventions had seemed brilliant in an evil gleeful sort of way when she'd come up with them, but now—with all these eyes trained on her—they seemed the most foolish things she'd ever designed. What had she been thinking?

She hadn't been thinking, That was obvious,

Jane decided. She tossed the little packets back into her briefcase.

As she reached to retrieve the banana and its spiked holder, Y asked sharply, "What are you doing?"

Jane paused and flushed. "I decided to skip this item. It's rather silly, and I thought I should just move on to—"

"No skipping," Y said firmly.

Mr. Manetrue nodded. "Even if an idea doesn't work out, Jane, it may spark another from someone else here, or even yourself. That's what these meetings are about, remember?"

Jane exhaled unhappily then replaced the banana and the spike on the table. She retrieved the small foil packets from her briefcase. "This idea . . . Well, my gran was telling me once about an agent friend of hers who was raped while on assignment. So, well . . . I thought—" Her face was flaming and she knew it, but she had no choice but to continue. Straightening her shoulders Jane blurted, "I c-came up with the B.L.I.S.S. Shrink-Wrap Condom."

Richard was not the only one to laugh this time, although most of the other laughs were embarrassed titters. Jane did her best to ignore them. She walked over to hand a packet to both Y and Mr. Manetrue, then she returned to her spot and opened the condom she'd kept for herself.

"As you can see, the label suggests this condom contains a Viagra-like substance to increase longevity, sensitivity and pleasure." She mumbled, wishing she'd never created the stupid prophylactics. "This is to make it appear more attractive to anyone who might use it, to entice a perhaps otherwise unwilling subject."

She removed the latex circle inside the packet and doggedly slipped it onto the banana, ignoring Dick's loud, uncontrolled mirth. "Once it's fully stretched out and applied, it reacts to human body oils and begins to constrict. Earlier I applied a special cream to the banana meant to emulate those oils, and as you can see the condom reacts quite swiftly."

The room had gone quiet again. Even Dick had stopped laughing. The condom shrank around the banana, forcing it to shrink too. When the peel actually burst, squirting pulpy mash out the bottom of the rubber, he along with most men in the room crossed his legs and grimaced.

"As you can imagine," Jane suggested, "this would significantly discourage any sexual interest or the possibility of rape."

Much to her amazement, Y burst out laughing. The woman eyed the banana mash leaking out all over the table from the now pencil-thin prophylactic. "Diabolical," she crowed. "Although it would probably have more use as a torture device to get information out of double agents or such. I doubt many men intent on rape would take the time to don a condom," she pointed out mildly. "Is there a way to stop it once it's activated?"

"Yes." Jane produced a small jar of cream from her case. "This will make the latex relax at once."

She opened the jar, scooped out some cream, then began smoothing it over the straining condom. As she'd predicted, the rubber immediately loosened around the shriveled banana peel.

Y nodded in satisfaction. "Anything else, Ms. Spyrus?"

Relieved, Jane smiled. She removed the shrink-wrapped banana, wiped up the mess left behind by her experiment, and put it all away. Then she peered at her last two items: The BMMLs.

Dismay again claimed Jane. Looking at the neon pink vibrator-missile launchers, she suddenly realized that every single item she'd brought today was sexual in nature. Even the Tracking Tampons had to do with reproductive organs! She had to wonder if that meant something. Was she desperate? Lonely? True; most of her time was spent alone in her workroom. As for a social life, she really had none of which to speak. She had the occasional coffee or pizza with her neighbor Edie, or the infrequent lunch with Lizzy, but she hadn't had a boyfriend in quite some time. There just hadn't seemed to be the opportunity since graduating from university. Was her repression releasing itself now through her inventions?

Jane had taken this job at B.L.I.S.S. right after she got her doctorate. For the past two years she'd worked long hours trying to prove herself. Much of that time had been spent alone in her D & C workroom,—there or on nights and weekends in the workroom she'd created in her apartment, which eliminated the need for a night nurse for Gran while still allowing Jane to tinker. Yet she still was working long hours even now. It was no longer out of a need to impress anyone, but simply because she enjoyed it. Jane had a passion for her work. She hadn't really felt a need for a social life—especially not one that included the emotional messiness of male-female relationships.

Not consciously she hadn't felt it, anyway. But now, standing here looking down at the contents of her briefcase, Jane began to suspect that subconsciously it was a different story. Perhaps she was inwardly yearning for something. And that something was possibly emotional, but most definitely sexual.

"Jane?" Ira Manetrue prompted, making her realize she'd stood silent an awfully long time contemplating the possibility that she needed . . . well . . . basically that she needed to get laid.

Sighing, she shoved her concerns aside and grimly lifted one of the BMML's out of her briefcase. The restless shuffling and soft murmurs that had begun to fill the room came to an immediate halt. Jane ignored the sudden silence and carried her invention down to the end of the table. There she handed it over to Y.

"Oh my." The woman turned the object over in her hand. "I hesitate to even ask what this is."

"A microphone," Dick spoke up with a laugh. As Jane returned to her seat and picked up the second BMML he added, "At least, that's what she appeared to be using it as when I stopped in to remind her about today's meeting so she wouldn't be late *again*."

Jane ground her teeth and began to twist the vibrator in her hands.

"Mind you," Dick continued, "She *said* she was *testing* it—but she may have had it at her mouth for another reason entirely." He waggled his eyebrows suggestively.

"This is the B.L.I.S.S. Mini-Missile Launcher," Jane announced to shut him up. She forced a calmer tone as she continued. "As you can see, it appears to be nothing more than your common everyday vibrator."

"So they're commonly neon pink, Jane?" Dick asked slyly. "And that shape?"

Jane's fingers tightened on her invention, unintentionally flicking its switch. The cylinder began to vibrate. Jane gave a start and dropped it. Fortunately, she caught it before it hit the desk, but she flushed even further as Dick burst into gales of laughter. Jane tried to shut it off. Unfortunately, in her agitation, she pushed down on the switch instead of flicking it off. Much to her horror, the BMML bucked in her hands.

The missile launched.

Chapter Two

It sailed right over Dick's head, the draft from its passing parting his hair dead-center. There was a tinkle as the missile crashed through the window behind him, but that was almost unnoticeable next to the loud percussion that followed. Jane stood completely still, not even breathing. Mr. Manetrue got to his feet and moved calmly to the window to peer out. Jane envisioned dead bodies strewn everywhere behind the building.

"Nice shot, Jane. You hit the explosion test-pit dead on," Manetrue announced. When he turned, his expression was curious. "That obviously isn't a microphone, and it has an excellent targeting system."

Relief poured over Jane. Her heart began to pump again, sending blood gushing through her veins. She even started breathing once more.

She hadn't hurt anyone! Thank God!

"No. Not a microphone," Y agreed dryly.

Jane glanced toward the head of B.L.I.S.S. who was now holding the other neon-pink BMML as if expecting it to explode at any moment. Grimacing, Jane hurried to retrieve it.

Y handed it back without comment, then Jane returned quietly to her chair, appreciating the sympathetic look Lizzy offered. This just wasn't her day, she supposed. Although, if she looked at it from a different perspective, perhaps it *was* her day. No one had gotten hurt by the malfunctioning BMML. And it *had* malfunctioned. She'd installed a fail-safe that should have prevented it from going off in such circumstances.

Jane's gaze slid along the table to Dick. He was no longer smirking or laughing; he'd gone silent and pale.

Everything had its up-side.

"Go ahead, Jane. Explain your invention," Mr. Manetrue suggested. He moved back to take his seat. He didn't appear the least upset that she'd very nearly beheaded one of her co-workers, blown a hole through the room's window, and launched a missile that might have killed them all. In fact, he appeared to be restraining a smile.

"Uh . . . yes sir." Clearing her throat, she held up the unused missile launcher. "The . . . er . . . B.L.I.S.S. Mini-Missile Launcher is highly non-threatening in appearance and easily c-carried in luggage into foreign countries. Made mostly of polymers, it will not set off airport alarms. Should it be discovered during a hand-search of luggage, it is unlikely to raise concern. In fact, most people would be too embarrassed to look at it closely. Even if they did, however, they will find a functioning vibrator." She'd remembered and fallen into the speech she'd prepared, and now she moved to flick the BMML's switch to on. Movement out of the corner of her eye made her hesitate.

Dick had finally snapped out of his stunned state, and he was moving to duck under the table, out of the way of the missile she'd unthinkingly turned in his direction. Jane bit her lip. Part of her wanted to smile at the obnoxious twit being sent to his knees that way. The bigger, better part of her felt slightly guilty.

"Er . . . I guess you don't need to see that part of it again," she remarked quietly. Then she glanced toward Mr. Manetrue and Y. "I did add a safety feature, though. It isn't supposed to fire unless you twist the base and tip in opposite directions first, then you push the button. The safety must have failed."

"You were twisting the base and tip while you were talking," Y mentioned gently. "But this indicates that a more complicated safety mechanism should be thought out. Otherwise, I think it's brilliant."

"Yes, yes." Ira Manetrue looked thrilled. "It will help avoid customs problems without having to reveal our agents to those countries who refuse to help us."

Y nodded. "I'll expect several new safety ideas for your BMML at the next meeting, Jane, and I want to be consulted as to the final design. Now, if that's all, I guess we can adjourn."

After a brief pause to be sure no one had anything to say, Y stood and left the room. Mr. Manetrue followed. The moment the door closed behind them, the room burst into activity. Everyone began to move at once, packing their things and preparing to leave.

Jane blew out a heavy breath, shaking her head at surviving, mostly, yet another monthly presentation. Then she opened her briefcase and set her BMMLs—spent and unspent—inside.

"Well," Lizzy said bracingly as she got to her feet. "That went well, I think."

"Ha ha," Jane muttered. Her friend grinned.

"No. Seriously. You had a little hiccup there with the . . . er, BM: whatever."

"BMML," Jane prompted, shrugging into her

jacket. "And nearly blowing off the head of a co-worker is hardly a hiccup."

"It is when it's Dick."

Lizzy and Jane had often agreed the man's parents had been prophetic, if cruel, in naming him. Jane's gaze moved along the table to the empty spot where Dick had been seated. "Did he leave already?" she asked hopefully. Jane rather supposed she owed him an apology, but she wouldn't be sorry to miss the opportunity if he'd left.

"I think he's still under the table. In a fetal position and sucking his thumb."

Mouth dropping open, Jane bent swiftly to peer under the table. Dick wasn't there.

"Janie, honey, you are so gullible!" Lizzy laughed good-naturedly.

Jane straightened, making a face and closing her briefcase with a snap. "It's part of my charm."

"Yes, it is." Lizzy grinned. "Want to stop for a drink and maybe a pizza on the way home?" They headed for the door.

"Can't. Jill has to leave early to pick up her daughter from the train station. She's skipping Friday's classes to come home from University for the weekend. I have to get straight back." Jill was the woman who watched Jane's Gran, and she was gold as far as Jane was concerned. She

340

was a hard worker, was always on time, was never sick, and most importantly got on with Jane's Gran. Which was no small thing. Maggie Spyrus could be a cantankerous mole.

Jane glanced at her wristwatch and frowned. "Actually, I'd better hurry about it too. Her daughter's train gets in at 5:30. It's already 5:00." She made a face. "This meeting *would* run late on a day I have to be home early."

"Hmm." Lizzy nodded. "That's the way it usually works. It would have gone faster if Lipschitz hadn't rambled on for an hour about his knock-out lipstick."

"Knock-out lipstick?" Jane asked. They started up the hall. She hadn't paid attention to Lipschitz's presentation. Or anyone else's for that matter. She really had to see someone about this fear-of-public-speaking thing.

"Yes." Lizzy pulled a small tube from her pocket and handed it over. "This is the prototype. He passed a couple around. We were supposed to give it back, but I forgot when he sat down and you opened your briefcase. I couldn't believe it when I saw those vibrators." She shook her head and laughed.

Jane smiled slightly and took the sample, managing to uncap it one-handed. The color was a hot red. Every man's dream, she supposed. "How does it work?"

"There's a clear stick in the other end. You put that on first like a base coat, then put the color over top. Kiss a guy, and poof!" She snapped her thumb and finger together. "He's out cold and you're fine, according to Lipschitz."

Jane pursed her lips. "I wonder if he tested it himself . . . And if he did, whether he was the kisser or the kissee."

"Good Lord, I hope he was the kissee! Lipschitz in lipstick is just not something I want to imagine."

Jane laughed. Closing the colored end of the lipstick, she turned it over to open the other and stared with interest at the clear glistening tube beneath. "Is the base coat an antidote, or does it just prevent the drug from touching the wearer's skin?"

"I'm not sure. I missed that part of his very long explanation. I kind of zoned out after the first fifteen minutes." Shrugging, Lizzy changed the subject. "So if Jill's daughter is home, who's watching your grandmother tomorrow?"

"I am," Jane managed to say without grimacing. "I took tomorrow off."

"Off?" Lizzy smiled. "You mean you'll work at home. As usual."

"Yeah, well—"

"Lizzy!" At the call, both Jane and her friend paused and looked back. Joan Higate, one of the three secretaries everyone in D & C shared, started down the hall after them. "You have a phone call. A Mark Armstrong."

"Damn. I have to take that," Lizzy muttered. "Well, I'll give you a call this weekend." She turned and broke into a jog back toward the phones.

"Oh wait! The lipstick." Jane took a step after her friend, but paused when Lizzy waved back at her not to worry.

Shrugging, Jane turned back toward the exit. Recapping the lipstick, she slipped it into her pocket. She'd give it back on Monday; she really had to get home now. The last thing Jane wanted was to piss off Jill. Who else could take care of her Gran? Maggie Spyrus had been an active, sharp-minded agent right up until six years ago. Then, after forty-five years in the business, one year before she would have retired, an assignment had gone awry. She had been training a rookie who'd made a terrible error—one that had cost the girl's life and landed Maggie in a wheelchair. She'd not taken the change well. She missed the action and adventure of her old job. She missed using her brain and body. And she got into all sorts of trouble—or had until Jane hired Jill.

Jill was the sixth nurse Maggie Spyrus had in the year after the incident, but she was also the last. The woman had once told Jane the secret to her success with Gran; She hid whatever sympathy she felt. When the old girl misbehaved, Jill berated her for acting like a child, accused her of being a nasty old witch feeling sorry for herself. Which was apparently what Gran needed. The last thing Maggie could handle was being pitied or treated like a senile old cripple, so Jill's attitude was perfect. Gran responded well to expectations, and Jill had a lot of them. She expected Gran to do what she could and to behave well. And for Jill, Gran did.

Jane paused at the door at the end of the hall, punched a code into the keypad, stuck her thumb on another pad so it could read her print, then pressed her eye to the retina scanner. A buzz sounded and the door unlocked. Jane immediately pushed it open and stepped out into a small lobby painted a soothing blue. It was very small, perhaps twenty feet wide. The wall facing her had three elevators. A small counter stood at either end of the room, a man in a security guard's uniform behind each. Jane gave a smile and waved in response to their greetings. As she crossed the short distance to the first of the three elevators, the doors slid apart almost at once, opened by one of the guards.

Jane stepped inside. This elevator was saved for D & C use only. The other two traveled up, carrying people to the higher floors and departments in the B.L.I.S.S. building, but this one was reserved for her department alone. It opened out into the main lobby or traveled down to the first and second basements, where all of the more interesting and dangerous experiments took place. Thus the security for it was very tight.

The doors at Jane's back clicked shut, enclosing her in the mirrored elevator. A moment passed during which, as well as traveling, she knew she was being x-rayed and what she carried was being recorded. Then the doors in front of her slid open.

Jane stepped out and crossed the large main lobby filled with B.L.I.S.S. workers coming and going. She pushed through the main revolving doors to the outside. Hurrying along the concrete sidewalk, she passed the large sign that read Tots Toy Development and had a laugh. It was a dummy sign. Camouflage. There was very little having to do with tots inside that building, unless you counted weapons against terrorists or counter-agents or threats to the world order as nifty children's games.

The sight of her little white Miata sports car made her smile. Jane unlocked its door, tossed her briefcase inside, then slid behind its wheel.

Catching a glimpse of herself in the rearview mirror, she grimaced. The light dusting of face powder and rose lipstick she'd applied that morning were long gone. Large naked green eyes peered back at her. Between that and the long auburn hair pulled back into its usual ponytail, she looked about ten years younger than the 28 she was. Someday she'd look her age, she was sure, but by then she probably wouldn't want to.

Jane glanced up at the soft top of her car and considered putting it down. It was November but unseasonably nice, and she loved to drive fast with no roof. She was running late, however, and the latch tended to give her trouble; so she merely undid her window, buckled up, and started the engine. Imagining herself a racecar driver, she shifted the stick-shift into gear and roared out of the parking lot.

It was only a twenty-minute drive from the B.L.I.S.S. building to the apartment she shared with her grandmother. Today she made it in sixteen. Grabbing her briefcase, Jane scrambled out of the car and hurried inside. The apartment building had been designed in a squarish C, with the entry way and lobby in the front opening into a long corridor that diverged both right and left for a good thirty feet before turning sharply into the wings. Jane and her gran lived on the first floor in the hallway on the right. Their apartment overlooked the street, so she wasn't surprised when she rounded the corner and found Jill waiting in the open door with her coat on.

"I'm sorry," Jane apologized as she rushed forward. "I meant to get here earlier, but my meeting ran longer than usual."

"That's okay. I saw you pull up and got ready," the slender, fiftyish brunette said. She held the apartment door so Jane wouldn't have to use her key. "I'll get there just in time."

Jane breathed a sigh of relief. "Good. Thanks, Jill. See you Monday." She raised her hand to hold the door herself, then watched Jill hurry off up the hall. When the woman was gone, Jane stepped inside and pushed the door closed. She dropped her briefcase so that she could lock the door, and removed her jacket.

"Janie?"

"Yes, Gran, it's me. Be right there." Hanging her coat on the rack by the door, she picked up her case and moved into the living room.

Maggie Spyrus, seventy years old but still lovely, smiled at her as she entered. "How did the meeting go, dear?"

"Other than firing my BMML and nearly taking off Dick's head, I think it went pretty well."

Gran's eyebrows flew up. "Firing the . . . What did Y say?"

"Nothing about nearly killing Dick, but she did say she thought the BMML was brilliant."

"Brilliant? My!" Gran marveled. "That is high praise from her."

"Yes, and she thought the shrink-wrap condoms were "diabolical" but would be more useful for torturing enemy spies than anything else. She didn't say much about the tampon trackers . . . but she did ask a lot of questions about them."

"She likes them then," Gran said with satisfaction. She absently petted the small white Yorkie in her lap.

Jane merely shrugged, weariness coming over her now that she was home. The stress was over. She wanted nothing more than to have a light dinner with Gran and maybe watch a movie. Tomorrow she'd start thinking up new fail-safes for the BMML. "How was your day?"

"Oh, well . . . I didn't die. But we can always hope for tomorrow."

"Yes," Jane agreed pleasantly. "I'm going to go change into something more comfortable, then see about dinner." The best way to fight Gran's depressive moments was to ignore them.

"Jill made a nice lasagna and salad. She said she put them in the fridge, and that the lasagna just has to be cooked for fifteen minutes or so at 325 degrees to warm it up."

"Jill is a jewel," Jane breathed. "Be right back."

She left Gran watching *Judge Judy* and walked down the hall to the bathroom. Stepping inside and closing the door, Jane realized she still carried her briefcase. She rolled her eyes at herself. Setting the case on the bathroom counter beside the sink, she began to dig things out of the pockets of her business jacket: a small screwdriver, a pencil stub, a pen, kleenex, a wad of saran wrap from her lunch. Lipschitz's Lipstick was the last thing she found. Frowning at the plain silver tube, she snapped her briefcase open and dropped the lipstick inside. She had to remember to take it back to the office on Monday.

Done emptying her pockets, Jane quickly stripped out of the rest of her clothes, tugged the elastic band out of her hair, then went to turn on the shower. She adjusted the water and stepped under the spray with a sigh. Simply standing under the pulsing stream, Jane enjoyed its pounding on her skin for several moments. At last she grabbed the shampoo and soap.

Ten minutes later, she was turning the water off and grabbing a couple towels from the rack. Jane wrapped the first around her long hair, turban-style, then quickly dried off with the second. It was when she stepped out onto the floor mat that she realized she hadn't grabbed anything to change into.

Wrapping the towel she'd used to dry off with around herself, Jane snatched up her dirty clothes and turned toward the door. Unfortunately, her jacket caught the edge of the open briefcase and sent it crashing to the floor. Its contents scattered across the bathroom's marble tiles.

Jane stared in dismay at the mess she'd made as one of her trackers rolled to a halt at her feet. The silver case that had held them had snapped open on impact. There were only two left in the case, the others were strewn across the floor.

Jane bent to begin picking them up; but a moment later decided against it. She was naked, cold and hungry. The mess could wait.

Leaving the steamy bathroom, she hurried to her room and dropped her towel. She dug a pair of clean joggers and a sweatshirt out of the drawer, then pulled on the pants.

"Jane?"

"Coming, Gran!" Jane called. She dragged the sweatshirt over her head, pulling it into place and hurrying along the hall to the living room. "Is something wrong?"

"Tinkle needs to go out, dear."

Jane's eyes dropped to the dog with resignation. The animal was whimpering and circling in Gran's lap: a sure signal she had to relieve herself.

"I don't know what is the matter with the silly animal," Gran fretted. "Jill took her out to do her business just an hour ago. I hope she hasn't got a bladder infection."

"I'm sure she's fine, Gran," Jane said. She

sighed. To be honest, she suspected the little dog really didn't have to go out at all. The little beast just wanted to annoy her. Tinkle seemed to have the uncanny knack of "having to go out" whenever Jane was in the shower or busy doing something important. The beast might look adorable with its long white hair and pink bow, but Jane was positive that cute exterior hid an evil soul.

She couldn't say anything to Gran, of course. The woman adored "her little Tinkle." The dog was an angel in her eyes. Of course, the dog did behave well around her for the most part. Tinkle saved misbehaving for when she was out with Jill or Jane.

"Poor baby," Gran crooned as the dog's whimpers increased in volume. She turned apologetic eyes to Jane. "Could you, dear?"

"Of course, Gran. I'll just get the leash."

"Thank you."

Jane detoured through the kitchen to turn the oven on, then grabbed Tinkle's leash from the hall. She took it out to her gran who put it on the small dog. Jane then scooped the dog up, making sure her hands were nowhere near the animal's mouth where she was likely to get bit. Carrying the beast into the kitchen, she set it on the floor and hooked the leash to the doorknob. Going to the fridge, she retrieved the lasagna Jill had made.

"What are you doing, dear?" Gran called when Tinkle's whining grew in protest at the delay.

"Just popping the lasagna in, Gran. That way it'll be ready when we get back." Removing the plastic wrap Jill had covered the pasta with, Jane matched action to words: she slid the dish into the oven.

"There. All done. We'll be right back," she announced, then stuck her tongue out at the dog. Unhooking the leash from the doorknob, she followed the little monster to the apartment door. As she pulled it open, however, Jane found her neighbor Edie Andretti standing on the threshold, hand upraised to knock.

"Oh, Jane! I have a big date tonight but . . . I was just coming over to see if I could borrow—"

"Is that Edie?" Gran's voice interrupted from the living room.

"Yes, Gran," Jane called, scowling at Tinkle. The beast had begun running around in circles, binding her up in its leash.

"Come on in, Edie dear, Jane will be back in a minute." Gran called. "You can keep me company."

"Oh, I can't stay long, Mrs. S.," Edie replied. She stepped past Jane into the apartment. "I have a date. In fact, he's picking me up in ten minutes. I was just going to borrow a couple of things from Jane."

"Oh my!" Maggie Syprus called. "A hot date is it, Edie dear? And on a Thursday night? You must come tell me all about it."

"Okay," the younger woman agreed. She turned back to Jane. "Can I—"

"Borrow whatever you want. You know where everything is," Jane answered, distracted trying to untangle herself from Tinkle's leash. Finally managing, she started out the door—only to halt abruptly as her head was suddenly jerked backward. Glancing around with a start, she saw Edie grinning at her, a damp towel dangling from the woman's hand.

"Damn," Jane growled. She'd forgotten all about it. Reaching up, she slicked the tangled mass of her wet hair back with her fingers, hoping that made it at least a touch less disreputable. "Go on in. I'll be back as quick as I can. If you have to leave before I return, borrow what you need and go. But I expect to hear all the details of the date tomorrow."

"You will." Edie grinned and closed the door behind her.

"Come on, Tinkle," Jane said glumly, heading for the elevator. She wasn't at all surprised when the beast decided it didn't want to walk and sat down in the hall to whine. Sighing, Jane picked up the Yorkie and carried her to the elevator. This was a sure sign that Jane wasn't going to get back before Edie had to leave. She suspected she'd be lucky to get back before the lasagna burned.

As she'd expected, Edie had already left when Jane returned with Tinkle. The lasagna had been in the oven longer than the recommended fifteen minutes, but it was still edible. Jane and her gran ate, then watched an old James Bond flick. It was eleven before the show ended and Jane saw to settling Gran and Tinkle in bed.

Quite ready for bed herself by then, Jane made her way to her bathroom, pausing at the sight of her briefcase sitting on the counter with its contents replaced neatly inside. Hadn't she knocked it to the floor and left it to clean up later?

Stepping forward, Jane peered inside. Edie had obviously taken the time to put everything back for her. Which was very nice, but Jane had to wonder why Edie had even been in the bathroom. Her neighbor was a good friend, but generally she borrowed clothes or jewelry rather than anything out of the bathroom. Well, really she tended to borrow mostly jewelry. Jane didn't have that great a wardrobe; it was made up mostly of a combo of business clothes and sweatsuits, and it was sadly lacking in the sexy slinky-type clothes one might want for a date. In any case, whatever clothes and jewelry Edie may have been interested in, they certainly wouldn't have been found in the bathroom.

Jane scanned the contents of her briefcase again. Everything seemed to be there: the BMML, the launched BMML, the shrink-wrap condoms. Jane counted those, terrified for a brief moment that the girl might have borrowed one. Wouldn't that have made for an interesting date, she thought ruefully. However, all of the little foil packets were present and accounted for. Even the knockout lipstick remained. She breathed another grateful sigh.

Shrugging, Jane started to close the briefcase, then paused as she realized what was missing. There was only one silver case of personal trackers—the lubricated ones, she saw upon snapping open the container. Setting it on the counter, she quickly shifted through the contents of her briefcase just to be sure.

No, the pack of absorbent tampon trackers wasn't there.

Jane raised her head to peer at herself in the mirror, only then noticing the Post-it stuck to the glass. It was orange and obviously from the pad in her briefcase.

Dear Jane,
    Borrowed some tampons. Hope you don't mind, but took the case. Knew you wouldn't need them

since you borrowed my last ones last week. Will re-
turn the case and spares tomorrow when I fill you in
on my date!
Toodles, Edie

Jane groaned, then started to laugh. This was her own fault, of course. She'd left the contents of her briefcase lying around rather than putting them in her workroom. She *had* also told Edie she could borrow anything.

She tried to cheer herself. At least with the trackers there wouldn't be any of the calamities that might have occurred had Edie borrowed the lipstick or the condoms. But damn those had been some expensive tampons, and her friend would never even know!

Jane briefly considered tracking Edie and getting a free test-run out of the deal, but quickly she pushed the thought aside. She couldn't take advantage of her friend that way. She would just have to call them a loss.

Shaking her head, Jane picked up her briefcase and took it to her workroom. She would have to be more careful in the future. She knew better than to leave things lying around! Wasn't that one of the first things they taught you at B.L.I.S.S.?

"At least she took the absorbent ones," Jane muttered as she closed the door of her work-room.

the Mermaid of Penperro
LISA CACH

Konstanze never imagined that singing could land someone in such trouble. The disrepute of the stage is nothing compared to the danger of playing a seductress of the sea—or the reckless abandon she feels while doing so. She has come to Penperro to escape her past, to find anonymity among the people of Cornwall, and her inhibitions melt away as she does. But the Cornish are less simple than she expected, and the role she is forced to play is harder. For one thing, her siren song lures to her not only the agent of the crown she's been paid to perplex, but the smuggler who hired her. And in his strong arms she finds everything she's been missing. Suddenly, Konstanze sees the true peril of her situation—not that of losing her honor, but her heart.

___52437-6 $5.50 US/$6.50 CAN

The CHANGELING BRIDE

LISA CACH

In order to procure the cash necessary to rebuild his estate, the Earl of Allsbrook decides to barter his title and his future: He will marry the willful daughter of a wealthy merchant. True, she is pleasing in form and face, and she has an eye for fashion. Still, deep in his heart, Henry wishes for a happy marriage. Wilhelmina March is leery of the importance her brother puts upon marriage, and she certainly never dreams of being wed to an earl in Georgian England—or of the fairy debt that gives her just such an opportunity. But suddenly, with one sweet kiss in a long-ago time and a faraway place, Elle wonders if the much ado is about something after all.

___52342-6 $4.99 US/$5.99 CAN

Dorchester Publishing Co., Inc.
P.O. Box 6640
Wayne, PA 19087-8640

Please add $1.75 for shipping and handling for the first book and $.50 for each book thereafter. NY, NYC, and PA residents, please add appropriate sales tax. No cash, stamps, or C.O.D.s. All orders shipped within 6 weeks via postal service book rate. Canadian orders require $2.00 extra postage and must be paid in U.S. dollars through a U.S. banking facility.

Name_____
Address_____
City_____State_____Zip_____
I have enclosed $_____ in payment for the checked book(s).
Payment <u>must</u> accompany all orders. ❑ Please send a free catalog.
CHECK OUT OUR WEBSITE! www.dorchesterpub.com